Breaking
All the Rules

by

Rachael Richey

Breaking All the Rules

Cover Art by *Tina Lynn Stout*

The Wild Rose Press, Inc.
PO Box 708
Adams Basin, NY 14410-0708
Visit us at www.thewildrosepress.com

Publishing History
First Champagne Rose Edition, 2017
Print ISBN 978-1-5092-1320-7
Digital ISBN 978-1-5092-1321-4

Published in the United States of America

Kate's mouth fell open as she found herself face to face with a tall, slim young man, his thick messy dark hair falling over his deep velvet brown eyes. Eyes that had always had the ability to turn her legs to jelly. She put a hand out to steady herself on the table and licked her suddenly dry lips.

"Sam," she managed, her voice emerging as a squeaky croak.

"Hello, Katy." He smiled at her, the deep brown eyes crinkling enticingly at the corners. "It's so good to see you."

"Sam," Kate repeated, unable to tear her eyes away from his. "What are you doing here?"

"I've come home." Sam grinned at her and ran a hand through his hair. "Thought it was time I settled down. Got a job, that sort of thing."

"You've been travelling all this time?"

"Yeah, pretty much." He glanced around him with interest. "It's kinda weird being back here, actually. This all seems so…so…"

"Boring?" Kate supplied the word. "So boring after India, and Australia, and wherever you've been the last eight years. Where *have* you been, Sam?"

"No, not boring." He ignored her question. "Just normal. Normal and sort of…well, just normal."

Kate stared at him, her heart pounding uncomfortably in her chest. Sam was the last person she had expected to see at the WI fête. The last person she had ever expected to see again. She had stopped hoping for that a long time ago.

Praise for Rachael Richey

"…another very entertaining book with a great mixture of love, suspense and drama."

~Portobellobookblog (4 Stars)

~*~

"This is the third installment in the NightHawk series and I was gripped yet again with the drama and romance in Abi and Gideon's life."

~Kraftireader (5 Stars)

~*~

"An exciting, suspenseful book that once again consumed me within its pages and never let me down."

~Whispering Stories (5 Stars)

~*~

"Rachael's writing style flows so easily that she effortlessly moves from past to present, revealing just enough information each time and leaving the reader clamouring for more."

~The Book Magnet (5 Stars)

~*~

Other books by Rachael Richey
Available from The Wild Rose Press, Inc.
The NightHawk Series:
STORM RISING
RHYTHM OF DECEIT
COBWEBS IN THE DARK
THE GIRL IN THE PAINTING

Dedication

To my gorgeous little granddaughter,
Harlie Eliza,
who was born the day I signed the contract.

Chapter 1

Sunday 28th June, 2015

"Katy?"

Kate grimaced and pretended she hadn't heard. No one called her Katy anymore, except a few of her older relatives and some of her mother's more annoying friends. Agreeing to help out at the WI fête was already proving to be a mistake, and she could certainly do without some interfering old biddy coming and telling her how ill, or thin, or worried she looked. She kept her head down and savagely buttered a scone.

"Katy? Is that really you?"

God, they weren't going to give up then. With a sigh she straightened up and pushed a strand of long dark hair out of her eyes. The butter knife still clutched in her hand, she glanced over her shoulder in resignation, prepared for the onslaught of criticism.

"I thought it was you. You haven't changed a bit."

Kate's mouth fell open as she found herself face to face with a tall, slim young man, his thick messy dark hair falling over his deep velvet brown eyes. Eyes that had always had the ability to turn her legs to jelly. She put a hand out to steady herself on the table and licked her suddenly dry lips.

"Sam," she managed, her voice emerging as a squeaky croak.

"Hello, Katy." He smiled at her, the deep brown eyes crinkling enticingly at the corners. "It's so good to see you."

"Sam," Kate repeated, unable to tear her eyes away from his. "What are you doing here?"

"I've come home." Sam grinned at her and ran a hand through his hair. "Thought it was time I settled down. Got a job, that sort of thing."

"You've been travelling all this time?"

"Yeah, pretty much." He glanced around him with interest. "It's kinda weird being back here, actually. This all seems so…so…"

"Boring?" Kate supplied the word. "So boring after India, and Australia, and wherever you've been the last eight years. Where *have* you been, Sam?"

"No, not boring." He ignored her question. "Just normal. Normal and sort of…well, just normal."

Kate stared at him, her heart pounding uncomfortably in her chest. Sam was the last person she had expected to see at the WI fête. The last person she had ever expected to see again. She had stopped hoping for that a long time ago. Slightly self-conscious, she hooked a strand of hair behind her ear and looked up at him.

"So you're back for good then?" she asked. "Does your mother know?"

"Of course she does." Sam grinned at her again. "I'm staying there for now. I'm off up country to see some friends tomorrow, and back again on Thursday. Then I shall get a job."

He sounded so pleased with himself, that Kate couldn't stop the corners of her mouth from twitching.

"A job? You have one lined up?"

2

"Maybe. I have a few possibilities." Sam moved a little closer. "We must have a proper catch-up. What are you doing on Friday night? I'll be back by then; let's go for a drink and a real chat."

"Friday? I can't do Friday. I'm going out."

"Cancel it. Come out with me. We have eight years to catch up on."

"I can't cancel it."

"Course you can. Who are you going out with? Is it Jenny? I bet you're still best friends."

"Jen will be there." Kate nodded. "But I can't cancel it; it's a party."

"A party?" Sam's eyes lit up hopefully. "Can I come with you? It'd be great to see all the gang again."

"You can't." Kate shook her head firmly. "It's a Hen Party."

"Oh, right. You mean like a proper Hen Party? For a bride?"

Kate nodded. "Yeah, a proper Hen Party. For a bride."

"Well, I guess I really can't come to that then." Sam smiled again and shrugged. "How about Thursday then? Safer than Saturday when you'll probably be hung over?"

"Thursday will be fine." Kate didn't hesitate. "But I don't drink much anyway these days, so I'll be fine on Saturday too. Where shall we go?"

"I'll pick you up at seven. D'you still live with your parents?"

"No—yes—yes, I do. But no, don't pick me up. I'll meet you somewhere." Kate thought fast. "By the park gates. At seven."

"All right." Sam looked at her quizzically. "By the

park gates at seven it is, then. Looking forward to it. We have a lot to catch up on." He winked at her and turned to go.

"And Sam," Kate called after him, "it's Kate now. No one calls me Katy any more."

Sam looked over his shoulder at her. "I do," he said with a lopsided grin, then disappeared across the grass through the crowds.

Kate's shoulders slumped, and she covered her face with her hands. She had not been expecting that. That Sam Somerville should turn up again after all these years. And now of all times. She exhaled, aware she had been holding her breath since he walked away, and turned back to the table of scones. Automatically she began the buttering again, her thoughts flying all over the place. She had just agreed to go out on a date with Sam Somerville. Well, not a real date, of course. Just a catch-up. But it would be just her and Sam. And he would want to know all about her. All about the things that had happened to her since he'd been gone. Since that dreadful day just after they left school. He'd ask all sorts of questions she wouldn't want to answer. And she would want to ask all sorts of questions *he* probably wouldn't want to answer. She stopped buttering the scone and stared out across the now muddy field. She would have to cancel. She couldn't risk—what? She laid down the knife and wiped her hands on her jeans. What couldn't she risk? Sam finding out...

"Kate, haven't you finished those scones yet?" Her mother's voice was mildly annoyed. "You spend far too much time daydreaming. Come on, they need them over at the tea tent."

"Sorry, Mum." Kate glanced over her shoulder. "Got a bit distracted. I'm nearly done. Here you go. I'll bring the rest in a minute."

"Thank you, darling." Helen Granger frowned at her daughter. "I understand you have a lot to deal with just now, but you must learn to concentrate better. The least little thing seems to distract you these days."

"Sorry, Mum." Kate felt her face flush, and she turned away in annoyance. "It's fine. I'll have them done in a minute."

"Well, stop daydreaming." Helen gathered up the plates. "You'll get them done much quicker then."

Kate stared after her retreating back, then looked down at the remaining scones. She had to get out of here. With a sudden burst of speed she slathered them with the rapidly melting butter, then piled them on a plate. She would deliver them to the tea tent. Then she needed to get away. She needed to think, and possibly to speak to Jenny.

The tea tent was heaving with middle-aged ladies all speaking at once, and Kate squeezed through them, attempting not to make eye contact with anyone, the last two plates of scones held above her head for safety. She arrived at the far side of the tent and deposited her load on the already creaking table.

"Thanks, darling." Helen smiled at her from where she was refilling the urn, her face red from the steam. "Are you staying to help serve?"

"I can't, Mum." Kate began to back away. "I promised I'd…" She tailed off as she realised her mother had stopped listening, and quickly made her escape from the claustrophobic environment. Back out in the fresh air, she paused for a moment, closed her eyes, and took a deep breath. She had to leave—now. With a final glance back into the tea tent, where she could just make out her mother deep in animated conversation, she ducked under the guy ropes and hurried away across the grass.

The field was only half a mile from their house, and to save getting her car bogged down in the mud, Kate had walked over. She picked her way carefully between the ancient cow pats that lined the path to the gate, and finally made it out onto the road, her flats only slightly muddy. Well, that was one event she was never going to again. No matter how hard her mother begged. She set off down the road just as an overloud voice announced the judging of the flower-arranging competition over the tannoy. Kate shuddered. She was never going to get old. Not if it meant spending one's Sunday afternoon in a muddy field with over-enthusiastic, tea-drinking women.

By the time she turned up the drive to the house, the first spots of rain were beginning to fall, and Kate couldn't help a tiny smile curling the corners of her mouth. Imagine the consternation at the fête! She inserted her key into the lock and decided she really wasn't a very nice person.

Kicking her damp flats into the corner of the porch, she padded through the hall and went straight to the fridge to get herself a glass of wine. She glanced at the clock. Nearly four thirty. Oh, well, she'd earned it. Sod the time. Now what was she going to do about Sam Somerville?

Leaning against the work surface, sipping her wine, Kate found her thoughts getting ever more befuddled. Sam turning up really shouldn't be affecting her like this. She hadn't seen him for nearly eight years. She hadn't even heard from him for about five. Her life was going pretty well. Why had seeing him thrown her into such a state? She took a very long slurp of her wine, walked through to the dining room, and went over to the window. Staring out at the darkening sky, she took a deep breath. She knew why, of course. She just didn't want to admit it. She really couldn't afford to let herself admit it. That would get far too complicated. Just for once her life seemed to be going in the right direction. Just for once things were going well. Allowing Sam Somerville to interfere with that would be madness. Yet she knew she was going to meet with him on Thursday.

Kate leant her head against the cool glass of the window and sighed. Why now? Why did he have to come back now? Any other time over the last eight years would have been fine. Any other time but now. She shivered as she remembered just how it had felt when he'd called her Katy. Her whole body had tingled, and she had felt lightheaded. Why did he still have that effect on her? It really didn't make any sense. She supposed she was going to have to tell Jen. She'd find out eventually anyway; his presence in the village was hardly going to be a secret. Especially not with his parents having such a pivotal role in the life of the community.

She turned away from the now rain-drenched window and fished her mobile out of her pocket. She tapped the screen, then held it to her ear.

"Jen? Hi. You busy? I need to talk."

"Kate! I was going to call you." Jenny's voice floated down the line. "Are you still at the fête worse than death?"

"No." Kate smiled despite herself. "I managed to escape. But something happened there. I need to tell you."

"Yeah?"

"Yeah. Sam Somerville turned up."

"What?" Jenny screeched in surprise, and Kate held the phone away from her ear. "What, at the fête? What the hell was he doing there? Did you speak to him?"

"Yes, of course I spoke to him. He came over to see me. He says he's come home to settle down and get a job."

"Sam, settle down? Never happen. What did you say to him? Did you tell him about—"

"No." Kate interrupted her. "There wasn't really the opportunity. He's going away for a day or so to visit some friends; then he'll be back on Thursday. I'm going for a drink and a catch-up with him when he gets back." Kate took a deep breath. "He wanted to go out on Friday, but I told him I couldn't."

"Of course you can't! What did you tell him you were doing?"

"I said I was going to a Hen Night."

There was a slight pause. "But did you tell him it was yours?"

Chapter 2

"Really, Kate, you might have stayed and helped out a bit." Helen laid her dripping umbrella in the sink and wriggled out of her raincoat. "You disappeared as soon as you'd buttered the scones. Did you not see how busy it was in the tea tent? I could really have done with your help."

"Sorry, Mum." Kate perched on the end of the kitchen table and watched her mother ease her feet out of her muddy Wellington boots. "I buttered hundreds of scones; isn't that enough? I had things to do."

"Wedding stuff, I presume?" Helen glanced up at her daughter and gave a little smile. "It's all right, darling. I understand. It's a very exciting time for you. A once-in-a-lifetime experience."

"Sometimes," Kate muttered under her breath, feeling her face begin to get hot. Suddenly the excitement of the wedding had become a little tarnished. For nearly a year she had been caught up in dress fittings, floral arrangements, choosing menus, catering for awkward guests who only ate nuts that had fallen from the tree, petulant flower girls, and bickering bridesmaids, and she had begun to feel that was the norm. Now the encounter with someone from her previous life had brought it all crashing down around her ears. She had remembered there was more to life than organising a wedding. More to life than actually getting married. "Some people do it twice. Or three times."

Helen glanced up at her. "What, darling? What are you talking about?"

"Nothing." Kate slid down off her perch and shrugged. "Jen's coming round in a minute."

"Now you haven't forgotten Richard and his parents are coming at seven, have you?" Helen was filling the kettle. "We're going to finalize the travelling arrangements."

"Does it have to be tonight?" The words were out before Kate could stop them, and she bit her lip in annoyance.

"Yes, it does." Helen looked at her in surprise. "It's been arranged for weeks. It really is the last chance for all of us to get together before the wedding. I'm doing a roast."

Kate glanced at the clock. "Mum, it's gone six now. How can you do a roast in that time?"

"Don't be silly Kate, we're not eating at seven. We'll be talking for about an hour, I'm sure. You know how Janice goes on. Anyway, I did all the veg before I went out." She nodded towards several large covered pans that were already on the stove. "And the turkey has been on for hours."

"Surely there isn't that much left to talk about, is there?" Kate was aware she sounded like a petulant child, and kicked at the skirting board crossly. "We've done nothing but talk weddings for months."

"There's a lot of organisation to a wedding." Helen frowned severely at her. "You'll find out soon enough when your first daughter gets married. It's a stressful time."

"Well, you should have just let us go away and do it on our own then. That's what I wanted."

"Now you know you don't mean that. And think about poor Richard. How would he have felt? He's invited a lot of influential people to the wedding. It could be very useful for him."

Kate sighed. "I guess. Well, Jen should be here any minute. I'll get rid of her by seven, if you insist."

"If you would. I don't know what's wrong with you tonight, Kate. Is it your time of the month?"

"Mum! No, it's not. Not that I'd tell you if it was. I'm just tired, and to be honest, getting fed up with wedding stuff. I just wish it was all over."

"Well, only four weeks to go now." Helen beamed at her. "Then you've got that lovely honeymoon to look forward to."

As Kate opened her mouth to reply, there was a tap on the back door, and a voice called, "It's only me. Can I come in?"

"Yes Jenny, come on in," Helen called back. "I've just boiled the kettle. Would you like a cuppa?"

"No, Mum, of course she wouldn't. She's not one of your friends. We'll go to my room." Kate caught her friend by the wrist and propelled her across the kitchen and upstairs to her bedroom. She slammed the door shut behind them and sat down on the bed. "Richard and his parents are coming at seven. You have to be gone by then."

"Okay." Jenny stared at her in surprise. "We'd better be quick then. Pity. I would have liked a cup of tea. What's going on? Why didn't you tell Sam about the wedding?"

"There was no chance." Kate looked down at her

hands, her fingers picking at a loose thread in her bedspread.

"Weren't you wearing your ring?"

"I was buttering scones in a field, Jen. Of course I wasn't wearing it! Richard's so bloody precious about how expensive it was, I don't even wear it to work in case I lose it."

"But you told him about the Hen Party?"

"I just said I was going to one. He didn't ask whose it was."

"Kate, why didn't you tell him? Do you still like him?" Jenny sat down next to her, concern in her eyes.

"No, of course not." Kate bounced angrily on the bed. "No. No. I haven't seen him for years. How could I still like him? He went travelling without me."

Jenny surveyed her friend silently for a moment, her blue eyes speculative. "You know why he went travelling."

"He still should have taken me. It was all planned."

"No, he shouldn't." Jenny shook her head decisively. "He needed to get away on his own. You know that better than anyone. You weren't even his girlfriend." She paused and brushed her long blonde hair back from her face. "The question is, why is he back now, and why do you care?"

"He's back to settle down and get a job." Kate shrugged. "That's what he told me. And I *don't* care. I was just surprised to see him."

"Yeah, you care. Even *I* care, and I wasn't madly in love with him in sixth form! Sam Somerville has that effect on people."

Kate flopped back on the bed and covered her face with her arm. "Oh, God, Jen, what am I going to do?

I'm going out for a drink with him on Thursday, and I'll have to tell him I'm getting married."

"Of course you will. D'you want me to come with you?"

Kate moved her arm off her face and raised an eyebrow. "No. Certainly not. I finally get a date with Sam Somerville, and I'm not going to share it with you, even if you *are* my best friend. It'll probably be the last time I can go on a date with anyone who's not Richard."

Jenny lay down on her stomach next to Kate and grinned. "And aren't you the tiniest bit concerned as to why that matters?"

"Nope. Everyone should have a final fling."

"Kate, you won't do anything silly, will you? Nothing you'll regret."

"Jen, I haven't done anything I'd regret for years." Kate sat up and groaned. "My life is so boring and predictable. I never do anything wrong, or silly, or dangerous." She pulled her knees up to her chest and linked her arms around them. "Or maybe I *have* been doing things I'll regret for years. Maybe my whole life is wrong. Maybe I'm living the wrong life. It certainly feels like it sometimes."

Jenny stared at her in amazement. "Kate! Seriously? How can you say that? You're engaged to a gorgeous, successful man, you have a good job, you're pretty… How can that be wrong? Please tell me you're not still yearning for Sam?"

"I don't know!" Kate buried her face in her knees. "No, of course not. I'm marrying Richard. I love Richard."

"Yes, you do," Jenny replied briskly, getting to her

feet. "You love Richard, and in four weeks' time you're marrying him. Tonight he's coming over for dinner, and you're going to be nice to him."

"I'm always nice to him." Kate reluctantly allowed herself to be pulled to her feet. "Well, mostly, anyway. I really do love him; of course I do. He's very nice to me."

"Well, that's not a good reason to love someone." Jenny frowned at her. "But I think you really do love him, so get out there and let him know. And forget about Sam Somerville. It's not going to do you any good to get hung up on him again. You know that."

Kate nodded slowly and turned to her wardrobe to find something more suitable to wear for dinner with her prospective in-laws. "I know. And he never really liked me anyway."

"He liked you as a friend. A best friend, even. But Kate?" Jenny caught her arm. "You must stay away from him. You do know that, don't you?"

"Rather hard when he's back in the village." Kate was wriggling out of her jeans. "But I'll do my best. Now what should I wear for Richard's parents? Does this look boring enough?" She pulled out a blue flowered dress and waved it at Jenny.

"That's nice. It suits you. But it's not boring. You must stop saying Richard's boring."

"No, not him. But his parents are. It's okay; I'm not marrying them." She tossed her top into the corner of the room and pulled the blue dress over her head. "Bloody good job, his mum drives me crazy. She's so stupid. Beats me how she managed to have such an intelligent son."

"Right. I'll leave you to it." Jenny grinned at her.

"Behave yourself tonight, and just look forward to the Hen on Friday. It's going to be awesome."

Kate squirmed round in an attempt to zip up her dress and peered suspiciously at her friend. "What d'you mean? What have you got planned? I'm trusting you, Jen. You're my chief bridesmaid. I don't want to end up half naked and chained to some railings."

"Honestly, Kate, what *do* you think I am?" Jenny tossed her hair back. "That's the sort of stupid thing men do. No, ours will be much more classy."

"Hmm. Hope so." Kate pulled open her wardrobe again and flung her discarded clothes inside. "I wish my sister wasn't coming, though."

"Kate, she's a bridesmaid, and your sister. Of course she has to come."

"I didn't want her as a bridesmaid. Mum said I had to." Kate pushed Jenny towards the door. "You know we don't get on."

"Is she coming tonight?"

"Oh, God, I hope not! Mum didn't say. I doubt it. She's usually out on the town on a Sunday night, with her friends." Kate glanced at Jenny. "Which is probably what I should be doing. Not sorting out the transport for a wedding."

"It's *your* wedding." Jenny gave her a little push. "Stop being negative. You love Richard. Now go and be nice."

Chapter 3

"Don't you agree, Kate?"

Kate looked up with a start as she heard her name. Richard's mother, Janice, was staring at her with her delicately drawn-on eyebrows raised.

"Kate. Did you hear what Janice said?" Helen frowned at her daughter and leaned over to tap her on the knee.

"Sorry, Janice. Just lost concentration there for a moment." Kate mustered a weary smile. "What did you say?"

"I asked if you were happy if the cars go back as soon as everyone has been dropped off at the church. That would be best, don't you agree?"

Kate stared at her in non-comprehension. "What else would they do?" she asked in surprise. "Wait around while we get married, and then do what? Drive you and Martin and Mum and Dad a hundred yards along the road to the reception? That's just stupid. Of course they should go away."

"Kate, that was a bit rude," Helen rebuked her and turned to their guests with an apologetic smile. "Sorry, Janice. I'm sure you understand she's been under a lot of pressure these last few weeks."

"Of course." Janice smiled sweetly at Kate. "I remember just what I was like when I was planning my wedding to Martin. I couldn't think straight for months.

It was all so exciting. Nothing else matters when you're getting married, does it?"

Kate glanced at her with barely concealed dislike, then turned to her father. "Can I have more wine, Dad?"

He leaned forward and topped up her glass, giving her a sympathetic wink as he did so. Kate smiled back and took a long slurp of her wine. Her dad was the only one who understood just how tedious she found all the wedding stuff. He knew she would much rather have had a quiet little family affair—or, even better, run off and told no one. As he'd pointed out to her more than once, that would also have made it much easier on his pocket.

"Another one, Kate? We haven't eaten yet." Helen pursed her lips in annoyance. "In fact, I think the roast will be nearly ready by now. Would you all like to go into the dining room?" She got to her feet and brushed some imaginary crumbs off her skirt. "Come and give me a hand, Kate."

Reluctantly Kate got to her feet and followed her mother into the kitchen. The heat from the cooker hit her like a wall, and she recoiled slightly. "Mum, it's far too hot for a roast. What were you thinking?" she muttered crossly, getting the plates out of the cupboard with a clatter. "We should have had salad or something."

"Nonsense, darling. Everyone likes a roast."

"Except Cousin Emil. He only eats nuts."

"What's that, darling?" Helen was bending down in front of the oven, her face flushed from the heat.

"Nothing." Kate watched as her mother placed the enormous turkey on a large oval serving plate. It looked big enough to feed at least twelve, and she began to feel a bit sick at the thought of eating anything.

"Take this in and give it to your father to carve." Helen handed her the plate. "Tell them the veggies are just coming. Then come back for the potatoes."

With a sigh Kate carried the steaming hot plate through into the dining room and plonked it in front of her father.

"That looks lovely," Janice enthused. "Doesn't it, Martin? Isn't Helen wonderful with her cooking?"

"It's only a bloody turkey," Kate muttered half to herself as she headed back to the kitchen. "Anyone can cook a bloody turkey."

"Try and cheer up, darling." Helen handed her two dishes of roast potatoes. "You're like a bear with a sore head tonight. Are you sure it's not your time of the month?"

"No, it's not," Kate snapped, snatching the dishes and stomping back into the dining room. She slammed them down on the waiting table mats, then went and retrieved her wine from the living room. She knocked it back in one go and stood for a moment with her eyes closed. She really needed to keep it together. It wasn't fair to her parents, or to Richard.

She took a deep breath, walked back into the dining room, and slid into her seat next to her fiancé. Richard reached for her hand under the table. Kate took it and gave it a squeeze, glancing up at him with a small smile.

"Sorry," she mouthed, feeling suddenly very guilty about her bad mood. He really was very good-looking. Thick light brown hair cut stylishly short, kind green eyes, and a very nice figure. His work as a lawyer necessitated him wearing a suit much of the time, but tonight he was more casually attired in cream chinos and a dark blue shirt, open at the neck. He smiled at her, his eyes crinkling at the corners, reminding her again that he was nearly thirty.

Leaning towards her, he put his lips to her ear. "Let's go for a walk after dinner. Get away from the parents for a bit."

Kate nodded and smiled her gratitude. He really was very caring. She must let him know how much she loved him. He smelled nice, too. She closed her eyes and inhaled his scent, reminding herself how she liked to smell it when they made love. They really needed to do that more. Then maybe it would be easier for her to remember why she was marrying him.

She abruptly let go of his hand and picked up her knife and fork. She was marrying him because she loved him. That was why. And she loved him because he was a lovely person. And he'd asked her.

"Cabbage, love?"

Kate took a spoonful of the soggy green leaves her mother was holding in front of her, and slopped them onto her plate. She really wasn't hungry, but she knew just how upset her mother would be if she didn't eat a huge plateful. With a sigh she reached for the gravy boat and poured a large quantity all over her turkey. She stared down at her plate. That hadn't helped. Now it looked as if she had even more food.

"You are a marvellous cook, Helen." Janice waved her fork in the air, and a tiny particle of potato wafted over and landed next to Kate. "I just don't know how you do it. You just conjure up these wonderful meals at a moment's notice."

"Well, thank you, Janice"—Helen smiled

politely—"but I did know you were coming. It was hardly a moment's notice."

"But with all the other things you do, I just don't know how you find the time, or energy." Janice sighed dramatically and took a delicate mouthful of cabbage. "I could never do what you do. Kate, I hope you appreciate what a wonderful person your mother is."

Kate shoved a large forkful of turkey into her mouth so she didn't need to reply, and nodded briefly. The woman was so stupid. And to think she was about to become her mother-in-law. Well, she certainly wasn't going to move in with them when she was old and incontinent. She was going into a home, whatever Richard thought of it.

"She's organized this wedding almost single-handedly," Janice went on, waving her fork in the air again. "You really owe her a lot, Kate. You'd never be in this situation without her."

Kate tried hard to swallow her turkey, at the same time forcing herself to keep staring at her plate so as not to show her feelings. She was aware of Richard stirring beside her.

"She knows that, Mum," he said quickly. "But Kate has done a lot of the wedding preparations herself, you know."

"Well, I know she's done *some* of it." Janice sniffed and speared a carrot. "I'm just saying how wonderful Helen has been…"

"I'm sorry, I feel sick…" Kate pushed her chair back with a clatter and hurried out of the room towards the stairs. Fully aware of five pairs of eyes following her, she took the stairs two at a time and burst into the bathroom, locking the door behind her. She leaned back against it and closed her eyes. It was partly true that she felt sick. The large mouthful of turkey was having a problem going down her throat, but the truth was, if she'd stayed there any longer she might well have done Janice some damage. The woman was just too infuriating! She made it perfectly clear that Kate wasn't good enough for her precious son, yet at the same time making out Kate's mother was some sort of domestic goddess. Which she really wasn't, as the dry turkey and soggy cabbage demonstrated.

Kate leant forward and spat the rest of the chewed turkey into the toilet, then wiped her mouth and pressed the flush. She stared at herself in the mirror. God, she looked a mess. It was surprising Richard even wanted to marry her. Maybe he'd change his mind. She closed her eyes and leant against the washbasin. Would she even care if he did? Yesterday she would have done. Wouldn't she?

"Kate?" A tentative tap on the door accompanied her mother's voice. "Kate, are you all right? Let me in."

"I'm fine, Mum." Kate sighed but made no move to open the door. "I'll be back down in a minute."

"No, let me in, Kate." Helen tapped again, this time more loudly. "I need to talk to you."

Muttering under her breath, Kate reluctantly unlocked the door and sat down on the edge of the bath. Helen came in and closed the door behind her. She surveyed her daughter severely.

"Really, darling, you can't just run off like that. It was very rude. Imagine how Janice and Martin felt."

"A lot better than if I'd thrown up on the table."

"You really felt sick?" Helen peered more closely at her. "Why?"

"Oh, I just put too much turkey in my mouth." Kate shrugged. "It was very dry."

"Hmm. That doesn't sound very convincing." Helen sat down on the edge of the bath next to her. "You can tell me, darling. It would certainly explain your bad mood."

"What?" Kate stared at her in surprise.

"If you're pregnant."

"Pregnant? Of course I'm not pregnant!" Kate got to her feet and stared at her mother in horror. "Wherever did you get that idea?"

"You've been moody and snappy all day." Helen shrugged. "And now you feel sick. You say it's not your time of the month, so what am I to think? It's okay if you are. You're getting married in a month."

"Well, I'm not!" Kate snapped crossly. "And the amount of time Richard and I actually get to spend together, I doubt I ever will be. Not that I want to be anyway. I'm just feeling a bit stressed. And Janice was driving me mad. Mum, she's so stupid, and quite obviously doesn't like me."

Helen stood up and tidied her hair in the mirror. "She is a little annoying, I agree, but of course she likes you. Mothers are often a bit possessive about their sons. That's all it is."

"But I shall be stuck with her as a mother-in-law for the rest of my life if I marry Richard. And then when she's old and incontinent she'll want to move in, and I shall say no, and we'll have a huge row…"

"*If* you marry Richard? Surely you mean *when*. It's a bit late for second thoughts. You're not having second thoughts, are you, Kate? Oh, please say you're not."

Kate felt her face begin to get hot and turned away

to look in the mirror. "No. No. Of course not. But I hate the idea of having that woman in my life."

"Well, that's not a good enough reason not to marry Richard." Helen put her hands on Kate's shoulders. "Now wipe your face, tidy your hair, and come back down again. You'll find a way to deal with Janice. When you're in love you can deal with anything."

Kate followed Helen slowly out of the bathroom and back down the stairs. Was she really in love? Or was she just in love with the idea of getting married? God, no, it certainly wasn't that. In fact, she could really do without the wedding bit. So it must be Richard. She really must be in love with Richard. Of course she was. What on earth was the matter with her? Just because she saw an old friend for an instant she'd started doubting her relationship? Her really solid relationship that she'd been in for three years. How shallow was that? Sam Somerville had never been interested in her like that anyway. And it wouldn't matter if he was. She was in love with Richard now. She was going to marry Richard and live as a lawyer's wife for the rest of her life. She paused on the bottom step. That was a very long time. She might live to be over a hundred. Great Aunt Hester had. She had lived to be a hundred and seven. That would be another eighty-one years. Eighty-one years married to the same person. She took a deep breath. Well, at least Janice would be long dead by then. And men didn't live as long as women, so she wouldn't actually be *married* for eighty-one years; she'd obviously be a widow for some of it. She had reached the dining room door, and paused again; was she actually wanting Richard to die before her? Well, obviously he would. He was nearly four years older, but she wasn't actually wishing him dead. She was just being practical. One needed to plan for these things.

Richard looked up as Kate walked in. "Are you all right, darling?" He pulled out her chair. "I was worried about you."

Kate sat down with a murmured apology, managing a small smile for Richard. He squeezed her leg gently and raised his eyebrows at her.

"I'm fine now. Sorry about that." Kate glanced around the table. "Just got a bit of turkey stuck. But I don't think I can eat any more." She pushed her plate slightly away from her, and sat with her hands in her lap.

"Well, I'm glad you're feeling better, Kate." Janice leaned around her husband. "But you're missing a treat here. This turkey is the best I've ever tasted. I hope you've been having some cooking lessons from your mother."

"She doesn't need to eat it if she doesn't want to." Helen frowned at Janice. "She's just been sick. And for the record, Kate can cook very well. She got an A at GCSE." She held out a dish. "Now would you like some more potatoes? They're beginning to go cold."

Chapter 4

"Oh, god, that was awful." Kate leaned back against the wall of the summer house and closed her eyes. "I'm so sorry, Richard. I didn't behave very well at all. I don't know what got into me. Now your parents will really hate me."

Richard chuckled and slipped his arm around her shoulders. "Stop worrying. They didn't like you anyway."

Kate's head shot up, and she stared at him suspiciously. "You're being serious, aren't you? I knew it…"

"Kate." He squeezed her shoulder. "No, of course I'm not being serious. But you know what they're like. No one's ever good enough for them. They can be very trying. Come on, let's walk down to the river."

Kate shook her head and brushed her hair back with a sigh. "Not now. I'm so tired. Can we just go and sit on the bench for a bit? Think I need an early night." She turned and led the way down the garden towards the wooden bench positioned to overlook the valley that lay behind the house. She sank down on the hard wooden seat and covered her face with her hands. "I shall be so glad when this is all over."

Richard sat down beside her and put his hand on her leg. "Not long now, darling. And once you've had your Hen Party, the time will fly by. This time next month we'll be lying on the beach in Barbados with nothing to think about except us."

Kate lowered her hands and leaned back. "I guess. But you'll still get e-mails from work, I bet. There's no way you'll be able to leave that behind, will you?"

"It won't bother you." Richard put his arm round her shoulders and pulled her closer to him. "I can't just abandon everything for two weeks, but I'll make sure it doesn't interfere with your holiday."

"*My* holiday? *My* holiday? That's the sort of thing I mean, Richard. It's *our* holiday. Our *honeymoon*. What is the point of having a honeymoon if one of the parties isn't fully committed to it? We may as well have a night in a cheap bed-and-breakfast and be done with it." Kate pulled away from him and got to her feet. "I'm going to bed. I'm far too grouchy to be good company, and if we keep talking we'll end up having a row."

"Kate, I'm sorry. I didn't mean it like that. Of course I'm committed to our honeymoon. We'll have a wonderful time. But you must understand I can't just abandon everything else. But I promise you it won't interfere." Richard followed her as she headed back to the house. "Please, Kate, I'm sorry."

Kate continued walking up the damp lawn and spoke over her shoulder. "I know. I know what you meant. But I meant what I said about being tired. I'm going to bed now, and we can talk tomorrow." She turned to look at him as they reached the back door. "And when can we next have a night together? It's been ages."

Richard caught her hands in his and pulled her close. "Soon, my love, soon. I'm so sorry I've been so busy, but it's that big case. We're in court all this week, and it may well spill over into next week, too, and you know I can't see you when it's like that." He bent forward and dropped a light kiss on her nose. "You'll have loads to do this week anyway, with the Hen Party and your sister coming over."

"Oh, right, bring her into it!" Kate pulled away and rolled her eyes. "Why she even has to be involved in the wedding I don't know. She'll only go and do something to ruin it."

"Why do you hate her so much?" Richard smiled at her in the darkness. "I get on fine with her."

"Well, you're the only one who does," Kate muttered darkly. "Even Mum and Dad find her difficult. You watch your back. If she's nice to you, it means she either fancies you or she's out to get you." She pushed open the back door and light flooded out from the kitchen. "Come on, I'd better say goodbye to your parents, I suppose. Then I really am going to bed, rude or not." Kate strode across the kitchen, leaving Richard to close and lock the door, and stuck her head around the living room door. Her parents were squashed together on the sofa, listening politely while Janice regaled them with some long-winded story. Every so often she appealed to Martin to back her up, and Kate couldn't help smiling at the expressions of complete bewilderment that adorned her parents' faces.

"I'm off to bed now," she chipped in when Janice paused for breath. "I'm still not feeling quite myself. Bye, Janice, bye, Martin. See you at the wedding."

"Oh, I'm sure we'll see you before then." Janice waved a hand in the air. "Still lots to sort out. And then there's your Hen Night, of course."

Kate stared at her in horror. Did the woman think

she was invited to that? Even her *own* mother wasn't coming to it. She licked her lips. "The Hen Night?" she managed. "What d'you mean?"

"Well, we'll want to hear all about it." Janice beamed at her. "Lots of pictures. And it's no good saying you'll put them on Facebook; you know Martin and I don't understand that. We want to see actual photographs."

"Right." Kate stared at her, wondering again how she could possibly have given birth to Richard. She backed out of the room. "Okay then. See you soon." She reversed into Richard, who caught her round the waist and kissed the top of her head.

"Night, darling. I'll call you tomorrow."

"Yeah." Kate nodded and gave him a tired smile. "You do that. Night." She scooped up her mobile from the hall table and made her way upstairs, pausing at the top to give a final wave to her fiancé. Then she walked into her bedroom and carefully closed the door behind her.

She stood for a moment savouring the tranquillity before she flung herself down on the bed and buried her face in the pillow. What the hell was wrong with her? The whole evening had been a nightmare, but she was well aware that her own behaviour had been atrocious. She rolled onto her back and stared up at the ceiling. The whole wedding thing had really got to her tonight. And that woman was just too much to bear. That she would be her mother-in-law if she married Richard was a very unsavoury idea. She pulled her knees up to her chest and hugged them tightly. There it was again. *If* she married Richard. Not *when* she married Richard. She was marrying him in less than four weeks' time.

Surely that was a "when," not an "if"? She loved him. She did. Even if his stupid job was driving her mad. They hadn't managed to spend a night together for nearly three weeks, due to his job, and she wondered just how many nights they would be spending apart after the wedding. Maybe he'd make her sleep in another room when he had a big case on? She sat up abruptly. That would never do. If anyone was going in a different room it would be him. She wasn't moving out of her own bedroom just because of his stupid job. He could sleep in the guest room. How dare he expect her to move out?

She got to her feet and pulled her dress over her head crossly, well aware that Richard hadn't, and probably never would, ask her to sleep in their as-yet-imaginary guest room. She knew she was being unfair and unreasonable, and decided that she really needed a good night's sleep to sort herself out. A really good night's sleep in which she definitely wouldn't dream about Sam Somerville and his gorgeous brown eyes. No, she would definitely not dream about him. She would dream about—she slid into bed and lay down, pulling the quilt up to her chin—she would dream about…anything except Sam Somerville. With a sigh she closed her eyes and reached out her arm to turn off the light. It would probably be better if she didn't dream about anything.

Chapter 5

Wednesday 1ˢᵗ July

"Kate, have you done those invoices yet?"

The voice cut through Kate's daydreaming and brought her back to reality with a jolt. Guiltily she rummaged through the papers on her desk, then peered intently at her computer screen.

"Nearly done," she called, frantically trying to locate the correct files. "I'll bring them through in just a sec."

"Well, if you would." The voice had a slight edge to it. "I did ask for them half an hour ago."

Kate rolled her eyes and began to fill out the invoices she had finally located. Oh, god, there were six she needed to do. Oh, why on earth hadn't she paid more attention? It was going to take her at least ten minutes, by which time her boss, quite rightly, would probably be breathing fire, and right down her neck. She sighed, hooked a loose strand of hair behind her ear, and got down to it.

Ever since the encounter with Sam at the fête on Sunday, Kate had been finding it hard to concentrate. She was loathe to admit, even to herself, that she had been affected by it so much, but she had barely been sleeping, and although she had assured her mother it was just pre-wedding nerves, she was pretty sure it was more to do with Sam.

She gritted her teeth as her fingers flew over the keys. And of course she hadn't seen Richard since Sunday either. That wasn't helping. With him absent, it left her mind completely free to focus on things it should really leave well alone. She finished filling in the invoices, pressed Print, then got to her feet and walked over to collect them when they came out of the printer.

Leaning against the wall while she waited, Kate wondered for the hundredth time whether she should look for a better job. She had been the sales secretary at the farm machinery outlet for five years now, ever since she finished at Uni, and she couldn't help feeling she was stuck in a rut. It was a very small firm, employing only about twenty people, and she knew them almost better than she knew herself. She knew when all their birthdays and anniversaries were, she knew who was sleeping with whom, who had a crush on whom, and in most cases what they were allergic to. Even her boss had the disconcerting habit of telling her all his marital problems, and she shuddered as she recalled the moment the week before when he'd opened up and asked her advice on his underwear. It seemed he felt it was inhibiting his sex life, and he valued her opinion. Kate had managed to escape fairly rapidly, but it had made her all the more determined to pursue a new career. But as usual she had done nothing about it.

With a sigh she rescued the invoices as the printer spat them viciously out and they floated towards the floor, then popped them into a folder and walked through to put them on her boss's desk.

"There you go." She slapped the folder down in

front of him. "The printer's playing up again. Shall I ask Gav to take another look at it?"

"If you would." The short balding man at the desk didn't even bother to look up. "And get me a coffee, will you, Kate? Thanks."

"Yes, sir," Kate muttered under her breath as she escaped the over-warm room out into the corridor. "And another job too, I think."

She wandered along to the staff room, heaved the door open with her bottom, and peered cautiously in. There was no one else there. Perfect. She could sneak a little break while she waited for the kettle to boil. She filled it with enough water to make both her and James, her boss, a coffee, then slumped down on the sofa and closed her eyes. Before she had time to get lost in her own thoughts, the door was flung open and someone bounced down onto the sofa next to her.

"Kate, what're you doing in here? Are you skiving?"

Wearily Kate opened her eyes to see the newest member of the office staff beaming at her. Holly had joined the firm straight from school a couple of weeks earlier, to work for the summer, and had only just turned sixteen. She was employed officially as assistant receptionist, but in reality she was a general dogsbody. She was nice enough but had a tendency to attach herself to Kate, who although ten years her senior, was the nearest in age to her. She was currently staring expectantly at Kate as if awaiting a bedtime story.

"No, Holly, I'm not skiving. I'm getting my boss a coffee. Just having a rest while I wait for the kettle. Why are you here?"

"Same." Holly nodded happily, her precariously

fastened topknot wobbling annoyingly. "I'm getting coffee for all the front office. They drink soooo much of it. I spend half my day in here."

Wondering silently how much that had to do with her co-workers need for caffeine and how much with their desire for a few minutes' peace, Kate smiled at the girl.

"Always the same when you're the new girl. You'll be running errands for everyone all summer."

The kettle clicked off, and Holly jumped to her feet. She carefully lined up four mugs and began to spoon instant coffee into them. Kate watched her for a moment, then made herself more comfortable on the sofa.

"Can you make mine too, Holl?" she said with a guilty grin. "I've just got comfy. Milk and sugar for James, and just milk for me."

"Course I will." Holly immediately rummaged in the cupboard for more mugs and spooned coffee into them. "I'm getting really good at making drinks." She poured the water in and stirred each mug rapidly, splashing a little coffee over the sides. "I bet you're really excited about your wedding now, aren't you? I'd be soooo excited I wouldn't be able to sleep." She turned round and beamed at Kate. "I mean, in less than a month you'll be committing yourself to spending the rest of your life with one person. Imagine that! The whole rest of your life! That could be—like—thirty years or something."

"Well, I hope it's a bit more than that," Kate murmured, shifting uneasily on her seat. "That sounds very final, when you put it like that. I see it more as—sharing my life with the man I love. Not being committed."

Holly handed Kate her coffee and bounced down onto the sofa beside her. "Wow. That sounds awesome. You must really love him. I can't imagine loving someone like that." She hesitated for a moment, her head on one side. "I think when I do—love someone, I mean—I think he'll be more interesting."

"More interesting than what?"

"Than your boyfriend. He's got a pretty boring job. I think I'd like to fall in love with an explorer or something. Or a sportsman, or an astronaut..." Holly blushed. "Oh, god, I'm soooo sorry. I didn't mean your boyfriend was boring. Well, maybe I *said* that, but I meant his *job* was boring. Oh, shut up, Holly!"

Kate gave a chuckle. "It's all right. Don't worry. I guess Richard's job isn't the most exciting in the world—well, not as exciting as an explorer, anyway—but I think it could be pretty interesting. He's my fiancé by the way, not my boyfriend."

"Oh, yeah." Holly took a long slurp of her coffee. "I guess he is. Sorry I said he was boring. I just think when I get married I want to travel the world with my husband, or something. Or go into space, of course."

"Of course." Kate couldn't help smiling. "Well, to be honest, if someone came along who could take me into space, I may well be tempted to go with him! Now I guess we'd better get back to work. Those coffees will be going cold."

****

Kate let herself in the front door and kicked her shoes into the corner. It looked like she was the first one home. She tossed her bag onto the hall table, headed straight for the kitchen, and poured herself a large glass of Pinot Grigio. She leaned back against the worktop and took a long, slow swig, closing her eyes and savouring the moment. Holly's words of earlier were still ringing in her ears, and she tried unsuccessfully to imagine Richard in the role of explorer, or even better, astronaut. He just didn't fit. He was a lawyer, and that was that. A very successful lawyer, she reminded herself. He was going to go far. He'd always told her that. But only far in terms of the law. He'd probably end up being a judge or something, and to be honest, that really didn't have the appeal of an explorer. He didn't even like the idea of a walk in the country very much, and she would certainly never get him to climb a mountain, or skate on a frozen river. Her eyes snapped open in surprise, and she took another swig of wine. Whatever had made her think of that? That had been a very long time ago. It wasn't very often one found a frozen river anyway. It had been pure fluke, that time when she and a few school friends had braved the unexpected cold spell and spent a brilliant hour or so sliding around on the river. She must ask Jen if she remembered it. That had been such fun. And of course Sam had been there. Sam was always up for a bit of fun.

She shook her head sharply, downed her wine in one gulp, and leaving the glass on the worktop, made her way upstairs to get changed. Her heart plummeted when she remembered her sister was coming down tonight. Her mother had arranged a final fitting for the bridesmaids' dresses, and both Vicky and Jen were coming over. Vicky had moaned about it, and Kate had had a moment when she actually thought she was going to refuse to be a bridesmaid, but unfortunately their mother had talked her round, and she had reluctantly agreed to pay them a visit for the evening. At least Jen would be there too, Kate thought as she pulled off her work clothes and rummaged in her cupboard for some jeans. The whole wedding thing was just becoming far too stressful, and the addition of her ghastly sister into the mix was just too much.

Angrily Kate pulled a blue strappy top over her head and wriggled into her jeans before freeing her hair from its clip and letting it cascade over her shoulders. She shook her head violently, then glanced at herself in the mirror. She looked nothing like the sensible secretary she had been all day, and nothing like the future wife of a judge. She looked far more like an explorer's wife, or better still an explorer herself. Why on earth did she keep thinking of herself in terms of someone's wife? God, it wasn't the nineteen fifties! She wasn't going to disappear and stop being her just because she was married. She would still be a person in her own right. Wouldn't she? Even her mother had a job. Maybe Richard would want her to give up work. Maybe he just wanted her to sit at home and look pretty for when he brought his colleagues home.

No. She scowled at herself in the mirror. She couldn't let that happen. If she decided to become an explorer, or take up extreme sports, then Richard couldn't stop her. Just like he couldn't make her sleep in the spare room when he had a big case on, or insist his mother live with them when she was old and incontinent. No, if she was going to marry him, it had to be on her terms.

With a sigh, she flopped down on the bed. There it was again. "If" she married him. The wedding was in less than four weeks. She probably ought to make up her mind.

With a frustrated snort, Kate leapt up again and glowered at herself in the mirror. Of course she was going to marry him. She loved him, didn't she? She'd just have to lay down a few ground rules before things went any further. She snatched up her phone and wrote a quick message to Richard.

Just to get a few things clear—I'm not giving up work when we get married, I'm not sleeping in the spare room when you have a big case, and your mother is not coming to live with us. Oh, and if I want to become an explorer, I will.

She pressed Send and watched until it said it had been delivered. There. That should put him right. So long as he agreed to all that, she would marry him. While she was still staring at the screen, his reply appeared.

Kate? Have you been drinking? Of course you mustn't give up work, we need the money. I would never throw you out of our bedroom. I shall sleep in the spare room when I have a big case, and why on earth would my mother want to come and live with us? I also think you may be better suited to being a secretary than an explorer. Love you, darling. See you soon.

Kate stared at the message in disbelief. He really didn't understand at all. Him sleeping in the spare room was just as bad, and how dare he say she couldn't become an explorer? How on earth did he know she wouldn't be very good at it? He thought she was better suited to be a secretary. Did she really think she wanted to be a secretary all her life? That was just a temporary job until she found her vocation. She paused and sat down on the bed again. A temporary job that had lasted five years. But it was still temporary. She could leave anytime she wanted. And she would. Very soon. That'd show him. Her phone bleeped again, and she glanced down at it. It was Jen this time.

Are you home? Can I come over now?

Kate sent an instant reply.

Yes. Please do.

Maybe she shouldn't reply to Richard just now. Not while she was feeling so annoyed with him. That probably wouldn't help anything. She'd talk it through with Jen, who usually knew what to say to make it all better. With a sigh, Kate got up and headed back downstairs to the kitchen. She retrieved her glass and topped it up until it was almost overflowing, then got another one out of the dishwasher, ready for Jenny. If only Vicky wasn't coming over, the evening might be rather fun. But as usual her sister would probably spoil it in some way. Just by being there. Thank god she didn't live at home any more.

Kate poured a glass of wine for Jenny, carried them both through into the conservatory, and curled up in one of the cushioned wicker chairs. She tucked her feet up underneath her and slowly sipped her drink. If she wasn't getting married and moving out anyway, it was probably time she thought about getting a place of her own too. Vicky had never moved back in after Uni, so although she was nearly two years younger than Kate, she had lived in her own place in Bristol for three years. Well, it wasn't really her place, of course. She shared it with three other girls.

Kate heard the front door knock, then open.

"Kate? I'm here."

"I'm in the conservatory!" Kate watched the door as her best friend appeared, lugging a large green carrier bag.

"I've brought goodies," Jenny announced, dumping the bag on the floor and flopping down onto a wicker chair. "Thought we might need more wine to survive Vicky. And chocolate."

"You're a life saver." Kate handed her the glass of wine with a grin. "I've been dreading tonight, but with you and lots of goodies it may just be bearable."

"She's not that bad." Jenny flicked her long blonde hair over her shoulder and took a large gulp of wine. "You shouldn't let her get to you so much. Is she staying the night?"

"Yeah. Mum insisted. She's going back first thing tomorrow, though. She has work."

"God, you sound really miserable. Is it just Vicky, or is there something else?" Jenny watched her over the rim of her glass.

"Oh, everything!" Kate wriggled in frustration. "I hate this wedding. And Richard's going to sleep in the spare room, and he thinks I should be a secretary forever and not become an explorer."

There was a short silence, then Jenny cleared her throat. "Okay. How many wines have you had?"

"Oh, god, not you too! That's what Richard said. I haven't been drinking. I'm just not explaining it very well."

"Probably not," Jenny agreed, her lips twitching. "I had no idea you wanted to be an explorer, and why is he sleeping in the spare room? I thought your parents were okay with him staying over?"

"No, no, not here. When we have our own house.

He's going to sleep in the spare room when he has a big case… It's a long story. And I don't really want to become an explorer, but that's not the point. He says I'd be a better secretary and I should keep doing that."

"Okay."

"No, it's not okay. I feel like I'm going to lose my identity if we get married. He'll want to turn me into a clone of his mother. I can't let him do that."

"Kate, calm down! Where on earth is all this coming from? And what d'you mean 'if' you marry him? Kate, you're not actually having second thoughts, are you? Is this to do with Sam Somerville? Tell me it's not!"

"Of course not." Kate closed her eyes and curled up even tighter in her chair. "Of course I'm going to marry Richard, but I don't want to stop being me. This is all Holly's fault."

"Holly?"

"The new girl at work." Kate opened her eyes and glanced over at Jenny. "You know, that really young one. She's just finished her GCSEs. Well, she said that when she gets married she wants to marry someone more interesting than Richard. Like an explorer or an astronaut. And that got me thinking about just how boring he really is. Am I ready to be a boring wife?"

"You don't need to be boring, just because Richard is." Jenny sat forward and stared at Kate. "You can still be you. He won't want to change you—he fell in love with you as you are."

"So you agree he's boring?"

"I didn't say that." Jenny ran a hand through her hair in frustration. "Well, maybe I did—but I didn't mean that. Richard loves you as you are, Kate. You know that. And he'd love you whatever job you did. He probably thought he was being nice, saying you were a good secretary."

"Yeah, well, that's the point. If he knew me at all, he'd know that wouldn't make me happy. Surely he knows I'm only doing that until I find my vocation?"

"Maybe he doesn't. Have you ever told him? You'd been doing that job for two years when you met him. He probably thinks you like it."

Kate stared at her for a moment, then picked up her wine and finished it in a single gulp. "I need chocolate. What have you brought?"

"Take your pick." Jenny held out the bag to her. "I got a selection."

Kate peered into the bag and pulled out a large bar of nut chocolate. She broke a piece off and stuffed it into her mouth. "D'you remember the skating?"

"What?"

"The skating on the frozen river. D'you remember it?"

"Yeah, of course. That was fun. Whatever made you think of that? That was years ago."

"Richard would never do that. He's just not spontaneous. And he doesn't really like doing outdoor stuff. He'd think it was silly."

"Kate, we were about fifteen. I'm sure he would have done it at that age."

"Maybe, but he wouldn't do it now. I would, you would. And Sam would."

"So this *is* about Sam. Kate, you mustn't go there. Leave him alone. He's not for you."

"It's not about Sam. It just made me compare them. I don't want Sam Somerville any more. That was all years ago, but he was always fun. Richard just isn't fun at all, really. He's too…grown up. Jen, I'm not ready to be grown up. I'm not sure I ever will be."

"You've just got pre-wedding nerves." Jenny was watching Kate closely. "You know you love Richard, and—be honest—would you really want him to be reckless and childish?"

"Maybe I would." Kate folded her arms sulkily. "That's the problem. I just don't know anymore. And I need to know. I'm getting married in just over three weeks."

"Yes, you are. And that's why you're feeling the way you are. It's just a panic. Perfectly normal. You know Richard is right for you. You've been planning this for a year now. Don't you think you'd have noticed before if he wasn't the right person for you? Every bride feels like this." Jenny nodded with confidence. "My sister did. And my cousin. And both of them are still happily married. Well, my sister is. And my cousin is too, just not to the same person…"

"Really, Jen, that's not helping." Kate leaned forward and rummaged in the chocolate bag again. "But I guess you're probably right. It *is* just nerves. Mum'll be back soon. I'd better get more in the wedding-y mood, I suppose."

"That's the spirit," Jenny said encouragingly. "You can't let Vicky see you're panicking. She'll never let you forget it."

Kate rolled her eyes and peeled back the wrapper from a Flake. "Oh, god, I'd forgotten about her. She'll be moaning all the time, of course. She doesn't like the colour or the style of the bridesmaids' dresses. I told her she can have what she wants at her own wedding, and she laughed and said she'd never do anything so lame as get married. And I still can't understand why Richard likes her."

Jenny giggled. "Well, she does look a lot like you. Maybe she's just his type."

"His type?" Kate snorted. "Yeah, right. She'd have him for breakfast. She can't stand any authority figure, and I'm pretty sure a lawyer counts as that. They do seem to be able to talk to each other, though. I hate that."

"She's just doing it to annoy you." Jenny got to her feet. "Now come on, I want to know what you're doing with your hair for the wedding. Can we go and play about with it before the others get here?"

"Oh, I don't want anything special." Kate stood up and scooped up the bag of chocolate. "I want it loose with some flowers in it. You know it's not me to have it all fancy."

"Okay, let's go to your room and have a play with it. I may wear mine up."

****

Kate stared at her sister with ill-concealed dislike. Ever since Vicky had arrived, late as usual, just as the dressmaker was about to give up and go home, the atmosphere had been charged with tension. As she watched the girls being pinned into their simple pale blue dresses, Kate had found herself wishing once again that it was just Jenny who would be preceding her down the aisle. It was true that Vicky did look like her, and to have a slightly taller, slightly thinner and slightly younger version of herself prancing before her into the church made her stomach churn. It would be Vicky that Richard saw first. Vicky that would be sticking in his mind when Kate finally appeared, and then he'd be disappointed. No wonder he liked talking to Vicky when she was so much younger, prettier, and thinner. And she had a better job. A proper career, not just a temporary job as a secretary.

"God, Kate, these dresses are such a cliché. No one wears stuff like this any more. Most people let their bridesmaids wear whatever they want."

Kate took a deep breath. "No, they don't, Vicky. You have no idea what you're talking about. If you don't want to wear the frigging dress, then go away and don't bother to come to the wedding. If you *are* insisting on coming, then shut up and do as you're told."

Helen glanced between her daughters and tutted loudly. "Girls, please. Stop bickering. Vicky, these are lovely dresses. Now stand still and let's get this finished. Kate darling, are you okay? You look a little flushed."

"I'm fine," Kate snapped. "Or I would be if *she* wasn't here. Does she *have* to stay the night?"

"Kate!" Helen frowned at her. "Of course she must stay the night. I thought we could all have a bit of a girly evening after this, and if Vicky was going to drive back, she wouldn't be able to have any wine. She can leave early in the morning."

"I've already had wine." Vicky twisted round and smirked at Kate. "Needed a glass before I had to see your face."

"Right, that's it!" Kate marched over and started to undo her sister's dress. "You are *not* being my bridesmaid. You are going to completely ruin my wedding, and I'm stressed enough about it already.

Take that off and get out."

"Kate!" Helen stepped forward and caught her hand as it was struggling with the zip on Vicky's dress. "What are you doing? Of course Vicky is going to be your bridesmaid. She's your sister. And if she's already had wine, I'm not letting her drive back to Bristol. Jenny, take Kate into the kitchen and sort out some snacks for after the dress fitting. We're nearly finished here."

Jenny finished slipping out of her dress and pulled her T-shirt and jeans back on. "Okay, Helen, and would you like a glass of wine?"

"Yes, please, love, that would be nice."

Sulkily Kate followed her friend into the kitchen and shut the door behind them. "I hate her, Jen. I truly hate her! I don't want her at my wedding. She's going to ruin everything."

Jenny handed her a very large glass of wine. "I know," she soothed. "She's a nightmare. But she won't spoil the wedding. She wouldn't dare, not with your mum and dad there. Where do you keep the bowls?"

Kate waved vaguely towards a corner cupboard and perched on the end of the table, cradling her wine in both hands. "Richard will see her first and then be disappointed when he sees me. That's what she wants. You know that."

"Chill out. You're just nervous." Jenny poured a packet of pretzels into a soup bowl. "Vicky always winds you up. She doesn't want Richard, and he certainly doesn't want her. And why on earth would you think he'd be disappointed when he sees you? You're gorgeous. Much prettier than Vicky. She wears too much makeup, and I think she's too thin."

Kate watched her over the rim of her wineglass. "Thanks, Jen. You always know what to say. I guess I *am* just nervous. It's all getting so close and so real now. And I just never seem to get to spend any time with Richard. It would be much easier to remember how much I love him if I ever saw him! We haven't had sex for weeks."

"Too much information!" Jenny held up her hand. "I may be your best friend, but there are some limits. When are you next seeing him?"

Kate shrugged. "Dunno. Not before the weekend, obviously. He's always so busy, and it's all a bit private, so he can't even talk to me about his cases. I know he has to go up to London sometime soon for some really high-profile one. I shall have forgotten what he looks like by the wedding."

"Better carry a photo around with you." Jenny giggled and poured a glass of wine ready for Helen. "How's your mum being with all the wedding stuff? Is she stressing you too?"

"She's been pretty good, really." Kate nodded. "She thrives on that sort of thing. The only problem with her is the fact that she seems to be convinced I'm pregnant."

"What? Why on earth does she think that?"

"Oh, it was at the weekend. I was in a weird mood after seeing Sam at the fête, and then we had Richard's parents over, and you know what they do to me. I got a bit snappy and stroppy, and then I was nearly sick during dinner. She followed me to the bathroom and told me it was okay if I was pregnant because the wedding was so soon. I couldn't seem to convince her I wasn't. She still keeps giving me knowing looks. We haven't had sex for so long that if I *was* pregnant I'd be showing by now!" She paused and stared at Jenny in horror. "Oh, god, maybe that's it. Maybe she thinks I look fat. Do I look fat? Is that what she meant?"

"Of course you don't look fat." Jenny giggled. "You're just right. And you wouldn't fit into your dress if you'd put on weight, and that still fits perfectly."

"Okay." Kate was slightly mollified. "Well, I just wish we could talk about something other than the wedding, or Richard, or periods, or pregnancy. I want to get on with my life. And I need a new job."

"As an explorer?"

"Don't take the piss. No, maybe not, but something more exciting than a secretary. Or even a secretary to someone more exciting. You know, PA to a millionaire or something. Someone with a yacht."

"Richard should be able to afford a yacht soon. Certainly by the time he becomes a judge or whatever these lawyers end up as. Can you imagine him in one of those silly wigs?"

"He already has to wear one of those small wigs when he's in court." Kate grinned. "I think they look even more stupid. Can't tell him that, though. Yeah, he makes a lot of money. Maybe we could get a yacht one day."

The kitchen door opened, and Vicky's head appeared.

"Sorry, Kate. I was just trying to wind you up, and Mum says I need to apologise. The dresses aren't that bad, I guess. Now Mum wants her wine, and can we eat something?"

Kate looked at her suspiciously, but nodded and picked up a couple of bowls of crisps and nuts. Jenny handed a glass of wine to Vicky, then picked up the one for Helen and ushered the sisters back towards the conservatory.

"That's better," she said. "Let's see if we can have a civilised evening, shall we? If Kate's going to survive this wedding, we all need to get on."

"Survive?" Vicky looked over her shoulder at Kate. "Not panicking, are you? It's meant to be a happy occasion, isn't it, not something to survive?"

"No, I'm not panicking, and I'm not pregnant, whatever Mum tells you. Just a bit stressed with all the arrangements. And I never seem to get to see Richard any more."

"Mum thinks you're pregnant?" Vicky stared at her in surprise. "Why ever does she think that?"

"It's a long story, but I'm not." Kate scowled at her. "And I never will be unless we can spend some time together."

"Do you want to be, then?" Vicky slumped down on the sofa and took a handful of peanuts. "Do you want babies?"

"Maybe one day." Kate curled up in her favourite chair and popped a pretzel in her mouth. "But not for years and years. I want a career first." She stared at Jenny, daring her to say anything about explorers.

"Yeah, you really should get a proper job." Vicky smirked. "Are you still pretending that secretary job is just temporary?"

"It is temporary." Kate scowled at her. "But I'm not going to argue with you tonight. That's not fair on Mum and Jen. Now have some more peanuts and shut up." She thrust the bowl at her sister, privately hoping she'd choke on them.

"Well, this is nice." Helen walked in and beamed at them all. "All girls together. Has everyone got some wine?"

"Yes, thanks, Helen." Jenny smiled at her. "What have you done with Peter tonight?" She peered around as if expecting Kate's father to be hiding in the corner.

"Oh, he's gone to the golf club with his friends. He won't be back till late. Gives us lots of time for girly wedding chatter." Helen glanced over at her daughters. "Are you two getting on now?"

"We're fine." Vicky smiled angelically. "I said sorry about the dress."

"Good girl. And Kate, are you feeling okay? You still look a bit flushed."

"Mum, I'm fine. It's a hot day." Kate wriggled uncomfortably and scooped up a handful of nuts.

"So what's happening on Friday, then?" Vicky was watching her with amusement. "Where are we going for this Hen do?"

"It's a surprise," Jenny said. "Kate doesn't know anything yet. I'll tell you later, on your own, if you like."

"Nah, don't bother. Is Richard having his Stag the same night? Hope you don't bump into each other."

"No, he's having his next weekend. They're going to Bristol for it, for some reason."

"Bristol? Maybe *I'll* bump into them, then!" Vicky chuckled, her eyes sparkling evilly. "Any idea where they're going?"

"None at all." Kate looked warily at her sister. "You can't join them. It's a Stag party, remember? Just him and his mates. I dread to think what they'll be doing." She paused and shrugged. "Although knowing

Richard, it won't be anything very exciting. They'll probably go for an Indian or something."

"Richard won't be arranging it, remember?" Jenny pointed out. "His best man will be. Maybe he'll book something more exciting."

"They could go skydiving," Vicky suggested.

"Yeah, right! Richard won't even go on the swings in the park."

"Well, he told *me* he'd always fancied skydiving." Vicky shrugged and popped a pretzel into her mouth. "Seems like a good opportunity to do it."

"When did he tell you that?" Kate stared at her in amazement.

"Oh, I dunno. Last time we were both here for dinner, I guess. Few months back."

"Well, I think he was probably joking." Kate leaned over and topped up her wine. "That's not his sort of thing at all. He was probably just being polite. Now can we talk about something else? Something not to do with the wedding?"

Chapter 6

Thursday 2nd July

Kate stared at herself in the mirror in frustration. Her hair had gone frizzy again. Why was it that every time it really mattered, her hair let her down? When she was at work it invariably looked lovely, but now when she was getting ready to go out it looked like she'd had an electric shock. With a sigh, she pulled the straighteners out of the cupboard and plugged them in. Good job she'd given herself plenty of time to get ready.

She knelt down on the floor in front of the long mirror and peered closely at her face. At least she had no spots, and so far her mascara hadn't smudged. Vicky's mascara never seemed to smudge. Vicky's hair never frizzed, either. She picked up the straighteners and tested the heat. They were pretty much ready, so she started with her fringe and set about making her hair presentable.

She was very happy with what she was wearing— faded skinny jeans and her favourite green strappy top. She would take a cardigan with her in case it got chilly later, but judging by the weather at the moment she probably wouldn't need it. It had been almost unbearably hot at work, and she had ended up taking several illicit breaks in the staff room, hanging as far out the window as she could safely manage. Holly had joined her once or twice and had succeeded in messing with her head again. She really had to stop talking to the girl.

And of course tonight was messing with her head too. She wasn't really sure why she was going. She knew full well she shouldn't be—borne out by the fact that she'd actually let Jen believe she wasn't. But how could she not go? The chance of a date with Sam Somerville—well, okay, it wasn't really a date—was too much to pass up. She had been waiting ten years for that, and however illicit it now was, she wasn't about to miss it.

She turned off the straighteners and glanced in the mirror. That was better. Her dark brown hair was now hanging tamed and glossy over her shoulders, her fringe just the right length for once, if a little uneven. She really ought to go to the hairdressers more often, and stop cutting it herself. Standing up, she slipped her feet into her green flats and posed in front of the mirror.

"You look good, girl," she murmured. "Even better than you did in sixth form. He won't be able to resist you." Grinning to herself and feeling extremely naughty, Kate slipped a couple of bangles onto her wrist, fastened a string of multicoloured beads around her neck, and put in matching earrings. She snatched up her bag and cardigan—just in case—and headed back downstairs. "I'm off now, Mum. Don't wait up."

Helen appeared in the kitchen doorway, wiping her hands on a tea towel. "Okay, love. Where is it you're going?"

"Oh, just out with a friend." Kate waved a hand vaguely and pulled open the front door. "I have my key."

"Well, be careful. Remember it's your Hen Party tomorrow."

"As if I'd be allowed to forget that," Kate muttered to herself as she started down the path, leaving the front door to bang shut behind her. But tonight she was going to do just that. Tonight was about her. Not about the wedding, not about the Hen Party, not about Richard. Certainly not about Richard. It was about her. And Sam Somerville. Of course she'd have to tell him she was getting married, but she could at least have a couple of drinks with him first. It didn't need to be the first thing she told him, and since she wasn't wearing her ring, he wouldn't have any reason to ask her.

As she set off down the road towards the park gates, her phone started to sing to her. She fished it out and glanced at the screen. It was Jenny. She turned it to silent and dropped it back into her bag. Sorry, Jen, can't risk you talking me out of this, she thought guiltily, mentally promising to confess to her the next day.

It was nearly five to seven when she arrived at the park gates, and the only people in sight were a teenage couple snogging in the trees. Kate leant against the railings and tried to steady her breathing. At least she had arrived first. She was bound to do that, of course; she was always early for everything. Quite strange, really, considering her normally disorganised lifestyle, but being on time seemed to come naturally. Maybe she *was* as boring as Richard. He was always early too.

She shook her head to get rid of the image of her fiancé and took a deep breath. Suppose Sam didn't turn up? Suppose he had forgotten? She was going to look really silly standing at the park gates for hours. Because how could she be sure he wasn't just going to be late? From what she remembered of him, he was usually late. She'd need to wait for quite a while to be sure. She glanced at the time. It was still two minutes to seven. He wasn't late yet. She closed her eyes and tried to think of something neutral. Buttered toast. That would do. Concentrate on buttered toast…

"Katy? Are you all right?"

Shocked back to reality by his voice, Kate's eyes snapped open, and she stood up straight. "Fine. Thank you. Just thinking about toast." She felt her face begin to redden as she realised just how gauche and stupid she must sound. "Hello."

Sam smiled down at her, his deep brown eyes crinkling alluringly at the corners. "Hello. It's so good to see you again. Properly this time. You look great."

"Thank you. So do you." Kate took in his ripped jeans, faded black T-shirt, open blue-checked shirt and very old black Converse, and her heart did a minor flip. He looked just as he had at eighteen. His hair was a bit longer, had got tucked into his collar at the back, and flopped over his forehead in a most distracting manner.

"Shall we go?"

"Yeah. Sure. Where are we going? We don't have to stay in the village, do we?"

"Not if you don't want to." Sam looked at her quizzically. "I thought we might drive out to a little pub I found the other day. It's in the middle of nowhere."

"Sounds great." Kate smiled up at him, finding it hard to tear her eyes away from his. "Do you have a car?"

"Of course." Sam chuckled. "I'm not eighteen any more. Come on, it's over here." He set off down the road towards a tatty green Land Rover that was parked at the roadside. "Here we are. Hop in." He pulled open the passenger door for her, then ran round and got into the driver's seat.

Kate stifled a smile as she noted the very old and tatty interior of the vehicle. Somehow it was typical of Sam. Just what she would have expected. She reached up to pull her seatbelt around her. It didn't move. She tried again. Still nothing.

"Sam?"

He glanced over, his eyebrows raised.

"The seatbelt won't work."

"Ah. There's a knack. Let me." He leaned across her and gave the belt a sharp tug, his thick hair brushing against her cheek. The belt gave way with a crunch, and he handed it to Kate. "There you go. Should be fine now."

She took it out of his hand and pulled it across her body, her face still tingling from the touch of his hair, and her body tingling from his familiar male aroma. God, he smelled good! She fastened the seatbelt, then leaned back in her seat and took a deep breath. This had been a Very Bad Idea. She'd better just have one drink, then ask to go home. She must think of an excuse. She had only been in his presence for about five minutes, and she was already behaving like a lovesick teenager and not the sensible engaged woman that she was. And she must tell him that. Immediately. She glanced sideways at him as he drove. His hair was flopping across his forehead again, and even from the side his eyes were compelling. She had forgotten just how attractive he was. Maybe she should make up an excuse right away. Before they even got to the pub.

"Have you eaten?" Sam's voice jolted Kate out of her reverie, and she jumped.

"What?"

"Have you had dinner, or shall we eat at the pub? Their menu is pretty good."

"Umm…well, no, I haven't actually had dinner…"

"Cool. I've been wanting to try the food there. My treat."

"Oh, no. I can't let you do that." Kate began to panic. It was suddenly turning into even more of a date. She couldn't let him buy her dinner. "Maybe I should just go home. If you're going to eat…"

Sam stared at her in surprise. "Whatever for? If you want to pay for yourself, be my guest. I didn't mean to make you uncomfortable. Is there a problem?"

Kate looked away. "No, no, of course not. I'm sorry. I just felt a bit… Take no notice. I'm just being silly. You can pay for dinner if you like. I never turn down free food."

Sam gave a bark of laughter and put his foot down as they left the village. "You haven't changed. You always seemed to be eating when we were at school. Surprised you never put on weight." He glanced at her again. "And I can see you haven't. You look just the same."

Kate gave a small smile and gripped her hands tightly together on her lap. She would have to have dinner with him now, then. But she would make her excuses straight afterwards. She really couldn't risk staying in his company for too long. He probably wouldn't want her to, once she told him about Richard, anyway. Or maybe it wouldn't matter to him. Maybe he just wanted to be friends. Maybe she was presuming too much. She leaned back and closed her eyes. Jen was going to be so cross with her. Perhaps she wouldn't actually tell her.

Ten minutes later they drew up into the car park of a low, rambling, thatched building covered in ivy. A chalkboard outside proclaimed they were serving food, and a small garden that ran down to the river, to the rear of the pub, was set with umbrella'd tables.

"This looks nice." Kate stared around in appreciation.

"I think so." Sam reversed the Land Rover into the corner of the car park and turned off the engine. "It's so hot. Shall we sit in the garden?"

"Yes, please. I've been too hot and cooped up in an office all day." Kate opened the car door. "I'd love to sit outside."

The inside of the pub was as nice as the exterior, and Kate very quickly chose lasagne from the menu, realising she was extremely hungry. Sam ordered fish and chips, then got them both drinks, which they carried back out into the garden and selected a table with a lovely view of the river and the fields beyond.

"I had no idea this was here." Kate gazed around her. "And it's so close to home."

"Yeah. Quite a find, eh?" Sam looked very pleased with himself, and Kate found herself grinning. He hadn't changed at all. He was still the carefree, relaxed, and totally gorgeous Sam Somerville he had been all those years ago.

Which was really rather a problem. Over the previous couple of days Kate had managed to convince herself she was completely unfazed by Sam's return, and that she was looking forward to marrying Richard.

Now she felt as if her world was turning upside down. If she still had feelings for Sam, how could she marry Richard? Was it fair to any of them?

She glanced over at him. Maybe it was just a crush, though. Like one had on a rock star. After all, he had made no suggestion that he actually wanted to ask her out. He never had done. The madly-in-love part had all been on her side. So it would be very silly of her to ditch Richard just in case her high school crush wanted to ask her out after eight years. And anyway, she loved Richard. Of course she did.

"Penny for them?"

"What?" Kate stared at Sam in confusion.

"Penny for your thoughts. You looked miles away."

"Oh, right. Yeah I was. A bit. This is so weird. And so nice too. You must have so many stories to tell about your travels. I really don't even know where you've been. I think you were in Australia last time I heard from you."

Sam ran a hand through his thick hair. "Wow. Yeah, Australia. That was a long time ago. Been loads of places since then. I'll tell you all about it while we eat. But what about you? What are you up to? Did you get your degree? I expect you have a glittering career by now."

Kate rolled her eyes. "Oh, you'd think so, wouldn't you? I leave Uni with a very good English Lit degree, and what do I end up doing? I'm a secretary for a firm that sells tractors. I took the job as a temporary thing until I found what I really wanted to do, and I'm still there five years later." She looked up at Sam. "It's still temporary, though. I don't intend to stay. I just haven't found my vocation yet."

"That's cool." He leaned back and stretched his long legs out in front of him. "Means you can leave whenever you want without worrying about it. You're much freer than if you were doing a job you cared about." He grinned at her. "So you could decide to explore the Amazon basin or something, and there'd be nothing to stop you."

Kate stared at him in amazement. How could he possibly know she had been thinking about explorers? Was he reading her mind?

"Yeah. I've been thinking about moving on. I'm really bored at the moment. Exploring the Amazon sounds fun."

"It is." Sam flicked his hair back off his face. "I was there about two years ago. Amazing place. You'd love it."

"You've explored the Amazon basin?" Kate could hardly get the words out. "You're an explorer?"

Sam threw back his head and roared with laughter. "Hardly! I just spent some time in South America, and that was one of the places I went to. Been to Machu Pichu, too. Bet you'd like that."

Kate felt her face flame as she realised just how gauche she must have sounded asking if he was an explorer. He'd never take her seriously now. He must think she was a complete idiot. Which of course is exactly what she was or she wouldn't be sitting in a pub garden with Sam Somerville just three weeks before her wedding.

"Katy? Are you all right?"

"Yes, sorry. Just realised how silly I must have sounded. I'd love to see South America, especially

Machu Pichu. Were you there long?"

"About eighteen months. It was one of my favourite places, actually. I managed to travel pretty much everywhere. Picked up quite a lot of Spanish, too."

The food arrived at that moment, and they spent a few minutes in silence, each concentrating on their meal. After a while Sam looked up.

"So apart from the boring temporary job, how are you?"

Kate swallowed a large mouthful of lasagne and washed it down with her wine. "Fine, thanks. Looking for another job, but fine."

"Still best friends with Jen, I guess?"

"Yep. Always will be, I reckon. She's good."

He paused for a moment and moved some chips around on his plate. "And…are you seeing anyone? At the moment. Anyone special?"

Kate carefully finished her mouthful and wiped her mouth on her napkin. Then she laid down her fork and took a deep breath. "No one special," she found herself saying. "Yeah, I am seeing someone, but it's not serious. I don't think it'll go anywhere."

Sam nodded and dipped a chip in the pile of mayonnaise on the side of his plate. "Okay. Good to know. How long have you been together?"

"Not long. I told you it's not serious. How about you?"

"No. No one. Not for a long time." Sam stared at her intently. "You seem a bit distracted. Are you sure you're okay?"

"God, you sound like my mother!" Kate scowled at him. "I'm fine. Just a bit tired. It's very nice to see you, though. And thanks for dinner."

"You can pay next time." Sam popped a chip in his mouth and raised his eyebrows at her. "Since you have a job and I don't. Hoping to get one soon, though."

"Next time?" Kate's heart began to thump painfully in her chest.

"Well, now I'm back, I hope we can hang out a bit? I've really missed you, Katy. I'm sorry I was away so long."

"I've missed you, too." Kate's throat felt tight. "But I understand why you went." *Without me*, her brain was shouting silently. *I understand why you went off and left me for eight years. But why did you have to come back now? Right now. The worst possible time.* Kate watched him as he wiped his plate clean with his bread. Or was it the worst possible time? Maybe it was just in the nick of time. If he'd come back next month, after she was married, it would have been even worse.

She bit her lip. What the hell was she thinking? This made no difference. She was still marrying Richard. In three weeks and two days. She would be Mrs. Cresswell and would cease to be herself. But she loved Richard. That was why she was marrying him. What she felt for Sam was just a crush. Just like it had been all those years ago. He hadn't wanted her then, and he wouldn't want her now.

She sneaked another glance at him, and he caught her eye. He grinned at her, and his deep brown eyes burned with some emotion she couldn't quite identify, but it made her stomach turn over. Suppose he really did want her now? What should she do? She really shouldn't have lied about Richard. She found it hard to believe she had actually done that, and her head began to spin as she visualised the possible repercussions.

"Well, that was nice." Sam put his knife and fork tidily on his plate. "I thought it would be. D'you want a pudding? I seem to remember you were obsessed with chocolate."

Despite the turmoil in her brain, Kate managed a smile. "Still am. Yeah, I could probably manage a small piece of cake or something. Will you have one?"

"Maybe. Let's see what they have." Sam got to his feet and headed off into the pub to get a menu. Kate watched him go, unable to keep her eyes off him. God, she was in a mess. How could she have let herself get into this situation? She was having dinner with the man she had had a crush on for years, three weeks before her wedding to one of the most boring men on the planet, and she'd lied about it. In a moment of panic, she fished her phone out of her bag and started to write a message to Jenny.

I'm having dinner with Sam. This is a mistake. I need your help. Think I've been stupid.

She pressed Send, then dropped the phone back into her bag. Although what she thought Jen could do she had no idea. Apart from agree she had been stupid. She could hardly work it out for her. That was something only she herself could do.

"There you go." A laminated menu appeared over her shoulder, and Kate reached up and took it. "They have several chocolaty things you might like." Sam sat down and grinned at her. "Personally, I fancy the treacle tart."

Kate scanned the card, her mind not really taking anything in. Eventually her eyes lit upon profiteroles and she pointed to them. "I'll have those," she said, handing the card back to Sam. "If that's okay?"

"Of course." He shrugged. "You can have what you like. You obviously never put on weight, so knock yourself out." He got up again and went back in to place the order, leaving Kate once more struggling with her feelings and her conscience.

She checked her phone, but there was no reply from Jen, and in fact she realised she had lost the signal and her original message still hadn't sent. She waved the phone around a bit, but it failed to register, so she dropped it into her bag and closed her eyes. She may as well just enjoy the rest of the evening. Everything would work out in the end. It usually did. Jenny would sort it.

By ten o'clock they had finished eating, talked about all the things that had happened to them in the last eight years, and generally had a very nice evening. Kate had begun to relax after her second glass of wine, and decided she would confess everything to Jenny in the morning and see what she thought. Her biggest crime was lying about Richard, and she realised it would get found out eventually, so she really needed to sort it. But not tonight. She didn't want anything to spoil tonight. She had waited ten years for a date with Sam Somerville, and she wasn't about to waste it by admitting she was engaged to someone else.

"This has been fun." Sam stretched and yawned. "We must do it again sometime. When are you next free?"

Kate felt her face begin to flame and made a pretence of looking in her bag. "Umm...not sure. Not tomorrow, of course."

"No, not tomorrow," Sam agreed. "You have that

Hen party, don't you? Is it anyone I know?"

"Er…no. No, I don't think so." Kate hurried to change the subject. "I'm free on Saturday, if you like. But you probably didn't mean that soon…"

"Saturday is good." Sam nodded. "I've still got loads to tell you about my travels. If you're interested, that is?" He suddenly sounded vulnerable, and Kate smiled.

"Of course I'm interested. I loved hearing about them tonight. Okay then, what do you want to do?"

"We could maybe come here again, if you like? Unless you'll be hung over from tomorrow?"

"Of course not." Kate sniffed. "I very rarely drink too much these days. Couple of glasses of wine will do me fine." She thought guiltily back to the night before, when she had polished off the best part of a bottle. But that had been Vicky's fault. If she hadn't been there, Kate wouldn't have needed any. Well, not so much, anyway. "I'll be fine for Saturday. Yes, let's come here again."

"Can I pick you up from your house, or do you want to meet at the park again?" Sam was watching her curiously.

"The park, please." Kate wriggled uncomfortably.

"Cool." Sam shrugged. "Fine by me. Seven o'clock again?"

Kate nodded, not trusting herself to speak. What the hell was she doing? Tonight had been a tremendous mistake, and yet she was organising another one. Tomorrow was her Hen Night. She was getting married in three weeks and two days. Why was she making a second date with another man? Oh, how she needed to speak to Jen!

"Shall we make a move?" Sam got to his feet. "Must admit I'm a bit tired. Only got back this morning, and it was a pretty hectic couple of days away. I'll go and pay."

This time Kate didn't watch as he walked away but pulled her phone out to check for a signal. Still nothing. Oh, well, probably better if she told Jen in person anyway. She stood up and pulled her cardigan on, then slung her bag over her shoulder and started towards the Land Rover.

She was leaning against it when Sam reappeared. He opened the doors, and they got in without speaking. As they drove back out onto the narrow country lane, Kate glanced at him.

"Thank you. That was very nice."

"Thank you for coming. It was fun. It's actually nice to be back. As nice as I hoped it would be."

Kate looked down at her hands. What did he mean by that? Oh, why was life so complicated?

They drove in silence until Sam pulled up by the kerb just along from the park gates.

"I take it you want dropping here, then?" He turned off the engine and glanced at Kate. "I'm not allowed to deliver you to your door?"

"Here is fine." Kate undid her seatbelt and rescued her bag from under the seat. "I can walk back from here."

"I'll walk with you." Sam got out and slammed the door.

"No—no, I'm fine. Really." Kate shook her head and began to edge away from the vehicle.

"It's all right. No one will see us." Sam caught her hand and pulled her towards the park. "We can cut through the park and across the fields that pass the back of your parents' house. I take it you don't want to be seen with me?"

Kate stopped walking and pulled on his arm. "It's not that. Not really…"

"But your parents know you're seeing someone, and you don't want them to see you with me in case they tell him? Maybe they're hoping he'll turn out to be 'the one'? Am I close?"

"Maybe. Sort of." Kate looked up at him. "Sorry that sounds so bad, but I just think it's better they don't see us together at the moment. I know we're just friends, but…"

"Of course. We're just friends. Good friends, I hope. Come on."

The full moon was high in the sky as they crossed the park and then scrambled over the dry stone wall that bounded the fields. Sam hopped over first, then waited while Kate caught him up. She stood on the top of the wall and stared up at the moon.

"It's so beautiful." She raised her head and let the rays shine on her face. "I love the moonlight."

Sam jumped back up onto the wall and stood beside her. "Me too. It makes you feel you're the only things in the world still awake. You should have seen it over the Sahara. That was really something."

"Is there anywhere you haven't been?" Kate smiled up at him.

"A few places." He slipped his arm around her shoulders and gave her a squeeze. "Need something to look forward to."

"You're going back travelling, then?" Kate was acutely aware of his body pressing close to hers, knowing she should move away but unable to do so.

"Sometime." Sam shrugged. "Not just yet. Might be nice not to go alone next time." He smiled at her in the moonlight. "Ready? We still have a field to cross."

Kate nodded, and together they jumped down into the field and set off towards the row of houses in the distance. As they approached, Sam slowed down.

"We're nearly there. I'll leave you here, if that's okay. Have a lovely time tomorrow night, and I'll see you at seven on Saturday. You can tell me all about the Hen Party. I've always thought it would be fun to be a fly on the wall at one of them."

Kate stopped walking and looked up at him. "Thanks again for a lovely evening. It's been fun catching up."

Sam stared at her for a moment, his eyes hidden by the shadows; then he bent his head and placed a light kiss on her lips. "See you on Saturday." He turned and with a quick wave jogged away back towards the park without a backward glance.

Kate's hand shot up to her mouth, and she stood staring after him, her heart racing. Life had just got even more complicated.

Chapter 7

Friday 3rd July

"Kate! Jenny's here." Helen's voice reached Kate as she lay in bed, the quilt pulled up to her chin. She really would have to get up, then. Helen's voice floated up to her again as she and Jenny moved into the kitchen.

"Come and have a coffee while you wait for her. She was home pretty late last night, and it took a while to wake her. Where are you off to first?"

Kate heard a door closing, and the voices dulled to a low murmur. With a sigh she threw back the covers and climbed out of bed. Her head was heavy from too much wine, not enough sleep, and stress about the night before, and she groaned when she looked in the mirror. Her hair was all on end, and she had huge black bags under her eyes. Not a good start to a busy Hen day. Apart from the evening with Jenny, three old school friends, and Vicky, she knew Jenny had something planned for during the day, and she realised she was going to have to wake herself up properly if she was going to enjoy it.

Pulling the door open, she padded downstairs, still in her pyjama trousers and old T-shirt, and walked into the kitchen, where she found her mother and Jenny sitting at the table, drinking coffee.

"Morning." She yawned and walked over to the kettle. "Didn't you make me one?"

"Didn't know you were ready, darling." Helen looked severely at her. "Jenny's waiting for you. I thought you were getting dressed."

"Oh, that won't take long. I need coffee first. And something to eat. Do we have any cake?" She pulled open a cupboard and began to rummage.

"Cake? For breakfast? Really, Kate, you must eat properly. Have some toast, at least." Helen got up and opened the bread bin hopefully.

"No, I want cake." Kate was firm. "Or chocolate. That would do. You all right, Jen?"

"Better than you, I think." Jenny was watching Kate, a speculative glint in her eye. "So where did you go last night?"

"Just out for a drink. Really, Mum, there must be cake. We always have cake."

"Oh, for goodness sake!" Helen opened a cupboard. "In here. There's some cupcakes in that box."

Kate pulled out the Tupperware container and helped herself to a cupcake. "Want one?" She held them out to Jenny.

"No, thanks. Just had breakfast. Proper breakfast." Jenny took a sip of her coffee and watched Kate over the rim. "Who were you out with last night?"

Kate turned round and fixed her with a warning glare, then grabbed a mug from the mug tree. "God, I really need a coffee. Finding it very hard to wake up this morning. I didn't sleep well at all last night."

"Wedding nerves." Helen smiled indulgently at her. "Only to be expected. Once the Hen Night is over, the next three weeks are going to fly by. You won't have time to be nervous. Now I must get on. We haven't all got the day off work. Have fun, you two, and I'll see you later." With a wave of her hand, she disappeared through into the hall, and they heard the front door open and close as she left for work.

Kate made a strong cup of black coffee and leant against the worktop, cradling it in her hands.

"Kate? Who with?"

"You know who with."

"Oh, Kate, you didn't! I thought you agreed it wasn't a good idea."

"It wasn't. And if there'd been a phone signal at the pub we went to, you'd have found that out last night. I sent you a text in a panic, but it wouldn't send."

"Oh, god, what happened? Why did you panic?"

Kate sighed and joined her friend at the table. She picked a second cake out of the box and took a large bite. "It was a lovely evening. We went to a little pub in the middle of nowhere, and he bought me dinner. That was my first panic. Suddenly it was like a proper date. But it was all nice, and he told me all about his travelling."

"So?" Jenny prompted her. "Why the panic text?"

"I realised I was enjoying myself too much. I liked his company far more than Richard's. I suddenly realised I was getting married in three weeks and I was on a date with another man."

"But you told him about Richard? Kate, tell me you told him."

Kate raised dark-rimmed eyes that spoke volumes.

"Oh, god, Kate, why didn't you tell him? Didn't he ask if you had a boyfriend?"

"Yeah. He asked if I was seeing anyone." Kate took a slurp of coffee. "I said I was. But that it wasn't serious."

"Jesus Christ! No wonder you had a panic. You know he'll find out, don't you? How could you possibly keep it secret? You live in the same village."

"I know, I know. You don't need to rub it in. I feel really guilty and really scared." She looked up at Jenny, the ghost of a smile on her lips. "But it was fun. And he walked me home through the park and across the field. In the moonlight."

"Good grief, this gets worse and worse." Jenny ran a hand through her hair. "Whatever were you thinking? Do you still like him, then? I thought you were over him."

"I dunno. It was nice. It felt fun and different, and I had to go just to see what a date with Sam Somerville would be like. He really hasn't changed since school. He looks just the same."

Jenny was staring at her in consternation. "Kate, this is dreadful. You mustn't have feelings for him. You have to marry Richard."

"I know." Kate sighed. "I know. He's not really a good bet for a relationship. He wants to go off travelling again. I doubt he'll ever settle down." She gave another little smile. "But he understands my need to be an explorer. Richard doesn't."

"How did that come up?"

"Oh, it doesn't matter. It just did. Anyway, I know I can't have him, and he probably doesn't want me anyway." She tried to push the memory of the kiss to the back of her mind. "So let's go and have the Hen day. Where are we going?"

Jenny stared at her for a moment. "This isn't over. But yes, we need to get going. I'm not telling you, but you do need to be dressed, and you might want to do something with your hair. It looks like a haystack."

****

"Jen, this is brilliant. Thank you so much for organising this. It's so relaxing. Just what I needed." Kate stretched out her legs and wiggled her toes. They had just had pedicures and were waiting for the manicurist to take over. Kate had had her toenails painted bright green to match the dress she was planning to wear for the evening.

"My pleasure." Jenny smiled sleepily. "Just doing my job as chief bridesmaid. It's supposed to relax you, ready for partying tonight."

"Well, it's really working. Are we going back home after this?"

"No. Oh, I may as well tell you now. We're having lunch at that new wine bar you like; then this afternoon we're having massages."

Kate stared at her in surprise. "Massages? Jen, that's brilliant. I've never had a massage before. What a great idea. Now I know why you're my best friend. Thank you."

Jenny smiled smugly. "Well, hopefully it will remind you that getting married is a good thing, and get you in the mood for tonight."

"I *am* in the mood for tonight." Kate smiled at her. "And so far managing not to panic about last night. I do need your help, though."

"What for?" Jenny narrowed her eyes suspiciously.

"To tell Sam I'm engaged."

"I'm not doing that! It's your mess; you need to

sort it. If you're going to tell such an enormous lie as that, you have to take the consequences."

"No, you have to help me," Kate wailed, grabbing Jenny's hand. "Please. I can't tell him now. It would be weird."

"Oh, so it wouldn't be weird if your best friend told him?"

"Well, maybe, but I can't. And I'm…" She bit her lip.

"You're what?"

"Nothing. I'm just embarrassed about it. Please, you tell him. Today."

"Of course I can't tell him today! When on earth will I have time to do that? And that wasn't what you were going to say."

"Yes, it was. Okay, then, tell him tomorrow morning. Please, Jen, if you love me."

Jenny looked suspiciously at her for a moment, then shrugged. "Maybe. If I see him. But I'm more concerned about why you lied to him. You *are* still going to marry Richard, aren't you?"

"Of course I am." Kate forced the words out, her body beginning to tingle as she remembered Sam's arm around her shoulders, and the touch of his lips on hers. "Of course I am. I love Richard. Sam was only ever a crush. I'm too old for crushes now."

"Okay. But I'm not convinced you're telling me everything. We still need to talk more about this. I can't risk you leaving Richard at the altar."

"I won't do that." Kate giggled slightly. "I love Richard. You know I do. And I don't mind that he's a bit boring. It's probably safer that way. He'll keep me grounded. Stop me going off to be an explorer."

"That's another thing we need to talk about." Jenny smiled as the manicurist arrived. "I really can't understand this new obsession of yours."

****

The girls arrived back at Kate's house just after five and let themselves in the front door. Helen appeared in the hall and beamed at them.

"Have a nice day, girls? Would you like a cuppa before you get ready?"

"That would be lovely." Jenny smiled her thanks. "We had a lovely time. Well, I did—I hope Kate feels the same?"

"It was awesome." Kate gave her friend a hug. "And all thanks to Jen. You really are the best friend ever. And we still have tonight, as well." She followed her mother into the kitchen. "I don't want tea, though. They gave us that at the nail parlour and the massage place. I'm all tea'd out. Jen, you must be getting old."

"Just lining my stomach before tonight." Jenny pulled out a chair and sat down. "Wouldn't hurt for you to do the same."

"Oh, stop fussing. I'll be fine. Milk's better to line your stomach anyway. I'll have a glass of that, to keep you happy." She fetched a glass and poured herself a drink of milk. "So are you going to tell me where we're going, then?"

"No. It can all be a surprise. I will tell you we're going to several places, though. It's going to be a busy evening."

"I hope none of you are driving." Helen placed a cup of tea in front of Jenny.

"No, we have a taxi booked for the whole evening. It's a people carrier, so we can all fit in. It's just going to be Kate, Vicky, and I, and Hannah, Maria, and Chelsea from school. The taxi firm gave me a very good deal."

"You must let me contribute." Helen reached for her purse. "How much was it?"

"No, Helen, it's fine." Jenny shook her head. "All the girls have chipped in. You and Peter are paying for the wedding—I've got this covered. It was a good deal, anyway, like I said."

"Well, if you're sure." Helen replaced her purse and smiled at the girls. "I'm sure you'll have a wonderful time. When is the taxi booked for?"

"It's picking us up here at seven, and we're meeting the other girls at the first stop. Except Vicky, of course. She's coming here too."

"Oh, god. I forgot that." Kate leaned forward and rested her forehead on the table. "And I was having such a nice day."

"Oh, she'll be fine tonight. Get a few drinks in her, and she's quite different." Jenny looked guiltily at Helen. "Sorry, Helen, not something you want to hear about your daughter."

"Oh, I know what my girls are like." Helen gave a small smile. "Both of them. Now off you go. I expect you're both wanting showers, and I know how long Kate takes to do her hair."

Muttering under her breath, Kate picked up her milk and followed Jenny upstairs to her bedroom. It was pretty much as she had left it that morning, and looked like a bomb had gone off. The bed was unmade, her clothes from the night before were strewn around the room, and all the cupboard doors were open.

"Jesus, Kate, what on earth were you doing in

here?" Jenny automatically began to pick up the clothes and dump them on the bed.

"I had to rush this morning, remember?" Kate tossed the clothes into the cupboard and pushed the doors shut. Then she quickly made the bed and grinned at Jenny. "There, that's all it needed. Now, what are you wearing tonight? I'm going to wear that new green dress. The one from New Look."

"I like that dress. What shoes will you wear?"

"These." Kate picked up a pair of very high black sandals and waved them in the air. "They're hell to walk in, but they look awesome."

"I love those." Jenny sat down on the bed. "You'll look great. And of course I have a few other things for you to wear, too."

"Oh, no!" Kate tossed the shoes into the corner and shook her head. "You're not dressing me up. No way. I want to look nice tonight."

"You will. Don't worry. But this is your Hen Night. It's tradition. I have some lovely—very tasteful—things to add to your outfit. We've all got something to wear. You won't be alone."

"Well, it better be tasteful. I'm not going clubbing, or whatever we're doing, in my underwear."

"It'll be fine. Chill out. We'll get you dressed up when Vicky gets here. Now hurry up, into the shower, and let's get ready."

Kate threw her a suspicious glance but peeled off her jeans and grabbed a towel. She stepped into the shower and turned the water on full, standing directly underneath and letting it cascade all over her body. She always found the shower a good place to think and sort out her problems, and she wondered if it was worth giving the Sam situation some thought. She poured shampoo onto her head and rubbed vigorously. No, Sam was not for now. Tonight was about her. And Richard, of course. It was about her wedding to Richard. Which was in three weeks. Tonight was all about her wedding.

Kate stuck her head under the water and washed the shampoo out. Her wedding. She suddenly realised just how scared she was. She was committing herself to Richard for life. Well, it was meant to be for life, and no one should go into a marriage assuming they could end it whenever they liked. What would be the point of that? But she had accepted his proposal because that was what she wanted.

Hadn't she? In fact she had rather pushed him into proposing, if truth be told. She had started to drop hints, and he had picked up on them rather faster than she had anticipated. It was definitely what she wanted. Until she realised just how boring he was. Until Holly said what she'd said about explorers and astronauts.

Until Sam Somerville had come back into her life. And kissed her.

Angrily Kate rubbed conditioner into her hair and screwed her eyes tightly shut as it ran down her face and into her mouth.

Why had he had to come back?

Why had she been so stupid as to go out with him, and why did she want him to kiss her again?

She rinsed her hair and pulled the towel down to dry her face. She needed to face this. She wanted Sam to kiss her again. Properly this time. A real, proper, long kiss.

She felt her lips tingle at the thought, and stepped

out of the shower. She needed to concentrate on tonight. She would sort out the Sam issue tomorrow. Or rather, Jen could do that for her.

She hung up her towel, took a deep breath, and walked back into the bedroom. Jenny was sitting in front of the mirror straightening her hair, and she glanced up as Kate entered.

"Nice shower? Did you work out what to do about Sam?"

"What? What d'you mean?"

"You always sort out your problems in the shower. You always have."

"Well, not this time." Kate wriggled into her bra. "Tonight is my Hen night. Nothing to do with Sam. Tonight is all about me."

"And your wedding. To Richard."

"Yes, and my wedding to Richard. Which is happening in three weeks, and nothing is going to stop it. Certainly not Sam Somerville."

"Glad to hear it." Jenny was watching Kate in the mirror. "So you're ready for some fun, then?"

"Too right." Kate pulled her dress over her head. "Can you zip me up? And when do I get to see this stuff you're going to make me wear? Will I look really stupid?"

"You're going to look amazing, Kate. You always do. There you go. This dress is really tight. You won't be able to eat much in that!"

"Just for once, I'm actually not hungry," Kate admitted with a grin. "I think I'm a bit nervous. Could do with a wine, though. We should have had some while we got ready."

"Plenty of time for wine later." Jenny returned to

the hair straighteners. "Don't want you pissed before we even leave the house. We'll dress you up when Vicky gets here." She glanced at her phone. "Which should be any minute, actually. It's nearly six."

Kate wandered over and looked out the window. The road below was quiet, and she watched as a small red car turned into the cul-de-sac and headed towards their house. "She's here," she said with a sigh. "Hope she behaves herself. I really wish she wasn't coming."

"She'll be fine. I'll keep her under control. Right. Help me do this top up, will you? I need to breathe in while you fasten it."

Kate moved over and helped her, then glanced up as her sister appeared in the doorway.

"Hi. You actually look quite nice, Kate." Vicky walked in and sat down the bed. "For now."

"What d'you mean?" Kate sighed.

"When we've finished dressing you up, you're gonna look very different."

"Vicky! Don't, or she won't agree to wear any of it. I've told her it's all very tasteful." Jenny frowned in annoyance. "Look, now you're here, we can dress her up." She pulled a large bag towards her and unzipped it.

"I really want my dress to show." Kate peered uncertainly into the bag. "I'm not wearing anything that covers it up."

"Stop fussing." Jenny produced a pink sash with "Bride To Be" emblazoned on it and slipped it over Kate's head. "Now you can't object to that, can you? And Vicky and I have sashes with 'Bridesmaid' on them, and the others have them saying 'Hen Party.' All very tasteful, just like I said."

Kate looked down at the sash and ran her fingers

over it. "Okay. This is fine. It's quite nice, actually. Is this all?"

"Not quite, but you need to do your hair first. Hurry up. The taxi'll be here in half an hour."

By the time Kate was satisfied with her hair, and Jenny and Vicky had added L Plates and a short veil to her costume, the taxi had arrived, and the three girls made their way outside. Kate's parents were standing in the garden to wave them off, and Peter thrust a twenty-pound note into Kate's hand.

"Have a good time, love," he murmured, giving her a quick kiss on the cheek. "You look lovely. Enjoy your last fling."

"Last fling? Dad, I'm not getting married for three weeks."

"I know, but isn't that what the Hen Party is? A last chance to let your hair down as a single woman? Go on, have a great time, and don't get too drunk."

"As if I would, Dad." Kate climbed into the back of the taxi. "I'm a good girl."

"Not like me!" Vicky leaned over her and grinned at her father. "I'm already drunk."

"Sit down, Vicky." Jenny pulled her back into her seat. "You okay, Kate? Ready for this?"

Kate nodded, her mouth suddenly dry with nerves as she watched her house and her parents disappear behind them.

What on earth was wrong with her? She was going out on the town with her friends. She was going out for a brilliant night, and suddenly all she wanted was to be tucked up at home in her PJs, with a bar of chocolate, a bottle of wine, and a good film. She gave herself a mental shake and summoned up a smile.

"Yep. I'm ready. *Now* will you tell me where we're going?"

"Okay," Jenny relented. "We're starting out at a really cool Italian restaurant in Exeter. Then we're going to a club—they're really good at Hen nights—and after that we're making our way back here with a pub crawl. I think we're going to about…six is it, Vicky?"

Vicky nodded. "Yeah, something like that. Not sure we'll have time for them all. Depends how good the club is, I reckon. I think we should just stay there, personally."

"Yeah, well, it's not your Hen do. Kate, would you rather stay at the club, or do the pub crawl as well?"

"I'll go along with whatever you decided." Kate smiled. "I think a pub crawl all the way back from Exeter sounds cool, actually. Clubs are fun for a while but can get a bit boring. Sounds like the perfect evening. Thanks, Jen."

"My pleasure." Jenny raised an eyebrow at Vicky. "Knew you'd like it. Now try and relax. It's about half an hour to Exeter, and definitely time for some of this." She produced a bottle of Prosecco from her bag and waved it in the air. "I even brought plastic glasses. You hold those, Vick, while I open it." With a practised movement, Jenny uncorked the bottle and poured the foaming wine into the cheap plastic glasses. She raised hers in the air. "To Kate. For a final fling as a single girl. And for a very happy married life."

They all swigged back the wine, and Kate wrinkled her nose as the bubbles tickled it. "Thanks, guys. Although I'm not sure about this final fling thing. That's what Dad said. It all sounds so—well, final."

"Like death." Vicky raised her glass again, her eyes glinting.

"For god's sake, Vicky." Jenny scowled at her. "What a thing to say! She's getting married, not facing a firing squad."

"Well, she doesn't look very happy about it. In fact, she looks positively terrified."

Kate finished her wine and held out her glass. "Is there any more? That was nice." She glanced at her sister. "Not terrified, just feeling a bit odd. Everything in my life is about to change. It's a strange feeling. It seems like I shall be a different person after I get married, and sometimes that's a bit hard to deal with."

"You will be. Mrs. Richard Cresswell. How middle-aged does that sound?"

"I shall be Mrs. Kathryn Cresswell," Kate corrected sharply. "We're not living in the nineteen fifties. It'll feel very different."

"Well, I'm never going to do it." Vicky sat back and crossed her long tanned legs. "Marriage is totally outdated. Really boring."

"And *why* are you here?" Jenny was getting annoyed. "Either get in the swing of things, or we're going to drop you off at the next bus stop, bride's sister or not."

Vicky had the grace to look slightly embarrassed, and slid down in her seat. "Okay. Sorry. I guess that was a bit crass. Sorry, Kate."

Kate shrugged. "S'okay. You don't like marriage, you don't have to get married. It's your life. This is my life. And scary though it is, I'm getting married in three weeks. And one day."

"Yes, you are." Jenny was watching her. "To

Richard."

"To Richard."

Vicky peered round Jenny. "Of course it's to Richard. I'm sure she doesn't need reminding. They've been together like forever. How long is it, Kate?"

"Three years and two months."

"Wow. I'd be dead of boredom if I'd been with a man that long." Vicky tossed back her hair. "We must be very different. Richard is okay, though."

Kate looked at her suspiciously. "You like him, then? I've always wondered what you talk about with him. He seems to like you. Much more than I do."

Vicky smirked. "Just stuff," she said. "We have stuff in common. We often talk about my job. After all, it is rather more interesting than yours. But I guess you'll just have babies once you're married. You won't need a career, so I s'pose it doesn't matter that you haven't ever really had one."

"Right, that's enough." Jenny held up her hands. "We are not going any further unless you two try and get along. Vicky, you know that was out of order. We're going out for a nice night to celebrate Kate getting married. She didn't want you here, but as you are her sister and her bridesmaid, you had to be. So, since you're stuck with each other, you *will* get along, or we all go back home now and cancel the whole thing."

"And the wedding," Kate murmured under her breath, sitting back and staring out the window.

"What?" Jenny looked at her sharply. "What did you say?"

"Nothing. Nothing." Kate shook her head. "Yeah, let's stop this, Vick. We need to get on, just for tonight.

And actually it's quite nice that you get on with Richard."

Vicky grinned. "Okay, let's have a ceasefire. Just for tonight. And maybe on the wedding day, too. Yeah, Richard's okay. Too good for you, of course." She saw Jenny's warning glance and laughed. "Only joking. You want to know what we talk about? Well, last time I saw him—when we all had lunch at Granny's, remember?—we were discussing one of his cases that had a connection to my firm. Boring for you, of course, but I was actually able to give him some information."

Kate looked at her in surprise. Vicky had qualified as an accountant fairly recently and was a very junior associate in a large firm in Bristol. Kate thought it all sounded very boring, but it probably was the sort of thing Richard would relate to. If she was honest, her conversations with her fiancé were fairly neutral and banal. They didn't often talk about very deep subjects. In fact, in recent times all they had talked about was the wedding and where they were planning on living. So once they were actually married, would they have anything left to say to each other? She felt a sudden wave of panic flood through her, and she turned to Jenny.

"Are we nearly there? I need another drink."

"Nearly, couple of minutes. Are you okay, Kate? You look a bit weird."

"She's probably having second thoughts." Vicky chuckled. "Bit late now, Katy. Only three weeks to go."

"Three weeks and one day," Kate snapped. "And don't call me Katy. I'm Kate now. Have been for years."

"Okay, okay. Don't be so touchy. So *are* you

having second thoughts, then? Have you realised I have more in common with your fiancé than you do?" Vicky flicked her long glossy hair over her shoulder and narrowed her eyes at Kate.

"Fuck off, Vicky." Kate reached round Jenny and slapped her sister on the leg. "No, I'm not having second thoughts, and Richard and I get on very well. We have loads in common."

"Right. We're here." Relief sounded in Jenny's voice. "Look, there are the others, waiting for us." She waved at the three girls standing on the pavement outside a brightly lit Italian restaurant. "Come on. Out you get, and please stop bickering." She turned to the driver. "Meet us back here at nine? That should be about right. Thanks."

She ushered Kate and Vicky out onto the pavement, and Chelsea, Maria, and Hannah rushed forward and pounced on Kate, dragging her towards the restaurant, all chattering together.

Chapter 8

"Kate! Kate, you still awake?" Jenny shook Kate's shoulder as the taxi drew up alongside the kerb. "We're back in the village. Just one more stop, then home."

Kate opened her eyes and smiled woozily. "Yeah, I'm awake. I'm fine. Ready for anything." She pushed open the door of the taxi and stepped out onto the pavement. As the cooler night air hit her, she wobbled slightly and caught at Hannah's arm to steady herself.

"You too, Kate?" Hannah hiccupped and giggled at the same time. "I can barely walk. Have you had fun, though?"

"Brill'ant fun." Kate nodded over-enthusiastically and found her head began to spin. "Should do this ev'y day." Still clutching on to one another, she and Hannah waited as the others joined them on the pavement. "Where we goin' now, Jen?"

"Our last stop. The Harlequin's Arms. Thought our local should be the finale."

"I like the Harlee…Harlequin—thingy." Kate nodded again, wishing the pavement would stop moving. "Lead on."

Laughing, the six girls wobbled their way along the main street of the village towards the large timbered pub that had pride of place on the village green. As they approached, Kate suddenly felt her face go hot and cold, and she grabbed Jenny's arm.

"Jen, Jen. I can't go in there." She was suddenly sober, her eyes wide with panic. "We can't go in there. Stop them."

"Kate? Whatever's wrong? Do you feel sick?"

"No, no. Of course not. I'm fine. I can't go in because of who owns the pub."

Jenny stared at her for a moment; then her hand flew up to cover her mouth. "Oh, shit. I never even considered that. Sam's parents."

"Yeah, Sam's parents. They own it, they live there, and he's staying there. They'll see me and tell him." Kate tried to pull away and turn around.

"Kate, come on!" Vicky was at the door of the pub. "It's your night, and this is the last stop. Hurry up. Oh, god, you're not going to be sick, are you? God, you're such a lightweight."

"No, I'm not going to be sick." Kate swung round again, her anger at her sister's words overcoming her reluctance. "I am *not* a lightweight. I just think maybe we should stop now…"

Her words were met with a chorus of disapproval from her friends, and before she could do anything about it, she found herself borne along to the entrance of the pub. Vicky opened the door and pushed her through, chuckling as Kate staggered a little and had to catch hold of a table to steady herself.

"Come on, girls, I'll get the drinks in. Shots everyone?" Vicky was already at the bar.

"It's okay, Kate," Jenny murmured in her ear. "Look, it's just bar staff. The Somervilles aren't here. Come on, just a quick drink to finish off the evening."

Kate looked around cautiously and nodded. "Okay, I guess it would look really weird if I went home. But keep me hidden if they do appear." She moved over to the bar with the others, several locals congratulating her as she passed, and took the glass Vicky held out to her.

As one, the six girls downed their shots and put the glasses back on the bar. Vicky laughed. "Again? Shall we get six more?"

Kate and the others moved slightly away, and Jenny suggested they take over the table in the corner. Kate was just about to sit down when Vicky's voice reached her.

"Kate, look. There's Sam Somerville! I thought he was abroad somewhere. Didn't you have a major crush on him at school?" Before either Kate or Jenny could stop her, Vicky had waved across the bar. "Sam! Hi, Sam, didn't know you were back."

Kate shrank back in her corner seat as she saw Sam appear behind the bar and wander over towards Vicky.

"Hello, Vicky. Up to no good as usual, I assume?" He stopped in front of her. "What can I get you?"

"Six more Tequila slammers, please."

"Six?" Sam turned away to get the glasses. "That's a lot, even for you."

"Stupid. I'm on a Hen Night. They're all over there. This is our last stop."

"Ah, the Hen Night. Yeah, Katy mentioned that. Are you having fun?"

"Yeah, it's been good. You back now, then?"

"Clearly." Sam put the drinks in front of her. "Never was any fooling you, was there, Vicky."

"Back working here, I mean?"

"For now. Until I get what I really want. So, where's the bride? Do I know her?"

Vicky stared at him and gave a short laugh. "Kate

told you about the Hen Night but didn't say who the bride was? That's priceless." She turned to the corner table. "Kate, get over here."

Kate shrank even further back in her seat and shook her head.

"Come on, Sam wants to see the bride."

Before she could protest, Hannah and Chelsea had moved out of the way, and Maria was pushing Kate along the seat towards the bar. Realising she had no choice, and that whatever she did, Sam was going to find out, Kate slowly got to her feet, straightened her L Plates, and walked as steadily as she could towards the bar. Sam was staring at her, a completely unreadable expression on his face. She stopped in front of him and stared back.

"Katy." He gave a slight nod. "You look nice."

"Thank you." Her voice just managed a whisper. Out of the corner of her eye she was aware that a grinning Vicky had taken her place at the table with the others. She took a deep breath and looked up at Sam.

"So is there something you want to tell me?" he asked, raising his eyebrows and leaning his elbows on the bar.

Kate shook her head. "No," she said. "If I'd wanted to tell you I would have. Now I don't need to."

"It's your Hen Party."

"Yes."

"So you're getting married?"

"Yes."

"To the person you're seeing on a casual basis?"

Kate looked down at her hands resting on the bar. "I think I want to go home now."

"Why didn't you tell me?"

She was silent for a moment, eventually raising her head and looking straight at him. Their eyes locked, and for a second Kate thought she saw something flicker. She shook her head.

"It's all right." Sam took pity on her. "I understand. Well, let me congratulate you and wish you every happiness."

Kate swallowed. "Thank you. Can I get a glass of water?"

Sam reached for a glass and filled it up, adding some ice and placing it on the bar in front of her. As she picked it up and took a long swig, he leant closer and murmured in her ear. "Are we still on for tomorrow night? Or…"

Kate put the water glass back on the bar and wiped her hand over her mouth. "Yes. If you want to. I can explain…this."

"Yes, I want to. See you at seven. Enjoy the rest of your party." He moved along the bar to serve someone else, and Kate slowly walked over to the table to join her friends.

She slid back into her seat and found five pairs of eyes staring at her. "What?"

"You told Sam Somerville you were going to a Hen Party but didn't say it was yours?" Hannah stared at her in amazement. "Why didn't you tell him?"

"Because I only saw him for a couple of minutes." Kate flashed a warning glance at Jenny. "It was at that dreadful WI fête last weekend. He suddenly appeared and said hello."

"And you told him about the Hen party, why?" Vicky was clearly enjoying her sister's discomfort.

"He suggested a group of us meet up tonight for a

catch-up. I told him I was busy, and he asked where I was going. I said a Hen party. And then he had to leave." Kate wriggled uncomfortably. "It's no big deal. He knows now. He's been away for eight years. It was a bit of a shock to see him, actually."

"I bet it was." Chelsea giggled, her blonde curls bobbing over her eyes. "He's just as hot as he was at school, too."

Vicky rolled her eyes. "God, did all your year fancy him, then? Kate had a real crush on him. Can't see what all the fuss is, actually. Not my type at all, far too scruffy."

"Did he go abroad straight after…you know? Straight after Cerys…" Maria tailed off, her face sombre.

"Yeah. Pretty much straight after." Jenny nodded. "And this is the first time he's been back, I think."

Kate wriggled a bit and yawned. "I'm getting really tired now. Can we make this the last drink? I'd love to get home and slob about for a bit. You're all coming, yeah?"

"Yeah, I'm getting a bit knackered too." Jenny immediately backed her up. "Shall we go back to Kate's and have snacks?"

"You're all so boring and old!" Vicky stared at them in disgust. "It's only just gone midnight. I'm staying here until they throw me out."

"You're welcome to." Kate stood up. "I didn't want you at my Hen night anyway, remember. Come on, girls, I'm the Hen, and I decide when we go home."

"Thought you'd all want to stay and ogle sexy Sam." Vicky picked up Kate's discarded Tequila and downed it in one. "Since you all love him so much."

"No, you're coming with us." Jenny caught Vicky's arm and pulled her to her feet none too gently. "Not having you stay here and make a fool of yourself. We're all going back with Kate. It's what she wants."

Grumbling audibly, Vicky allowed Jenny to propel her towards the door, and they all made their way out into the clear night. At the door, Kate turned and glanced over at Sam. He caught her eye, and she detected the hint of a wink, then he went back to serving his customer. She followed the others outside and joined them on the pavement.

"Thanks for tonight, girls," she said, putting her arms around Jenny and Maria. "I've had a totally brilliant time. You are the best friends ever. You don't mind if we go back now, do you?"

"Not so long as you have snacks and wine," Hannah said with a giggle. "Or maybe coffee!"

"We have all that." Kate smiled and started off down the road. "And Mum and Dad will be in bed. They know we're all coming back, so they'll keep out of the way. We can have another party."

Jenny caught her arm as they made their way along the road towards Kate's house. "You okay?" she whispered.

"Ish." Kate gave a lopsided smile. "That was awful in the pub, but at least he knows now. That's let you off the hook!"

Jenny laughed. "Yeah, right. Like I was actually going to tell him anyway! I only agreed to that to shut you up."

Kate giggled and slapped her arm. "Bitch," she said affectionately. "Love you, Jen."

"Love you too, Kate."

Chapter 9

Saturday 4th July

"Kate, are you asleep again?" Helen shook Kate's shoulder. "Honestly, what time did you get to bed last night anyway?"

Kate stretched and uncurled herself from the wicker chair in the conservatory. "Dunno. 'Bout five, I think."

"Good grief! I heard you all come back here about twelve thirty. What on earth were you doing after that?"

"Oh, not much. Talking. Drinking, eating. We played a few silly Hen Night games. That was fun." Kate grinned up at her mother. "I have lovely friends."

"You do. You're a lucky girl. Lovely friends, a caring fiancé, and of course, the best parents in the world."

Kate grinned again. "Of course, Mum. Hannah and Maria went to sleep first, but they both had to work this morning. They left long before I woke up."

"I know. I gave them breakfast." Helen looked smug. "Well I tried to, anyway. They actually only managed coffee and a piece of toast, but at least I tried. They did look a bit worse for wear. Chelsea and Jenny have both gone now too, haven't they? Or are they tucked away in some corner and I haven't noticed them?"

Kate giggled. "They've gone. Jen has a date tonight, and Chelsea has to go to her grandmother's birthday party. Has Vicky gone? I do hope so."

"Kate, when will you two learn to get on?" Helen sighed in annoyance. "But yes, she went about an hour ago. She's going somewhere or other tonight, I think. She always seems to be out socialising. I'm surprised she can keep up with it all, with that demanding job of hers."

Kate closed her eyes and sank down in her chair. "Oh, bloody Vicky and her bloody job," she muttered. "She's so bloody perfect."

"Kate, language!" Helen frowned at her. "I do wish you two could get on. And Vicky has done very well for herself with that job. I heard her telling Richard all about it last time they were both here. He seemed most impressed."

Kate stood up and flounced over to the window. "Oh, bully for Vicky. Maybe Richard should marry her instead, then."

"Kate, now don't be silly. You mustn't be jealous just because your sister has a better job. You'll find what you want to do soon, I'm sure. Vicky has always been more focused. Now I'm just going to make a cuppa. D'you want one?"

Kate shook her head and stared out down the garden. "No. Thanks. What time is it anyway?"

"Nearly six. You've been asleep for ages."

"Six?" Kate swung round. "How the hell did it get that late? I must get ready."

"Ready for what?" Helen's voice floated back from the kitchen. "Surely you're not going out tonight, are you?"

"Yes." Kate was bounding up the stairs, two at a time. "No time to talk now. Got to leave in forty-five minutes."

She ran into her bedroom and stood looking round in a panic. In an hour she was meeting Sam. What on earth should she wear, and more importantly, why on earth had she agreed to go out with him again? She moved rapidly around the room, picking up clothes, then discarding them. Her mind was still befuddled from the night before, and she had no clear idea what she was even doing. In desperation she flung herself down on the bed and started to text Jenny. As her hand hovered over the screen, about to ask for advice on what to wear, she remembered she had actually not told Jen she was going out with Sam again. She could hardly ask for help unless she told her, and she really doubted that was a good idea. She dropped her phone down beside her and buried her face in her pillow. What on earth was she doing? In three weeks' time, she would actually be married. Sam now knew that, and yet she was still going out on a date with him. Not that it was really a date, she told herself. It was still just a catch-up. He hadn't told her everything about his travels yet. That's all it was, just a catch-up of old friends. Nothing more.

Slowly she dragged herself off the bed, pulled off her T-shirt and sweat pants, and got in the shower. She really needed something to wake her up. She pulled on a shower cap, turned the water on full power, and stood underneath, letting it run all over her. Should she wear jeans? Or maybe a skirt would be better. She had that really nice blue one she got in the charity shop. She looked nice in that. But if she wore a skirt, should she wear heels? And if she wore heels, that might make walking back across the field difficult. And she really wanted to do that again.

With a sigh she turned off the shower and started to dry herself. Jeans were probably the best option. Then she could wear flats, which would be easy to walk in, and one of her skimpy strappy tops. The green one. She smiled to herself and stepped out onto the bath mat. Yeah, that would all look very nice. She cleaned her teeth, rinsed her mouth with mouthwash twice, and applied a large quantity of deodorant. She wanted no lingering odours from the previous night's party to remain.

As she wriggled into her jeans and pulled her top over her head, she realised she hadn't actually eaten all day and was, in fact, ravenously hungry. She hoped they were going to the same place as they had on Thursday. That food had been very nice. She sat down in front of the mirror and sighed when she saw her hair. It quite honestly looked like she'd been caught in a tornado. She tugged her brush through it while she waited for the straighteners to heat up, and peered at her face.

She had black bags under her eyes, and her cheeks looked sunken and sallow. Well, that needed some work. She put down the hairbrush, applied a lot of foundation, and eventually achieved a look that she felt wouldn't actually scare Sam away. She dealt with her hair, straightening her fringe and fastening the rest up messily in a large clip. She pulled some tendrils out to hang down on either side of her face and surveyed the final result. She'd do.

Glancing at her phone, she saw it was nearly six

forty-five, so she threw a breath freshener into her mouth, gathered up her bag, phone, and an oversized checked shirt to throw on over the top if it got cold, and made her way downstairs.

"I'm off now, Mum," she called, walking swiftly towards the front door. "Don't wait up. I've got my key."

"Hang on there, young lady." Helen appeared in the doorway. "Have you had anything to eat? You can't go out drinking on an empty stomach. I'm not sure you should be going out tonight anyway. You seem very tired."

"Mum, stop fussing." Kate jiggled the door handle in annoyance. "I'm not going out drinking, as you put it. I'm going out for a meal, and I'm fine. I'm twenty-six. Why on earth would I be tired? I can manage more than one night out in a row, you know."

"Well, this will be three in a row," Helen pointed out. "Just being a mother. Who are you out with tonight? Not Jenny, I assume. You said she had a date."

"Yeah, she has. No, just one of the girls who couldn't come last night. Sarah—you remember her? She's been away and only just got back. Haven't seen her for ages."

"Oh, give her my love." Helen smiled. "I liked Sarah. I often see her mother in Tesco. Have a lovely time."

Her heart sinking as she realised she had probably picked the wrong friend to use as her cover, Kate started to open the front door.

"Oh, and you'll never guess who else is back." Helen's voice halted her in her tracks. "Sam Somerville. You remember Sam, from the pub? You liked him when you were at school, didn't you?"

Kate nodded, not trusting herself to turn around. "Yeah, I know. He was serving in the pub last night."

"Nice boy." Helen sighed. "That was a bad business with that girl—what was her name—when you'd just left school?"

"Cerys. Her name was Cerys." Kate pulled the door open. "Must go now, Mum, or I'll be late. Bye." She escaped out into the still warm evening and hurried down the path as fast as she could. Oh, why had she said she was meeting Sarah? She had forgotten that their mothers were friends. And how on earth did her mother know about Sam being back? Things were getting even more complicated.

It was very nearly seven when she arrived at the park gates, but Sam wasn't anywhere in sight. Kate leaned against the railings and breathed deeply. Why did everyone keep mentioning Cerys? That had been eight years ago. It had been the reason for Sam's departure, but surely enough time had passed now. She glanced down the road just in time to see his Land Rover round the corner. He drew up next to her and wound down the window.

"Hop in."

She opened the door and climbed in, remembering this time how to work the seatbelt. Sam took off almost before she had finished fastening it, and they drove in silence for a few minutes. Eventually Sam spoke, his eyes never leaving the road.

"Nice time last night?"

"Yes, thank you." Kate looked down at her hands. which were clasped tightly in her lap. "Bit tired today."

"And hung over, I'm sure." He flicked the

indicator and turned off the main road. "Evil things, shots."

"I'm fine. Just a bit hungry."

"We'll be eating, don't worry."

"Are we going to the same pub as Thursday?"

Sam shook his head. "No, not tonight. But don't worry. There'll be food." He indicated again, and they turned down an extremely narrow lane bordered with high hedges. "I think you'll like it."

Kate sat back and stared out the window. She hadn't been paying attention and had absolutely no idea where they were. They had been travelling for about twenty minutes, but she didn't recognise any of the scenery.

"Where are we?" She turned to Sam, unable to help a little flutter in her stomach as she watched how his hair flopped over his forehead as he manoeuvred a tight bend. "Is there a pub down here?"

"Wait and see."

Kate sat back again and attempted to peer through the dense undergrowth to either side of them. They were in a very wooded area and were travelling rapidly down a very steep hill. Sam didn't seem to think it necessary to brake for bends, and Kate found herself clinging onto the seat with one hand and the door with the other.

Eventually they slowed and turned right down a narrow path that opened out into a wide grassy area dotted with trees and bisected by a wide stream. The early evening sun glistened off the slow-moving water, and the long shadows from the trees cast beautiful patterns on the grass.

Sam parked the Land Rover under a large tree and

turned off the engine. "Do you like it?" He didn't look at her.

"It's beautiful."

"Good. I thought you would. Come on, help me get the stuff out." He jumped down onto the grass and walked round to open the back of the vehicle. Kate followed, her curiosity fully aroused. Sam held out a folded tartan blanket. "Here, take this, and this." He handed her a zipped-up cool bag. "Find somewhere nice to sit."

She stared at him, and her face broke into a wide grin. "We're having a picnic. That's brilliant!"

"Thought it might be more fun than just another trip to a pub. Now I'm back living in one, it gets a bit boring. How about just over there?" He pointed to a flat area that jutted out into the stream. "That looks a nice spot."

Kate carried the rug and the bag over and laid them on the ground. The heat from the sun was still very strong, and the glistening water, although only about six inches deep, looked very inviting. She kicked off her shoes and rolled the bottoms of her jeans up as far as she could get them.

"Come for a paddle," she called to Sam as she stepped gingerly into the water. Despite the hot day, it was icy, and she gasped as it gently licked around her ankles. "Wow, cold!"

Sam placed a large basket on the grass and spread out the rug Kate had carried. He glanced over at her and laughed. "You have fun. I'll just sort the food out."

Kate picked her way carefully along the little stream, keeping one eye on Sam. She could hardly believe he had done this for her. He had organised what looked like a very sumptuous picnic in the most glorious place imaginable.

It was really very romantic. Richard had never done anything like that. Richard's idea of romance was to buy her something expensive. Very nice, of course, but he didn't really need to put a lot of thought into it. Sam had gone to a lot of trouble for this. For her. And he knew she was getting married.

Feeling suddenly very guilty, Kate turned and waded back to their makeshift camp, where she could see Sam arranging something on the rug. As she stepped out of the stream and back onto the grass, he looked up and smiled at her.

"Nice paddle? I never thought to bring a towel. You'll just have to dry in the sun. Come and sit down."

Kate joined him on the rug and sat with her damp legs stretched out in front of her. Sam handed her a plastic cup of something fizzy and sat down next to her.

"Not alcohol, I'm afraid. Thought you could probably do with a night off after last night, and I'm driving, so just fizzy grape juice." He raised his cup and looked thoughtfully at her. "What shall we drink to? Old friends? Your wedding? What do you think?"

"Old friends," Kate said at once, feeling her face begin to get hot. She took a sip and turned her head away. "Not my wedding. That's not for now."

Sam fell silent, and Kate sneaked a glance at him. He looked almost unbearably good-looking, and she caught just a glimpse of vulnerability in his eyes as he stared out across the stream to the woods on the other side.

He turned to face her, and it was gone.

"Old friends, then. But I think we may need to

discuss your impending nuptials at some point. Don't you?"

"Why? You know about them now. What's to discuss?" Kate pulled her knees up to her chin and hugged them tightly.

"Well..." Sam watched her, his head on one side. "Maybe the reason why you failed to tell me the Hen party you were going to was your own, even though we spent the whole of the previous evening together. And arranged another date. I can't help feeling there may be something to discuss there."

"Is this a date, then?" Kate rested her chin on her knees and watched him out of the corner of her eye.

"Don't change the subject." Sam lay down on his back and closed his eyes. "Why didn't you tell me you were engaged?"

"I meant to." Kate stared out across the stream as she tried to find the right words. "I really meant to. But it was so lovely being with you. So lovely hearing about your travels. So much more exciting than..." She tailed off as she realised she had said too much.

"Than what?" Sam opened one eye and looked up at her. "Than your fiancé? What's his name anyway?"

"No, I didn't mean that..." Kate felt herself going red again. "It's Richard. Richard Cresswell."

"Ah. Right. And what does Richard Cresswell do, then, that's so boring?"

"I never said that," Kate protested mildly, hugging her knees even tighter.

"You didn't need to. I've known you for a long time, Katy. I know what you're thinking." Sam propped himself up on his elbows. "Although I must say I hadn't picked up on the whole getting-married thing. You hid that extremely well."

"I'm sorry."

"No need to be sorry. You're under no obligation to tell me anything. Just seems a little odd that you wouldn't mention it when I asked you out again."

"Well…" Kate kept her face turned away. "Well, I didn't really know if it *was* a date. I thought we might just be catching up as old friends. That's all we were in school, after all."

Sam sat up and topped up their glasses. "Were we? Is that all it was? I had a feeling it might have been something more."

"So why did you go travelling without me?" The words were out before Kate could stop them, and she bit down hard on her lip to prevent herself from saying any more.

"You know why." Sam spoke quietly. "Everything changed."

"I'm sorry." Kate moved slightly closer and tentatively put her hand on his arm. "I shouldn't have said that. I know why."

"Do you want something to eat?" Sam moved away and started rummaging in the basket. "We have pizza, and quiche, and lots of nice cheese. Here, have some pizza. I know you love it."

Kate accepted the paper plate he held out to her, watching him miserably, well aware she had crossed a line. She was rather afraid she had spoilt everything. He wouldn't want to see her again. She took a bite out of the still-warm pizza and curled her legs up under her. But then, she had rather spoilt everything just by being engaged. Of course he wouldn't want to see her again. He had only gone through with tonight to find out more about her fiancé. Her eyes followed Sam as he piled his plate high with some of everything, then settled down cross-legged on the rug, a discreet distance between them. Kate took another bite of the delicious pizza. But why the picnic? If she had spoilt everything by being engaged, and he had only taken her out to find out why she hadn't told him, then why the picnic? That seemed to have been well planned and designed to please her. It really did seem like a romantic gesture. Did he realise she was having second thoughts about Richard? He said he knew what she was thinking. Kate stuffed the last of the pizza into her mouth and sat very still. *Was* she having second thoughts about Richard? What had made her suddenly think that? True, she had spent the week wondering if he was too boring, and she had got very annoyed when he had pooh-poohed her idea of becoming an explorer—but she still loved him. Didn't she?

She glanced sideways at Sam. His thick dark hair was flopping over his forehead again, and the sinking sun was glinting off his lean tanned arms. She gave a little shiver. He was so different from Richard. Richard would never sit on a rug by a stream, eating with his fingers. He wouldn't go paddling in icy water on a whim. Richard liked things to be well ordered and organised. And very boring. Kate sighed. He really was very boring. Why had she not noticed before? She had been with him for three years. Maybe she was boring, too, and that was why she hadn't seen it.

"D'you like the pizza?" Sam was watching her, his eyes narrowed against the evening sun.

"It's lovely, thanks. Did you bring it from the pub?"

"Yes, but I made it." He held out another piece to her. "I'm pretty pleased with it, actually."

"You made it?" Kate accepted the second slice and took a bite. "It's really nice. When did you learn to cook?"

Sam shook his hair back and grinned at her. "I've been away eight years, Katy, travelling the world. I'm bound to have picked up a few new skills." He topped up her glass again. "I learnt to make pizza in a tiny Italian village in the mountains, taught by a very old man who couldn't speak any English."

"That sounds amazing. You're so lucky. And all I've done is get a degree and get stuck in a job I don't like and didn't really want."

"And get engaged to a boring man you seem to be ashamed of."

"Ashamed of?" Kate frowned and wiped tomato sauce off her mouth. "What d'you mean?"

"Well, most girls can't wait to tell their friends about their fiancés. If I hadn't found out by accident, I doubt you would have told me yet. I can only assume you are either ashamed of him or having second thoughts."

"It's not like that." Kate wriggled uncomfortably and looked away from him. "I'm...I'm just a bit nervous, that's all. Just wedding nerves. I love Richard."

Sam watched her for a moment, then shrugged. "Well, if you say so. But just make sure you really do, before you commit yourself to him forever. That's a long time."

Kate pulled her knees up to her chin again and hugged them tightly. "And eight years away is a long time," she muttered, attempting to change the subject. "We were going to go away for three months. Instead you go on your own and stay away for eight years." She looked sideways at him. "I understand why you left, but why did you stay away so long?"

"You don't understand why I left." Sam got up onto his knees and began to pack away the food. "You don't know the whole story. Now come on, the sun's gone behind the trees now, and it's getting cooler. I think we should get back."

Kate's shoulders sagged. "Already? And what d'you mean I don't understand why you left? Of course I do. I was there, remember? I know what happened that night, and I know how you felt afterwards. Of course I understand why you went—and without me—but why for so long?"

"Not now, Katy. I should get you back."

Reluctantly Kate helped him pack up the picnic, well aware that she had probably spoiled the whole evening. Sam could barely look at her, and they packed the rest of the things up in silence, then loaded them into the back of the Land Rover. As she climbed into the passenger seat, Kate glanced over at him.

"Thank you for tonight," she said quietly. "I'm sorry I spoilt everything."

Sam turned on the engine and smiled at her. "You didn't. But something just wasn't quite right tonight. We'll do it again another time, when it will be right."

Kate fumbled with the seatbelt while she tried to imagine what he meant. She had to agree things had not been quite right between them. Firstly talking about Richard, and Sam suggesting she was having second thoughts, and then her faux pas of referring to the past.

But what did he mean about doing it another time? As everyone kept pointing out, she was getting married in three weeks. They could hardly go on a romantic picnic together after she was married, so he must be suggesting they go on another date fairly soon. She sat back in her seat and closed her eyes. Why would he even want to do that?

Things really did seem to be getting more and more complicated, and for once there wasn't really anyone she could discuss it with. Jenny must not know of her second date with Sam, and Jenny was really the only person she ever discussed things with.

She opened her eyes and sneaked a look at Sam as he drove. And what had he meant about her not understanding—not knowing the whole story? Of course she did. She had been there. What else could there be? What had he been running away from other than the heartbreak they all knew about? She would have to try and get him to tell her.

But not tonight.

As they pulled up to the kerb outside the park gates, Sam turned to her with a chuckle. "Of course it all makes sense now why I had to pick you up here on Thursday. I did think that was a bit odd. Come on, I'll walk you back across the field again."

Kate slid down onto the pavement and slammed the door behind her. "It's all right. You don't have to," she said half-heartedly. "I'll be okay on my own."

"Nonsense. I want to make sure you get home all right. Come on." He reached out, caught her hand, and pulled her towards the park entrance.

Desperately aware of his flesh touching hers, Kate stumbled along behind him, trying to make sense of his behaviour. She was fairly sure he liked her. In the same sort of way she was afraid she still liked him.

But if so, he was taking the news of her engagement rather too well. Unless—she frowned as a thought occurred to her—unless he just wasn't taking it seriously. Didn't actually believe she'd go through with it.

They had reached the wall that bordered the field, and Sam vaulted effortlessly onto it, holding out his hand to pull her up beside him.

"I *am* going to marry Richard," Kate said, as they watched the last rays of the setting sun disappear below the horizon.

"Of course you are."

"No, really. I am. It's all booked and paid for. It's cost my dad a fortune."

"I know." Sam jumped down into the field and waited for Kate to join him. He caught her hand again, and they set off through the long grass towards the houses.

As they got closer, Kate found herself automatically slowing her pace so as to delay their separation. She really couldn't imagine Sam wanting to make another date with her now he knew about Richard. And to be honest, she really shouldn't be considering it herself. It would most definitely be wiser for her to stay well away from him until after the wedding. She corrected herself—and stay away from him after the wedding, too. The thought made her suddenly feel very depressed, and she slowed almost to a stop, pulling on Sam's hand.

He turned, and she saw his eyes gleam in the growing dark. "Are you okay, Katy?"

Kate stopped walking altogether and stared up at him. "Yes. No. I don't know. Not really. What do we do now?"

Sam looked down at her quizzically. "Well, I shall go home to bed, and I suggest you do the same."

"That's not what I meant."

He grinned at her. "I expect you'll be pretty busy with the wedding for the next few weeks. Not much time for picnics." He had moved very close to her and put his hands on her shoulders. "But you know where I am, if you have a spare evening." He lowered his head and fastened his lips onto hers, this time lingering for a few seconds before pulling back and letting go of her. "See you soon."

With a wave, he turned and started back across the field towards the park, leaving Kate standing bemused and confused, her heart beating just a little faster than usual.

Chapter 10

Friday 10th July

"I really don't see why you have to go to Bristol for your Stag anyway." Kate gripped her phone under her chin while she attempted to struggle into her dress. "What's wrong with Exeter?"

She listened for a moment and rolled her eyes. "Well, do you have to do what they say? It's your Stag do. You should have an input." She listened again and frowned in annoyance. "Well, no, Jen organised it all, but that's not the point. You'll probably end up chained to a lamppost, or on a container ship bound for the Antarctic, and you won't get back till three weeks after the wedding. Anyway, I have to go now or I'll be late. I just wish we could have seen each other this week. You must come over on Monday and tell me all about it. Well, all the stuff I won't have already seen on Facebook, that is!"

She rescued the phone from under her chin and pressed it close to her ear while she slid her shoes on. "What? Oh, great. So do I not get to see you again before the wedding? Honestly, Richard, this is too much. How long will you be in London?…The whole week! Great. Well, you'd better send me a picture, then, or I'll forget what you look like. Got to go."

She disconnected the call and tossed the phone

onto her bed. Really, it was too much. What was the point of her having a fiancé if he was never there? She had really needed to see him this week to reassure herself that she wasn't having second thoughts, but he had been tied up the whole time.

And now he was off on his Stag weekend—how come he got a weekend when she only got a night?— and then straight off to London for a big case for the whole of the next week.

Kate picked up her bag and stomped downstairs. That would take it to just one week before the wedding. She really needed to see him before that. If only to confirm that the wedding was taking place. Which of course it was.

"Just off now, Mum. See you later." Kate pulled the front door open, hoping to escape outside before Helen responded. She was too late.

"Where are you going tonight?"

"Oh, just out with Jen. Haven't seen her all week. Need a bit of a catch-up."

"That's nice. Don't be too late."

"Mum, I'm twenty-six! It's not a school night, and I have a key." Kate rolled her eyes dramatically. "Stop fussing."

"You may be all grown up and getting married," Helen retorted, "but you're still my baby. Now have fun."

With a smile and a wave, Kate disappeared through the door and out into the garden. The weather was still very warm, and she was pleased with her choice of clothing for the evening. She was wearing a brand new, bright red dress she had only bought that day. It had caught her eye in the window of the clothes shop opposite her work, and she had succumbed to its charms in her lunch hour. She knew she looked good in it, and set off down the street with a spring in her step.

Since the picnic with Sam nearly a week ago, Kate had spent most of her time trying to put him out of her mind and concentrate on the wedding. The task had not been made easier by her not being able to see Richard at all, and now she had found she wouldn't be seeing him again for another week. At least she was seeing Jen tonight. Maybe she should confess about her second date with Sam. But not about the kiss. That was too confusing.

As she reached the centre of the village, she made sure she gave the Harlequin's Arms a wide berth so as to lessen the chance of seeing Sam, and hurried on along the road towards the village's only other pub, the very small Plough and Sickle. It was the pub most favoured by the older generation in the village, and normally she and Jen wouldn't have spent the evening there. However due to her present predicament with Sam, Kate had refused to go to the Harlequin's, and since neither of them wanted to drive, it was the Plough or nothing. As she approached the main entrance, Kate saw Jenny hurrying along from the opposite direction.

"Hi." Jenny waved as she got closer, wobbling dangerously on her heels on the uneven pavement. "Sorry, running a bit late."

"It's all right. I've only just got here." Kate grinned. "I wasn't early for once. Why are you wearing those shoes? No one's going to see you."

"*I* can see me," Jenny retorted, putting out a hand to steady herself against the wall. "I like these shoes, and I think I look good in them. We don't always have to dress to please other people, you know."

"I know." Kate laughed and pushed open the door of the pub. "But I bet you take them off to walk back home!"

The interior of the pub was dark, with low-beamed ceilings and heavy wooden furniture. It was split into two bars, a tiny lounge that was carpeted with a worn, red, patterned Axminster, and a larger public bar equipped with a pool table and darts board. The latter was relatively full, mostly of middle-aged farmers, while the lounge was completely empty.

Kate glanced back at Jenny. "Lounge, so we can talk?"

Jenny nodded and stepped carefully over the raised wooden step. "Yeah, too noisy in the other one. What are you drinking?"

"I'll get these." Kate was at the bar. "Wine?"

"Okay, ta." Jenny glanced around. "I'll grab a table before they all go, shall I?" she asked with a chuckle, crossing the room in two steps and sliding behind a small corner table.

Kate joined her with two glasses of white wine and a couple of packets of crisps, and sat down opposite. "There we go. Get stuck into that. Or did you want proper food?"

Jenny shook her head. "No. I had dinner before I came out. The food's pretty shit here anyway."

"That's what I thought." Kate opened her crisps and shoved a handful into her mouth. "That's better."

"So, how's your week been?" Jenny leaned back and surveyed Kate closely. "I feel you have something to tell me."

Kate narrowed her eyes. "Why?"

"The way you were on the phone. You saw Sam again, didn't you?"

Kate shifted uneasily in her chair and took a long swig of wine. "Why would you think that? He knows I'm engaged now."

"I still think you saw him again. I know you too well."

"Bloody hell, not you as well." Kate scowled in annoyance.

"As well?"

"Sam said that too." Kate sighed. "Okay, yes, I saw him again on Saturday night."

"Kate! Why?"

"I thought I owed it to him to explain about Richard, and try and explain why I didn't tell him. I actually thought that was why he wanted to meet up."

"And it wasn't?"

"Well, sort of. He did want to know why I hadn't told him, but…"

Jenny raised her eyebrows. "But?" she prompted.

"But he could have done that anywhere. Like the pub we went to on Thursday. I thought that's where we *were* going, actually."

Jenny sighed in frustration. "Get to the point, Kate! Where did you go?"

"He took me on a picnic. By a lovely river. And he'd made proper Italian pizza for me." Kate glanced up. "It was kinda romantic. He didn't need to do that."

Jenny sat back in her chair and whistled. "Phew! Kate you've got to stay away from him. Has he called you since?"

Kate shook her head. "No. And I haven't called him."

"Good! I should hope not. So it was a proper date, then? What did you talk about?"

"He wanted to know about Richard and why I had agreed to go on a date with him when I was engaged." Kate shrugged. "I said I wasn't sure it *was* a date, and maybe it was more of a friend thing. Then I messed it all up and mentioned him going travelling without me."

"I don't think there's anything *to* mess up here, Kate." Jenny frowned at her. "You can't have a relationship with Sam. You're getting married in two weeks."

"And one day."

"Don't be pedantic! Why did that mess things up anyway? You knew why he went."

"I know. That was a bit weird, actually. He said I don't know the whole story, but he wouldn't tell me. I don't know what he means. We were all there when it happened. What else could there be to know?"

"No idea. But Kate, that really doesn't matter. What matters is you went on a romantic date with Sam Somerville just three weeks before your wedding. And I can tell you want to go again."

"No, I don't. He hasn't asked me again. He knows I'm marrying Richard."

"But are you?" Jenny sounded genuinely worried. "Are you having second thoughts? If you have feelings for Sam, and not just high school crush feelings, then what about Richard? Do you still love him?"

"Yes, of course I do." Kate wriggled impatiently. "I love Richard. But I guess I do have feelings for Sam. Can I do that?"

"No! Of course you can't. You have to choose, and if you say you still love Richard, and the wedding is all organised and paid for, then I think you should marry him and keep well away from Sam."

"I know." Kate sighed and stared out the window. "But he'd let me be an explorer. In fact he'd come with me. But I don't even know if he likes me like that." She bit her lip as she guiltily remembered the kiss, and realised she was actually quite sure how he felt about her. But maybe he just wanted to have a fling with her. He might not be a good long-term bet. Kate closed her eyes. What was she turning into? She was twenty-six and thinking like a fifty-year-old. She shouldn't be worrying about a "long term bet," she should be out having fun like Vicky. Why was she even marrying Richard in the first place?

With a sudden movement, she picked up her wine and downed the lot. "Jen, I need your help."

"Of course, what is it?"

"Major panic attack here. Why am I getting married? I'm too young to settle down. Why did I ever agree?"

"Because you love Richard. You get on very well, and he loves you. Until Sam came back, you didn't even question it."

"But maybe I should have done. Maybe Sam is just a catalyst to show me what a mistake I'm making. I've just realised how boring Richard is, remember? And now I'm worrying that I didn't notice before because I was just as boring. What the hell am I going to do? The wedding is all paid for. I can't let Mum and Dad down!"

"Kate, you love Richard. You said you still love him You need to see him, talk to him, remind yourself why you're marrying him."

"That's easier said than done." Kate pushed her chair back in frustration. "I haven't seen him since the day of the fête, the day Sam came back, and I shan't be seeing him for at least another week."

"Why? That's a long time."

"He's in Bristol this weekend for the Stag. That's okay, I guess, but then on Monday he's off to London for the whole week for some big case. I shan't see him till this time next week, at the earliest. Jen, that will only be one week until the wedding. I need to see him before that. I'm forgetting what he's like. I need to have sex with him."

"God, Kate! I don't need to know that."

"No, that's always been really good. I need to do that to remind myself of the good things about our relationship. We've always really clicked in bed."

Jenny wrinkled her nose. "As I said, I really don't need, or want, to know that. But Kate, you can't marry someone solely because they're good in bed. That's no basis for a relationship."

"Whose side are you on?" Kate stared at her desperately. "I thought you wanted me to marry him. Now you're confusing me."

"Of course I want you to marry him, but only for the right reasons. You must marry him because you love him and want to spend the rest of your life with him. Not because he's a good shag!"

Kate giggled. "I know. He is, though. But I think if we spend some time together and have sex, I'll remember why I love him. That's what I mean. I think I've only been looking at Sam because I haven't actually had Richard here for so long. I know I love him, really. We get on very well."

"Okay." Jenny looked at her doubtfully. "Well, find some way for that to happen, then, and quickly. You don't have much time. Could you go and join him in London, maybe?"

Kate nodded slowly. "Maybe. I'd just have to turn up, 'cause I know he'd tell me not to come. He gets so precious about his work, but I'm sure he must get some time off. If I took a couple of days off mid-week, I could go up and surprise him. It needn't interfere with his work. We could just spend the evening together, but it would give me a chance to reconnect with him."

"That sounds like a good plan." Jen nodded with approval. "You really do need to see him. Get this sorted once and for all. And for god's sake, keep away from Sam." She picked up the glasses and headed back to the bar for refills.

"I will." Kate sighed. She just wished she didn't have to. She picked up her phone and logged onto Facebook. Richard and his friends should be out on the town in Bristol by now, and she wondered if they had posted any pictures. Maybe if she saw him having fun, that would reassure her. She scrolled down the page, and suddenly there was a picture of Richard, a top hat on his head adorned with the words "Future Slave" and with a large plastic ball and chain attached to his ankle. He was, thankfully, grinning widely, and his friends were all crowded around him. Clearly someone had thought to take a selfie stick, not something Kate would ever have associated with her fiancé.

Jenny arrived back from the bar and deposited the drinks on the table, followed by some packets of peanuts.

"Look, Jen, I found a pic of Richard at his Stag.

They've dressed him up. He looks pretty happy, though."

Jenny took the phone and grinned when she saw the picture. "Did it help, seeing him?"

"I guess." Kate shrugged. "He *is* very good-looking. Even dressed like that."

"Ooh, they've just posted some more…" Jenny held the phone out to Kate and moved round so they could both look.

"Well, it does look like they're having fun." Kate scrolled through the small collection of pictures that had appeared, a smile beginning on her face. "I've not seen him enjoy himself like that for ages." She peered more closely at the screen. "There's a girl in this one. God, I hope they haven't got him a stripper!"

Jenny was looking over her shoulder. "That's not a stripper. That's your sister."

"What the fuck?" Kate's grip tightened on the phone and she peered more closely at it. "Bloody hell, it is. What the hell is she doing there? I told her to keep away, but I never really thought she'd try and join them. God, I hate her! She spoils everything I ever do."

"She does live there. Maybe she just bumped into them," Jenny suggested reasonably. "She might have done."

"Yeah, right." Kate gave a snort. "You know my sister. This was deliberate. Look, they've added more photos. Bet she's in all of them." She began to scroll through the ten new photos that had appeared on Richard's page. In each one, the four boys were joined by the grinning figure of her sister, in most cases with her arms draped around at least one of them. Kate's eyes flashed as she got to the end of the photos, and she slammed her phone down on the table. "That little bitch," she muttered through clenched teeth. "She's done this just to spite me. I specifically told her not to go and look for them. How can we even be related? She's not being a bridesmaid. I shall refuse to let her in the house…"

Jenny patted her on the shoulder. "Calm down, Kate. What's she actually done wrong here? No, hear me out. She lives in Bristol, she knew the Stag was happening there, and she probably just wanted to go along and say hello. I agree that appearing in all the photos was probably designed to annoy you, but let's face it, she's not trying to steal Richard. He's there on his Stag with his best friends. There's no way they're gonna let any woman molest him. Let alone your sister. They all know her, don't they?" Kate nodded. "Well, there you are, then. They'll know what she's like. Stop worrying and drink your wine. This is supposed to be our night. Don't let her spoil it." Jenny sat back down and watched Kate across the table.

Kate took a deep breath and slipped her phone back into her bag. "Okay. I guess you could be right. I shall try and forget it."

Jenny looked at her speculatively. "Well, at least that showed one thing."

"What?"

"You do still care about Richard. If you didn't, you wouldn't care what he was up to."

Kate wrinkled her nose. "Maybe. Yeah, I guess so. I was really angry. Vicky does that to me, though. Would I have cared as much if there was some other woman draped all over him?"

"I think you would." Jenny took a sip of wine.

"And you know what I think? I think you should definitely go up to London next week. You really need to see him. Can you get the time off work?"

Kate shrugged. "Probably not. I have three weeks booked off for the wedding and the honeymoon. I guess I could pull a sickie."

"Right, well, really do it. You need to sort this. Will you tell him you're coming?"

"No. He'll tell me not to, but if I just turn up, he's stuck with me, and he'll have to talk to me. I guess it would be a good idea. I can't wait another week to see him, not feeling like this."

"Good girl." Jenny nodded. "It'll get you out of Sam's way for a day or so, too."

"That's not a problem." Kate shook her head. "It really isn't. He was just a crush." With amazing lips, her mind continued silently. With amazing lips that had the potential to be even more amazing, given the right situation.

"Kate? Are you all right?"

"Yeah. Of course. Just remembered something. Come on, let's have another drink and a good gossip. If you want to come back to mine after, we could watch a film. I have lots of chocolate."

Chapter 11

Tuesday 14th July

Kate stared out the window as the train hurtled through the countryside on its way to London. She had managed to convince her boss she had a bad headache, due to wedding stress, and would need the day off. He had been surprisingly sympathetic, and she had had a tiny qualm of conscience about deceiving him. Then she remembered his heart-to-heart with her about his sex life, and decided he could manage without her. She had taken an overnight bag in case Richard was delighted to see her and she was able to stay in his hotel with him. If so, she would of course need another excuse for missing work tomorrow. She'd cross that bridge when she came to it.

She had very nearly told Richard she was coming, but they had ended up having a row via text messages, and she decided not to. When she had confronted him—quite calmly, she thought—about the presence of Vicky at his Stag, he had got surprisingly annoyed, for him, and accused her of paranoia.

He assured her Vicky had come across them by accident and had in fact only stayed with them while they took the photos that Kate and Jen had seen. He claimed she had then left with a group of her own friends and they hadn't seen her again.

Maybe she was paranoid, but Kate was pretty sure he was lying, and in a couple of later photos, she could swear that Vicky was in the background. Richard had been quite condescending to her—no mean feat by text—and she had ended up shouting at him in capital letters, then terminating the conversation. That had been on Sunday night, and it was now midmorning on Tuesday.

She leaned back in her seat and closed her eyes, the rhythm of the train beginning to make her drowsy. She had only managed to get a rather slow train that stopped at nearly every station, and the journey still had another two hours to go. She may as well try and have a nap. It was going to be a long day.

No sooner had she started to doze than they pulled into a station, and she was jolted awake by an overloud announcement. She wriggled into a more comfortable position and leaned her head against the window, carefully keeping her bag on the seat next to her, to deter other travellers. Luckily, the train was relatively empty, and she was confident she should be able to keep the seat vacant. She watched as the two newly arrived passengers took their seats, then with a judder the train set off again, picking up speed as it left the town and once more sped through the countryside.

Kate sighed. She wasn't going to get to sleep; her mind was far too active. Why on earth had she decided to travel to London? She already knew that Richard was going to be annoyed with her for surprising him, but hopefully he would also be pleased that she cared enough about seeing him that she had taken the trouble to travel all the way from Devon to London on a whim. Of course, he wasn't spontaneous, so he might not understand at all. Richard always had to have things planned in advance, and had always abhorred Kate's propensity for random actions. He usually viewed these events quite indulgently, and as Kate thought about it, she realised he could actually be quite patronising when he wanted. If she was going to marry him, that would have to change. She sighed. There was that "if" again. Still, in a way that was what this trip to London was about. She had to be totally certain she ought to be marrying him. And she needed to be well away from home, and Sam Somerville, when she made that decision. As her thoughts strayed to Sam, Kate found to her dismay that her lips started to tingle again. She rubbed her finger across them, unable to prevent her memory replaying the two kisses. However wrong it was of her, she was also unable to stop her mind wondering just what a proper snog with him would be like.

With an annoyed sigh, she turned to stare out the window. How did her life get this complicated? It should all be so calm and easy. She should be happily preparing for her wedding to the man she loved, looking forward to the rest of her life in his company. The rest of her life committed to him.

That was the word that was bothering her. Committed. Why did people keep using that word? It seemed so final, so formal and, if she was honest, scary. Maybe she was scared of commitment? Could that be the problem? She didn't *think* she was, but maybe that was it. She did love Richard, of course she did, but the idea of being stuck with—no, *committed to*—him for the rest of her life was scaring the shit out of her.

She let her mind drift away for a moment and

found herself in the field behind her house, Sam's lips on hers. He didn't scare her. He didn't bore her, either. Kate closed her eyes and pressed her face against the window.

But she was in love with Richard, and the wedding was all paid for. Sam had only just arrived back in her life, after eight years away. She didn't even really know him any more. Just because he was a good kisser—she stopped herself.

Just because the mere touch of his lips on hers had very nearly caused her legs to give way was no reason to cancel her wedding to a very suitable, sensible man who loved her. Sam hadn't said he loved her. He hadn't asked her not to marry Richard. In fact, he had seemed to accept the fact of her engagement quite phlegmatically, so he obviously wasn't that bothered.

Kate scowled at the passing countryside.

No. She was marrying Richard. She just needed to see him again before she was totally committed. There was that word again. What she really needed was to have sex with him. He was good at that.

She curled up in the corner of the seat and closed her eyes again. Yes, he was good at that. Maybe if they'd been doing more of that lately she wouldn't be feeling the way she was. As she began to drift into a light doze, she found she was wondering just how good Sam would be in bed.

****

Kate pushed open the door of the court building and walked into the large entrance hall. She ascertained from Richard's office where his case was being heard, and roughly what time he was expected to break for lunch, and had decided to take a chance and wait for him. Her heart was beating over-fast as she realised it probably hadn't been one of her better ideas. He didn't like surprises at the best of times, and to have his very stressed fiancée turn up while he was in the middle of an important case—a fiancée demanding a night of passion—probably wasn't high on his wish list.

Kate bit her lip. Maybe she should just go back home and never tell him she was there. But then she'd never be sure. She had to be sure. She perched on the edge of a blue plastic chair, partly concealed by a large rubber plant, and took a deep breath. What did she have to be sure about? Marrying him? She had to marry him. It was all paid for. Everyone was coming. The food was all ordered, even the nuts for Cousin Emil. She'd be letting everyone down if she didn't marry him. Including him. And of course she loved him, so she couldn't let him down, either. She just needed to do something to cement that love, and sex seemed to be the best way. She just hoped he felt the same.

The sound of a door opening to her left, followed by footsteps coming closer, brought Kate to her feet, and she peered nervously around the plant. The door to the courtroom Richard was in was propped open, and several people were coming through it. As she watched, half a dozen members of the public, accompanied by a bewigged barrister, passed her and headed towards the main door.

She glanced behind them just in time to see Richard emerge from the court, deep in conversation with a stout man in a shiny grey suit. The man was wiping his balding head with a white handkerchief while attempting to shake Richard's hand. Richard patted him on the shoulder, murmured a few words in his ear, then moved away in Kate's direction. As he approached her, she stepped out from behind the plant and smiled at him.

"Hello, Richard."

He stopped short and stared at her in amazement. "Kate. You're here. Why… What on earth… Kate, why are you here?" He sounded very harassed, and Kate felt her heart plummet.

"I've come to see you," she whispered, all her confidence ebbing away. "I was missing you. I thought maybe we could…" She realised her suggestion of an afternoon of passion wasn't going to be well received.

Richard stared at her for a moment longer, then moved towards her and gave her a quick hug. "I'm sorry. That was rather rude of me. I've had a very stressful time in court this morning, and I have to go back after lunch. I'm sorry, Kate, but it's not really very convenient for you to be here. I have to meet some clients for lunch, and I have no idea what time I'll be finished this afternoon." He put his hands on her shoulders and smiled down at her. "I'm sorry, darling. Did you come all the way up here just to see me? I think you may have wasted your time. Even when I finish here tonight I have a dinner with some other clients. I'm sorry. I've missed you too."

"Have you? Really?" Kate looked up at him, her face serious. He was still just as good-looking. But he did look silly in that wig.

"Of course, darling. It's been hell not being able to see you these last couple of weeks. How are the wedding preparations going?" He glanced over his shoulder as he spoke, and nodded to a tall man in a dark suit who was standing by the main door.

"Okay." Kate sighed. "Go on, you need to go. I should have realised you'd be too busy to spend time with me. My own fault. I didn't think it through."

"My impetuous Kate." Richard smiled indulgently at her and dropped a light kiss on her head. "I really do have to go, I'm afraid. I should be back by Friday. We can do something then. Okay?"

"Okay." Kate nodded. "I'm sorry I disturbed you."

"That's all right, but I really do have to go. See you soon. And remember, it won't be long before we'll be together all the time." As he turned to leave, a tall grey-haired barrister appeared at his side.

"Richard, are you off for lunch? We need to have a chat."

Richard paused. "Yes, Tom, just off now, running a bit late, but I can give you a couple of moments. Hang on. Just need to speak to someone. This is my fiancée, Kate." He moved away to speak to the man by the door, and the newcomer held out his hand to Kate.

"Hello again."

Kate took his hand and frowned. "I'm sorry, have we met? I'm usually pretty good with faces…"

"Yes, a couple of times at parties, I think. Once was in Mayfair a few weeks back. Do you not remember? Well, I thought it was you. I'm so sorry, maybe I'm mistaken. What did you say your name was?"

"Kate, I'm Richard's fiancée." She watched him closely. "I don't think it could have been me. I've never been to a party in Mayfair. Or any parties in London with Richard."

The man looked a little uncomfortable and shook his head, peering more closely at her. "I'm so sorry.

Must have been someone who looked like you. I don't think I knew her name anyway. Sorry, don't know why I thought it was you. Are you here to see Richard?" He gave a short laugh. "Well, I assume you must be."

Kate nodded. "Yes, I popped up on the off chance, but he seems to be really busy today. I shall be going back to Devon later."

Richard appeared at Kate's side and gave an apologetic smile. "Sorry about that. Just needed to say I'd be a little late for lunch. Tom, I can give you five minutes. Will that do?"

"Fine, fine. Nice to meet you." He nodded to Kate and moved a few feet away.

Richard smiled down at her. "Sorry, darling, need to go now. Must sort this out and then try and make it to lunch. I'll see you on Friday." He blew her a kiss, turned to join Tom, and they walked around the corner to talk.

Kate sank down onto the blue plastic chair again. She'd got it wrong. As usual she had been too impetuous. She had even thought he might be pleased to see her, but although he had hidden it well, she could tell Richard had been slightly annoyed by her intrusion. She had to admit it had been a long shot, but she had hoped she might at least be able to spend the evening with him. It was probably better he never knew she had brought an overnight bag.

She got to her feet, shouldered her bag, and headed back out onto the street. She was in London now, so she may as well make the most of it. She had already checked out the return trains, just in case her little plan backfired, and she knew that the fastest evening one left Paddington at eight thirty. If she aimed for that one, it gave her all afternoon to do a bit of sightseeing. She very rarely got to spend any time in London, and almost never on her own. She could actually do whatever she liked.

Whipping out the little street map she had been careful to bring with her, Kate worked out where she was, and was delighted to see how close Trafalgar Square was. That was always a good place to start; there was usually something fun going on there. And then she could pay a visit to the National Gallery, and the Portrait Gallery as well. She stuffed her map back into her pocket and set off along the crowded pavement, a little feeling of excitement stirring inside her at the thought of a day doing what she wanted in London, and skiving off from work. It wasn't often she did things like that.

As she walked, Kate considered her situation. It was true she was impetuous, up to a point. She often did things without thinking them through properly, but it was very rare for her to "misbehave." Skiving off from work was something she had never actually done in all the five years she had been in the job. Maybe she *was* as boring as Richard. Maybe that's why she'd never noticed until recently that he was.

Until Sam Somerville had returned and tempted her to misbehave by going out with him, to be more precise.

Kate smiled to herself. That had really been misbehaving to a huge degree. Not the first date, of course. That had just been meant to be a catch-up with an old friend, but the subsequent date, and the fact that she never mentioned she was getting married? That had been misbehaviour. The kisses hadn't. She had had no control over them. It would have been rude to pull away.

So maybe she wasn't quite so boring after all, and that was why she had suddenly noticed that Richard was. He had looked very handsome in his court clothes, she had to admit that. Apart from the stupid wig, of course. But he wouldn't be wearing that in bed.

She shook her head. God, she was getting obsessed with sex! That was probably all that was wrong with her. She was frustrated because she and Richard hadn't been able to sleep together for weeks now, and the unexpected kisses from Sam had reminded her just how long it had been.

She smiled again as she hurried towards Trafalgar Square, remembering his lips on hers, and wondered just how bad it would be if she misbehaved again and met up with him before the wedding. Immediately she dismissed the idea and mentally shook herself. That would be A Very Bad Idea. She was going to marry Richard—of course she was—and consequently she needed to keep as far away from Sam as was possible. She didn't need anything else to sway her resolve.

As she passed the huge bronze lions that guarded the square, Kate found herself gazing around like a child at all the street performers and artists who were out enjoying the gorgeous weather and entertaining the thronging tourists. She paused for a moment or two to watch some jugglers. Then, since her stomach had been suggesting it might be lunchtime ever since she got off the train, she headed for the National Gallery with the intention of eating in their café.

Climbing the steps, she pushed open the heavy glass door and walked into the welcome coolness of the gallery entrance hall. She smiled to herself; she loved the gallery, and it had been several years since her last visit. Picking up a plan of the exhibits, Kate made her way straight to the café, where she found a table by the window and ordered a Brie and cranberry panini, a chocolate muffin, and a pot of tea.

She felt almost guilty having the tea and glanced furtively around, just in case her mother had followed her and was lurking in the corner. She would never let her live it down if she knew she had voluntarily had a cup of tea. She took a grateful bite out of the panini and planned the rest of her visit while she ate.

****

By the time Kate had finished her lunch it was nearly two thirty, so she left her overnight bag in the cloakroom and set off on a delightful wander around, rediscovering all her favourite paintings. If she hadn't studied English Literature at Uni, she would definitely have done History of Art, and she was fairly knowledgeable about several periods. Her particular favourites were the Impressionists, and she spent a happy hour browsing those rooms before heading over to the Sainsbury Wing, where her second favourites, the Early Renaissance works, were housed.

Her mind completely absorbed by the art, she found she had no time to think about the wedding, or Richard, or Sam, or even sex, and by five o'clock she was once more starving and in need of a sit down.

She decided to go back to the café, have some more cake, then pop over to the Portrait Gallery next door for a quick look. She was fairly sure it closed at six, so she didn't linger over her cake and more illicit tea before collecting her bag and walking the few yards to the gallery.

After a quick run around, she found herself being herded to the door with the few remaining tourists when it reached six, and she emerged into the still busy Trafalgar Square.

It was a beautiful evening, and since there were still a couple of hours before her train left, Kate sat on the wall by one of the fountains and soaked up the atmosphere. She realised that the day had actually done her a great deal of good. Although it hadn't achieved her original purpose, that of an afternoon of passion with her fiancé, it had allowed her to relax and completely leave behind all her stresses and worries. She felt miles better, and actually fairly well disposed towards Richard.

She totally understood his annoyance at her arrival, and of course she shouldn't really have expected him to drop everything on a work day and take her to bed. But it had been nice to see him and realise he was still just as good-looking.

She trailed her fingers in the cool water and gazed around her. It was so good to be away from home. Away from the little village where she seemed to spend her entire life. Where everyone knew her, and everyone knew each other's business. She realised she had been pretty lucky that no one seemed to know of her trysts with Sam. That would really put the cat among the pigeons.

How could she have been so stupid? Just because she had had a crush on him back in high school, why had she behaved like a teenager when he returned? She really needed to grow up. In less than two weeks she would be a married woman.

A responsible married woman.

A tiny flicker of something fluttered in her stomach, and she stood up, suddenly determined to ignore it. Nothing must spoil her lovely day.

Glancing at her phone, she saw it was nearing seven and decided to head towards Paddington, ready for her train. She always liked to get to the station earlier than necessary. Slinging her bag over her shoulder, she turned, and with a last look around the square, headed for the nearest underground station.

As she picked her way through the crowds and hurried across the busy roads, Kate couldn't help glancing into some of the brightly lit restaurants, wishing she had left more time to go and get a proper meal. She would need to get something at Paddington to take on the train. That would be fun anyway. Bit like a picnic. That made her think of Sam, and she started walking faster in an attempt to banish his face—and lips—from her mind.

As she was forced by the sheer volume of pedestrians to slow down passing a very smart Italian restaurant, a familiar figure caught her eye, and she stopped in surprise. Richard was just disappearing through the door with a group of people. Not that surprising, since he had already told her he was out to dinner with some clients, but Kate stared after him, her mouth going suddenly dry. He had his arm around the waist of a woman. A tall thin woman with glossy, shoulder-length, dark brown hair.

Kate only caught a glimpse of her back view, but there was something slightly familiar about her. She started to move towards the restaurant, then checked. What was she doing? If she went in to confront

Richard, what on earth was she going to say? And what would the outcome be?

Slowly she moved over to stand against the window of the next building, out of the way of the hurrying pedestrians. It could all be completely innocent. She could be a client and he was just putting his arm around her to guide her through the door. People did that. Didn't they? Or he could be having an affair.

Kate leaned back against the window and closed her eyes. Whichever it was, if she charged in and accused him of anything, she could end up looking very silly. She really had to just walk away and talk to him about it as soon as she could.

Slowly she began to walk towards the station again, her head thumping painfully and her stomach in knots. Richard wouldn't have an affair. He was far too boring and sensible. If either one of them was going to have an affair, it was going to be her.

And if she had managed to resist Sam Somerville, then there was no way Richard would succumb to some random woman. He loved her.

But they hadn't had sex for weeks. Maybe she was a prostitute. Maybe he'd got desperate and couldn't wait any longer.

Kate stopped walking again, and three people cannoned into her. She had to text him. Right now.

Standing stock still in the middle of the pavement, the commuters muttering as they were forced to go around her, she wrote a quick text and pressed Send.

I'm on my way to the station. Are you okay? What are you doing now?

She didn't want to sound suspicious, but just

wanted to see what he said. A few moments later her phone bleeped.

Travel safely. I'm fine, just tired. Out for that dinner now with a group of clients. Boring. See you Friday. Love you.

Kate started walking again as she read it. Well, he wasn't trying to pretend he hadn't gone out to a restaurant. And there had been a whole group of people with him. Not just the woman with the nice hair. She slipped her phone back into her pocket and picked up speed. Well, nothing she could do about it now; she had a train to catch.

It wasn't until much later, when she was on the train tucking into a very large tuna baguette and a diet cola, that she remembered the man at the court who had thought he'd known her. Did that mean Richard had been taking other women to parties? Or was the man just getting confused? He had been fairly old.

She took a large bite of her baguette and chewed thoughtfully. She would have quite a lot to discuss with Richard when he got back on Friday.

Chapter 12

Wednesday 15th July

"So where were you yesterday, Kate?" Holly turned round as Kate walked into the staff room. She carried on spooning coffee into four mugs. "Were you skiving?"

"Of course not." Kate turned her face away in case it betrayed her. "I had a headache."

"Oh, right."

Kate glanced at the girl suspiciously. "Why do you say it like that? Don't you believe me?"

"Well, you may have had a headache, but you certainly didn't stay home all day." Holly grinned at her as she slopped milk into the mugs. "My mum saw you at Tiverton Parkway last night. Coming off the London train."

Kate sat down on the sofa and closed her eyes. "Oh, whatever," she said wearily. "Are you going to tell anyone?"

"Course not!" Holly sat down beside her. "I wouldn't dob someone in. I'm sure you had a good reason for skiving. Did you go to see your boyfriend?"

"Fiancé," Kate corrected absently. "Yes, I did. He's been in London all week, and we haven't seen each other for ages."

"So you went all the way to London just to see

him?" Holly's heavily mascaraed eyes were wide. "That's soooo romantic! What did you do there? Did you go out for a meal? Did he take you dancing?"

"Nothing." Kate gave a short laugh. "I hadn't told him I was coming, and he was really busy and had to work all day. Then he had a business dinner in the evening." She frowned as she remembered the girl at the restaurant. "So I went sightseeing and caught an evening train home."

"Oh." Holly looked disappointed. "So you didn't go to a hotel and have an afternoon of passion?"

"You read too many romance novels." Kate walked over to the kettle, careful to keep her face turned away from the girl. "That's not real life." She got two mugs out of the cupboard and placed them on the work surface, aware that her colour was higher than usual. How very perceptive of Holly to come up with that idea!

"I think real life *should* be like that. When I have a boyfriend—sorry, fiancé—we'll do stuff like that. When we're not in space."

"Or exploring the Amazon?" Kate glanced over her shoulder.

"Or that." Holly nodded. "My fiancé won't be too busy to make love to me."

"Holly, that's enough." Kate slammed the milk bottle down and took a deep breath. "Hadn't you better take those coffees back before they go cold?"

Nervously Holly put the mugs on a small tray and backed out of the room, her eyes never leaving Kate. As the door slammed shut behind her, Kate let her head drop forward, and she supported herself on the work surface on her elbows. That girl talked too much, and now her words had done much to undermine the good the trip to London had done. With a sigh, Kate finished making the coffees and carried them back to her office. Her boss had disappeared, so she put his down on his desk, then carried hers over to the window.

It was raining for the first time in a couple of weeks, and the light drops pattered gently on the glass, trickling down and pooling on the windowsill. Kate stared down at the yard. The half dozen second-hand tractors that stood hopefully to attention were shiny from the unaccustomed shower and gleamed as the weak sun attempted to fight its way back through the clouds.

A large puddle had formed in the middle of the yard, and Kate had a sudden vision of putting on her wellies and jumping right into the middle of it. The thought brought a small smile to her face, and she turned away from the window. Richard would never do that. He might watch indulgently while she did, but he would make no secret of the fact that he thought the act to be childish.

Suddenly annoyed, Kate put her mug down none too gently on her desk and picked up her phone. She wrote a quick text.

When it rains I like to splash in the puddles. I always have and I always will. Deal with it.

She pressed Send, and the message winged its way to an unsuspecting Richard, still battling it out in court in London.

That'll show him, Kate thought, scowling to herself. She was still going to be her, even after she was married. No one could take that away from her. Which, to be fair, Richard probably didn't want to do. But she couldn't afford to take any chances. This was her whole life she was putting on the line with this wedding. There needed to be some ground rules.

She sat down at her desk and moved a few papers around randomly. Her mind was definitely not on her work, and she had absolutely no idea what she was supposed to be doing. To be honest, she wasn't really being much use to anyone, and it would be better all round if she went home, but having skived the day before, she felt duty bound to stay and attempt to do some work. As of Friday night, she was on holiday for three weeks, so she really ought to try and leave the office in some semblance of order for the temp.

With a sigh, she picked up the pile of papers in her in-tray and began to sort through them. If she could just get rid of those, she wouldn't feel so bad leaving the place for so long. Although why she felt bad at all she wasn't sure. She didn't even like the job, and once they were married she was definitely going to look for another one.

They would be living in his flat to start with, which was considerably further away from her job, and Richard had also mentioned they may need to move nearer to London, so she'd actually be forced to leave it in that eventuality.

She stopped sifting through the papers and stared ahead of her. Move nearer to London. She hadn't really considered what that would mean.

She had always lived in Devon. She had always considered it her home, and imagined she always would. Going travelling for a period of time would be fine, like she had been going to do after school, but to move to London…that was different.

No. She mustn't come up with more obstacles to her marriage. She really needed to man up, if the thought of leaving her home village freaked her out to that extent. It would be an adventure. Not quite like exploring the Himalayas, or canoeing through a rain forest, but an adventure nonetheless. The sort of adventure one would have with Richard. A sort of safe adventure, with lots of home comforts. Richard was not the type to want to rough it. He had been horrified when she had suggested a caravan trip a couple of years ago, and she hadn't even dared mention the camping trip she really fancied.

No, Richard may be good in bed, but he wasn't very adventurous out of it. She doubted he even owned a pair of wellies.

Now slightly annoyed, Kate gathered up her papers again and dumped them all back in the tray. Tomorrow would do for them. Right now she needed some food, and the canteen should be open. A nice bacon roll and a cupcake should do the trick. As she left the room and headed towards the stairs, her boss appeared.

"Kate, where are you off to?" He peered at her closely. "You don't look well. Have you still got a headache?"

"A bit," Kate thought quickly, and let her shoulders droop. "It's still niggling."

"You should go home. Take the rest of the day off so you're better tomorrow." He patted her on the shoulder. "I need you on top form tomorrow. We have that meeting with the directors."

Kate smiled weakly at him. "Really? You think I should go home? Well, I do still feel a bit odd. Is it really all right?"

"Yes, now off you go, but make sure you're back in full health tomorrow. No point hanging around here if you're not on top form."

Kate stepped back into the office, collected her bag, and scurried out and down the stairs before he could change his mind. She had got the rest of the day off without having to skive. She'd only had to tell a tiny lie, and in fact her head did feel a bit muzzy.

She walked out into the drizzle and hurried round to her car, still concerned lest he change his mind and call her back. Two illicit days off in a row. She really *was* learning how to misbehave! She must think of something fun to do with the rest of the day in order to make the most of it.

****

As she drove back into the village, Kate had a sudden craving for nut chocolate, so she pulled her car alongside the pavement opposite the village shop. Grabbing her purse, she headed inside and scooped up a couple of bars of chocolate and two packets of crisps. That should keep her going for her afternoon of skiving. She smiled to herself as she left the shop and started back towards the car. She was really beginning to get the hang of this misbehaving. It was rather fun.

"Katy!"

Sam's voice stopped her in her tracks, and she paused on the edge of the pavement. "Hi." She watched as he approached her from the direction of the pub. He looked as hot as ever, and he flashed her a heart-stopping smile as he joined her.

"Where are you off to? Shouldn't you be at work?"

"Got sent home." Kate grinned at him. "My boss thought I looked ill."

"But you're not?"

"No. But he thought I was yesterday, so it was easy to make him believe it."

"So you're skiving?" Sam looked down at her, his head on one side. "Why did he think you were ill yesterday?"

"Oh. No reason." Kate looked away, suddenly realising she didn't want to tell Sam where she had been the day before.

"You skived yesterday too?"

"Never mind that." Kate tossed her head impatiently. "What are you up to?"

Sam narrowed his eyes at her and took a step closer. "Hmm. Okay. Not much. Glad I ran into you. I was hoping to see you again soon."

"You were?" Kate looked up at him, suddenly acutely aware of his proximity.

"Haven't seen you at all since our picnic. I was hoping we were okay."

"Of course we're okay." Kate looked at him in surprise. "Why wouldn't we be?"

"Just checking." Sam looked down at her. "I was hoping we might be able to try the picnic again sometime. If you like." He looked away, and Kate caught a hint of vulnerability in his eyes.

Resisting the temptation to reach out and touch him, she shook her head. "I would love that. But I don't know when. I seem to be really busy at the moment, so unless it was right now I'm not sure when I could fit it in."

She heard the words leave her mouth and marvelled at her own weakness. Here she was admitting to Sam that she wanted to see him again, just twenty-four hours after her ill-fated trip to London during which she had resolved to keep away from him.

"Now sounds good to me." Sam grinned at her. "Or at least it would if I wasn't supposed to be working in the bar."

"What, now? You're supposed to be behind the bar now?"

"Yeah. I just popped out to speak to you when I saw you go in the shop." Sam looked a bit sheepish. "It's not very busy in there."

"You'd better go back." Kate smiled. "I should get home, really, I suppose. I *am* meant to be ill."

"Come in for a drink first." Sam smiled hopefully. "Just a quick one?"

The sane voices in her head screaming at her to refuse, Kate nonetheless found herself saying, "Okay. Just a quick one, then," and falling into step beside him as he headed back to the pub. What the hell was she thinking? She had decided she must avoid all contact with Sam until the wedding, and in fact after the wedding, but here she was going for a drink with him. It would have been easy for her to refuse.

And she had also told him she wanted to go on another picnic with him. Was she actually losing her mind? Jen must definitely not hear about this little aberration!

Sam pushed open the door of the pub and stood back to allow Kate to go through. "What d'you want to drink? On the house."

"Just a diet cola, please. Thank you."

Sam walked round behind the bar while Kate slid onto a high stool and rested her elbows on the bar. Glancing round cautiously, she noted there were only a couple of people in the lounge, and she didn't recognise any of them.

"There you go." Sam placed a tall glass in front of her. "Don't worry, no one will report back to your fiancé."

"I didn't think…" Kate felt her face flushing. "I'm allowed to come to the pub for a drink. Specially when I'm friends with the barman."

"Of course. We're friends." Sam's voice was neutral, and Kate looked up to find him watching her. "So you don't think you'll have time for another picnic before your wedding, then? That's a shame."

Kate took a long drink of her cola, watching Sam over the rim. She was finding it hard to interpret his mood. "It's all a bit hectic. And much as I'd like to, I'm not really sure I should."

"Maybe you shouldn't really like to, then." Sam moved away to serve another customer, and Kate stared after him. What had that meant? And why did he have to be quite so gorgeous? It really wasn't making her plan to stay away from him any easier. In fact, he was making it harder. Why was he asking her out again when he knew she was getting married in less than two weeks?

Less than two weeks. Kate felt her head start to swim, and she took another long drink. In less than two weeks she would be married to Richard. Forever. No chance of any more picnics. Was that why she was actually considering going on another one? Because it was her last chance?

She drained her glass and placed it on the bar. She really had to leave before she misbehaved again. Coming into the pub was proving to be another of those

Very Bad Ideas she kept having.

"Sam," she called down the bar to him. "I need to get back now. Thank you for the drink."

Sam moved along the bar and stopped in front of her. "Must you go? This is nice."

"I think I must." Kate tried to keep her eyes from straying to his lips. "I really think I must."

"Okay." Sam shrugged. "If you say so. You know where I am if you change your mind."

"Change my mind? About what?" Kate's heart leapt into her mouth.

"About the picnic, of course." Sam was watching her closely. "What did you think I meant?"

"Oh. The picnic. Yes. Okay. I know where you are." Kate managed a small smile and headed towards the door.

"Bye, Katy. See you soon."

Sam's words followed her as she stepped back out onto the pavement and walked towards her car. He was really messing with her head. Did he know how she was feeling? Even she wasn't sure how she was feeling. Now she was even more confused.

****

Hey Jen, I'm bored. Can you skive off work and come over?

Kate sent the message and lay back on her bed with an exaggerated sigh. Since she had returned home following her drink with Sam, she had been feeling very unsettled. She had had a bath, eaten a lot of cakes, watched a bit of daytime TV, and was now nearly climbing the walls with boredom tinged with guilt. It was all very well skiving when you got to spend the day in London, but to be stuck at home pretending she had a headache hadn't turned out to be much fun, particularly now she was even more confused about her feelings for Sam. And Richard.

Her phone bleeped, and she rolled onto her stomach to look at it.

Why are you home? Are you ill?

Boss sent me home, said I looked ill. Come and play with me!

Kate watched as her reply sent, then rolled onto her back again. This time next week it would only be three days until the wedding. Three days until she was committed. But she still needed to speak to Richard about that woman in London. Maybe he *was* having an affair and the wedding would be off. There was no way she was going to marry him if he'd been unfaithful.

She rolled onto her stomach again, and her fingers went up to her lips. Did Sam's kisses count as unfaithful? It wasn't as if she'd *asked* him to kiss her. And it would have been rude to pull away. No, they didn't count, which was a good thing, because there was no way on earth she was going to tell Richard about them.

She wasn't going to tell him about the dates, either, or the fact that she wanted to go on another one. Maybe starting a marriage with secrets wasn't the best idea in the world, but she couldn't help feeling it would be even worse if she did tell him. He would either be very forgiving and she would then feel really guilty, or he would break up with her. She rather thought he would be forgiving, which in itself was rather boring.

Her phone bleeped again, and she picked it up.

I'm stuck here till four. I'll come over then if you like?

Kate smiled.

Please do. And bring cake. She added a smiley face and pressed Send. So only another two hours and then Jen would arrive. She could probably cope with that.

Maybe she should be useful and do some housework to take her mind off things. She quickly dismissed that idea, and getting to her feet, pulled open her cupboard doors and surveyed her clothes. Now might be the time to go through them and chuck out the stuff she never wore. She'd been meaning to do that for months.

With a sigh she shook her head and closed the doors again. Too much like hard work. She'd just go back downstairs and watch some more daytime telly. That should pass the time. And maybe even have a cup of tea.

In the end, the two hours passed fairly rapidly, and by the time Jenny arrived, Kate was tucked up on the sofa, a packet of crisps open on her lap and an empty mug by her side.

"Well, you look comfy." Jenny flopped down on a chair and kicked her shoes off. "What are you watching?"

"*Jeremy Kyle*." Kate took a mouthful of crisps and grinned. "Some guy was shagging his sister and didn't know it. Usual stuff."

"Remember how we used to watch that when we were revising for our A levels?" Jenny rummaged in the large carrier bag she had brought in. "I got some cupcakes, and a bottle of Pinot. Is it too early, d'you think?"

Kate sat up and turned the TV off. "It's never too early for cakes," she said firmly, "and on this occasion I don't think it's too early for the wine, either. Get some glasses, will you? I don't want to get up."

Tutting noisily, Jenny disappeared into the kitchen, returning with two large wine glasses and a couple of plates for the cakes.

"So are you really ill, or just skiving again?"

"I'm not skiving. James told me to go home. I just didn't argue with him." Kate grinned. "He asked if I still had a headache, and I said, 'A bit.' It was nearly true. I was being no use at work anyway. I just couldn't concentrate."

Jenny handed her a glass of wine and a cake, and sat down again.

"So what happened yesterday? I assume you didn't get to stay the night. No night of passion, then. Did you manage an afternoon of it?"

"No passion at all." Kate bit into her cake. "He was too busy. He was actually annoyed at me for turning up. He didn't show it, but I could tell." She took a swig of wine. "Can't really blame him, actually. I mean, I just turned up at the court without warning. He had to be in court all day, have lunch with a client, and then have dinner with some more." She fell silent and stared into her wine.

"Kate? Did something happen, or are you just pissed at missing the afternoon of passion? You look a bit weird."

Kate took another sip of wine and leaned back against the cushions. "Something sort of happened," she said slowly. "I'm not sure if I'm being paranoid or not."

Jenny looked at her expectantly. "Go on. Is this to do with Richard?"

"Yeah." Kate put down her wine glass. "You know I said he had to go to dinner with some clients? Well as I was heading back to the tube, I passed him going into an Italian with a group of people."

"So?"

"One of them was a woman."

"And?"

"He had his arm around her waist as they were going through the door."

Jenny was silent for a moment. "Like what?"

"How d'you mean?"

"Well, was he actually holding her, or was he just guiding her through the door? Were there other people about?"

Kate nodded. "Yeah. They were in a group. I don't really know. That's what I wondered. He could have just been guiding her in. I just don't know."

"What did you do?" Jenny took a sip of her wine.

"I texted him."

"You texted him? Why?"

"Well, I nearly followed them into the restaurant, but then I stopped and thought about it. I mean, what was I actually going to do that wouldn't make me look stupid? If it was all innocent, I'd look like a complete idiot and Richard would be furious—and patronising— and if he was having an affair, well, I didn't really want to discuss it in public and feel humiliated. So I texted him."

"Fair enough. What did you say?"

"I just told him I was on my way home and asked what he was up to."

"Nice. And?" Jenny curled her legs up under her and got comfortable.

"He said he was having dinner with his clients and to travel safely. And he loved me."

"Okay. Well I guess that's good. He didn't lie."

"I know. But it still felt weird. And the woman looked slightly familiar. I only saw her from behind, but there was something."

"Have you met any of his clients before? Maybe it was one of them."

"I guess. Although I haven't really met many." Kate fell silent and bit on her lip. When she looked over at Jenny her eyes were troubled. "There's another thing. Bit weird, actually."

Jenny raised her eyebrows. "Come on, then, spill."

"When I spoke to Richard in the court, before he went off for lunch, he introduced me to some man— another barrister—and then left me with him for a minute while he spoke to someone. The man thought he'd met me before. At some parties in London. One of them in Mayfair."

"And you didn't know him?" Jenny's eyes had lit up.

"No, of course not. When did I ever go to a party in Mayfair? Richard never takes me to those things. So, what I want to know is, has he been taking other women to parties, or was the old man just mistaken?"

Jenny grinned. "Can you honestly imagine Richard taking someone else to a party? I can't even imagine him *at* a party! Lots of girls look like you. He was probably mistaken."

Kate scowled at her. "Are you saying I look boring?"

"No, not boring, but you're average height, slim, with long brown hair and blue eyes. Nothing too unusual. That could describe half our friends."

Kate sighed. "I guess so. So d'you think I should worry? D'you think he's having an affair?"

Jenny shook her head. "Not for a minute," she said firmly. "If either of you two had an affair, it would be you, not him. He's way too boring."

"Jen! What a thing to say. You make a fuss when I say he's boring. He's very attractive. Other women probably like him."

"So you're bothered about him being boring, but not by the fact that I said you'd be more likely to have an affair?" Jenny smirked at her.

"Of course I won't have an affair." Kate felt her face redden. "If I've managed not to so far, I'm not going to now."

"Has it been that much of an effort, then?" Jenny helped herself to another cupcake.

"No. No, of course not." Kate finished her wine and put the glass on the floor. "I don't mean that. I'm too boring too. Although…" She glanced at Jenny cheekily. "I have been misbehaving recently."

Jenny gave a short laugh and sprayed cake crumbs everywhere. "Misbehaving? What do you mean? Oh, Sam, I suppose."

"Well I realised I never do anything wrong. I've always been good and done what I was supposed to. Until recently. I went out with Sam—twice—when I really shouldn't have done. I lied to him—well, I concealed the truth anyway, and then I skived off from work for the first time ever, to go to London. Maybe I'm not as boring as I was, and that's why I think Richard is boring."

"Are you going to tell Richard about Sam?" Jenny

was refilling their glasses.

"No. There's nothing to tell. I went for a drink with an old friend."

"Hmmm. If you say so. What d'you think Richard would say? Do you really want to start married life with a secret?"

"Jen, stop being all chief bridesmaidy! I've actually thought this through." Kate glared at her. "If I tell him and he forgives me, I shall feel guilty, and he'll be all patronising and condescending and making out he's better than me. Or he'll break up with me. So I reckon I shouldn't tell him."

Jenny looked puzzled. "I don't see there's anything to forgive, really, and certainly nothing to break up over. All you did was go out for dinner with an old friend. Twice. It's not like anything happened..." Her hand shot up to cover her mouth. "Kate! What happened? What are you not telling me?"

"Nothing happened."

"Kate, I always know when you're lying. Tell me, now!"

Kate looked down at her hands and felt her face flame. "Ummm, well, Sam...Sam...might have kissed me. Just a little bit."

"Kathryn Granger, I'm shocked!" Jenny stared at her in amazement. "How could you not tell me that? That's huge! How, where, what happened? What was it like?"

Kate giggled, despite her discomfort. "It wasn't like a snog or anything." She sighed. "When he walked me home the first time, he gave me a very quick kiss on the lips before he left. No lingering."

"Okay." Jenny nodded. "Fair enough. He didn't

know you were engaged, and no lingering, that's kinda acceptable for friends. But?"

"The second time he walked me back, on the Saturday, when he did know I was engaged, he did it again and lingered. Not for long, but it was enough."

"Oh, Kate. Why didn't you tell me? How did you feel? Is that why you've been so weird?"

"I'm not weird." Kate sniffed in annoyance. "But I have been feeling strange about it. Jen, it was really nice. Am I a bad person? I want him to do it again."

"Well, he mustn't." Jenny stared sternly at her. "In ten days' time you're marrying Richard. You can't just go gaily around kissing other men. Especially Sam Somerville."

"I know." Kate's shoulders slumped. "God, it was nice, though. But you see why I can't tell Richard? He might forgive me, which to be honest would be boring and a bit weedy, or he might break up with me."

"Would you mind if he did?" Jenny watched her intently.

"Break up with me? Yes. No. I don't know!" Kate wailed, burying her face in a cushion. "That's why I went to London. I wanted to have sex with Richard to remind me how good that was. I thought that would make me forget the kisses. But it never happened. Nothing happened. He didn't even kiss me. And then I saw him with that woman."

"But that bothered you, didn't it?" Jenny sipped her wine thoughtfully. "So you must still care."

"Yes." Kate nodded slowly. "Yes, it did bother me. So I guess I must. I think I need to talk to him at the weekend. And have sex, of course."

"Enough with the sex." Jenny waved her hand at

her. "Keep that between you. But yes, you do need to talk. Are you still going to marry him?"

"I thought you said I had to." Kate stared at her. "I don't have a choice, do I? It's all organised and paid for. If I don't marry him, it will be because of Sam, and to be honest, he doesn't want me. If he did, he would have asked me not to marry Richard."

Jenny looked at her doubtfully. "Okay, but you must be sure. I know I said you had to marry him, but I didn't know you'd kissed Sam."

"That doesn't really count." Kate's lips began to tingle as she remembered the kisses. "He kissed me. I didn't have a choice. I wasn't being unfaithful." She looked over at Jenny. "I guess I'd better tell you. I had a drink with him again."

Jenny stared at her. "What, Sam? A third date? Kate! When? I thought we agreed you had to keep away from him."

"I know. We did. And I really meant to." Kate leaned back and closed her eyes. "It wasn't really my fault. I stopped in the village to buy chocolate, and he appeared. He asked me if we could go on a picnic again, and then I went and had a drink with him. Then I kind of panicked and came home."

"What, this was today?" Jenny was staring at her in horror. "He asked you out again, to a picnic? Kate, you mustn't!"

"I know. That's why I came home. But I really want to, Jen. I don't know what's wrong with me. Is it because I know that after I marry Richard I can't ever go out with anyone else again? Is that it?"

"I don't know, Kate, but you really must keep away from him. You have to marry Richard. You do still want to, don't you?"

Kate sighed. "I suppose so. I can't let Mum and Dad down now anyway. And I *do* still love Richard. Nothing has really changed. I think it's all just commitment nerves."

She curled up in the corner of the sofa. "I don't really know Sam anymore. I think he's just exciting because he's done interesting things. But I don't really need to be an explorer. I'll be better off with Richard. As the wife of a lawyer. We'll be rich enough to buy a yacht, remember? I'll be fine. Once we've had sex on Friday, I'll be fine."

Chapter 13

Friday 17th July

"Kate! Richard's here."

Her mother's voice reached Kate as she was attempting to brush the tangles out of her hair. The weather hadn't improved, and she had got caught in a very heavy shower, which had caused her hair to puff out like a clown's wig. She sighed, put down the brush, and clipped all the hair up on top of her head. No time to sort it now. At least she'd managed to smooth her fringe. She got to her feet, checked her reflection in the mirror, and headed for the stairs.

Richard was standing in the hall, chatting to Helen, and he looked up as Kate appeared at the top of the stairs.

"Darling, there you are. I'm so sorry we couldn't spend time together on Tuesday. It was probably the worst day you could have picked, actually. I was tied up with one thing or another until nearly midnight." He stepped forward as she reached the bottom step and pulled her to him. "But it was a lovely thought to come and see me."

Kate stood on the bottom step and stared into Richard's eyes. "It was my fault," she said sadly. "I should have thought it through. I just realised how long it was since we'd seen each other, and thought I'd do something about it. Sorry if I embarrassed you."

"Embarrassed me?" Richard's eyebrows shot up. "Why on earth would you have embarrassed me? You hardly spoke to anyone."

"That friend of yours at the court? Tom, wasn't it? I spoke to him."

"Ah, Tom's okay. Bit of an old fusspot, but a good barrister. You hardly had time to talk to him, though."

"He said something odd, actually." Kate stepped off the bottom stair and led the way into the conservatory. "I need to ask you about it."

Richard followed her, and they sat down on the sofa, looking out across the valley. "What did he say? He didn't upset you, did he?"

"No, no. Nothing like that." Kate hesitated. "Well, actually, I guess it disturbed me a little." She glanced up at him. "He thought he already knew me. Seemed to think he'd met me a couple of times at some parties in London. One of them in Mayfair."

Richard stared at her, a frown furrowing his brow. "So? He was obviously mistaken. What's the problem?"

Kate shifted uncomfortably. "I thought maybe—maybe you'd been taking other women to parties."

Richard stared at her, and for just a second, an odd look flashed into his eyes. Then he started to laugh. "Honestly, Kate, you really are the limit. There are lots of girls who look like you. Tom's not the youngest person in the world, and I've been thinking his memory was a bit off lately. You do know there are women at the parties I go to, as well as men, don't you? And I do talk to them. There were women at the dinner I went to on Tuesday night, too. Are you going to suggest I'm up to no good with them too?"

Kate looked away, her face feeling hot. How could she tell him now what she'd seen at the restaurant? And yet she had to. She turned to face him. "Yes, actually. Yes. I was walking past that restaurant you went to on Tuesday night, on my way to the station, when I saw you going in. You had your arm around a woman. What was that about?"

Richard looked momentarily shocked and ran a hand through his hair. "What? What d'you mean? My arm around her?"

"Yes. You were just going through the door of the restaurant, and you had your arm round the waist of some skinny woman with shiny hair."

"Ah. Yes. I was just guiding her through the door. Honestly, Kate, you've seen me do that before. I didn't have my arm around her, I had my hand on her waist, guiding her through the door, as I said. You didn't really think I was being unfaithful, did you?"

"I didn't know what to think," Kate muttered miserably. "That's why I texted you. To see what you said. Who was she anyway?"

"You texted me to check up on me?" Richard's face had gone a little pink. "Don't you trust me, Kate? We're getting married in a week. Do you honestly think I'd be going on a date with another woman?"

Wincing slightly, Kate turned away again and stared down the garden. "No. I guess not. But who was she?"

"A client. Well, to be exact, a friend of my client. There was a whole group of us. I told you that."

Kate sighed. "I'm sorry. I didn't really think you'd be unfaithful. I should have realised it was all quite innocent."

Richard moved closer, put his arm around her shoulders, and pulled her towards him. "It's all right. You're under a lot of stress. Perfectly normal just before your wedding. It's nice to know you care, anyway."

"Of course I care." Kate's voice was muffled by his arm. "It's *our* wedding, not *mine*."

"Of course." He smiled down at her. "Are we all right now, then?"

"Yes, we're all right. Can we go to bed now?" Kate looked up at him, her hand beginning to stroke his chest.

"What, now? It's half past seven!"

"Yes, now. And bugger the time. I'm not suggesting we go to sleep." She stood up and held out her hand to him. "To do what I actually went to London for."

"Kate!" Richard pulled her down onto the sofa again. "Sex? Now? Your mother is just getting dinner. Both your parents are in the house and wide awake. I'm not sure now is the best time."

"I can be quiet, and you can be quick. Come on, we can get it over with before dinner." She stood up again, pulling on his hand.

"Get it over with?" Richard got to his feet and stared at her. "Honestly, Kate, that's not the way to look at it…"

"It is this time." She was pulling him towards the stairs. "We haven't done this for weeks, Richard. It won't take long, but I need to do it now. We need to connect. Come on."

Still protesting mildly, Richard followed her up the

stairs and into her bedroom. She gently closed the door behind them, sat on the bed, and grinned at him expectantly. With a little laugh, he sat down beside her and leaned in to kiss her.

****

"You look very tired, Kate." Helen handed her a plate of chilli. "Are you feeling all right?"

"I'm fine, Mum. Don't fuss." Kate frowned and scattered salt on her dinner. "Just glad it's the end of the week."

"And glad to see Richard, I'm sure." Helen smiled at her future son-in-law. "You've been a stranger lately. I think Kate has been pining for you."

"Mum!" Kate felt her face flush with annoyance and embarrassment, and took a long swig of her wine. "Don't be ridiculous."

"Well, I hope you've been pining a little bit." Richard smiled at her. "It doesn't bode too well for our marriage if you've been perfectly happy these last few weeks without me."

"I've missed you, of course I have—that's why I went to London—but I think pining is a little strong. I don't think I've ever *pined*, Mother."

"More wine, Kate?" Her father held out the bottle to her, his eyes sympathetic.

"Please, Dad." Kate gave him a little smile. He was on her side as usual. God, she wished her mum didn't fuss so. Pining for Richard, indeed. She glanced sideways at him. He was tucking into his dinner with unaccustomed zeal, and she couldn't help wondering if their few minutes of passion in the bedroom was to blame for his appetite. She herself just felt sleepy. She was glad they'd done it. As usual, it had been very

161

good. Quick, but still very good, and she felt rather more well disposed towards him. She had been right. Sex *was* what she needed. She must remember to tell Jen.

"You haven't forgotten you have to go to church on Sunday, have you?" Helen looked pointedly at Kate. "For the banns."

"What?"

"They're reading the banns for your wedding on Sunday. You ought to be there."

"Do we have to?" Kate sighed, and laid down her fork. "Haven't we already done that?"

"They have to be read three times, Kate. I explained all that to you." Helen sighed also. "This is the last time. You really should be there if you can be. And since Richard is here this weekend too, it would be nice if we all went."

"Oh, god, all right. Why make such a fuss about it, though? Why are we even getting married in church? We don't believe all that stuff."

"I'm afraid that was my mother's idea." Richard looked apologetically at her. "And you know how hard it is to argue with her when she gets a bee in her bonnet."

Kate nodded. "Oh. Right. I remember now."

Peter topped up Kate's wine again. "I think your grandmother thought it would be nice in a church, too. More traditional. And she *is* helping to pay for it."

"Oh. I forgot Granny was paying for some of the wedding. I told you we'd elope. We could have avoided all this."

"Kate, this is all part of the tradition of marriage." Helen put more rice on her plate. "You should be enjoying it. Savour it. You only get to do it once."

Kate looked up and caught her father watching her. He raised his eyebrows. She shook her head slightly and managed a small smile, then applied herself to her dinner.

She would be so glad when it was all over. She had completely forgotten that Granny was helping to pay for it. Yet another reason she couldn't change her mind at the last minute. No, she would definitely be marrying Richard in one week. And one day.

She sneaked another glance at him. He had dressed hurriedly after their little tryst in the bedroom, and the collar of his shirt was askew. She smiled to herself. That actually made him look a little bit more interesting. She would just have to keep remembering how interesting he could be in bed. And anyway, whatever her mother said, people did get married more than once.

****

Sunday 19th July

"I publish the banns of marriage between Kathryn Anna Granger of this parish and Richard David Cresswell of the parish of Tiverton. This is the third time of asking. If any of you know any reason in law why they may not marry each other, you are to declare it." The vicar stopped speaking and glanced briefly around at the sparse congregation.

Kate found she was holding her breath just in case someone came in and declared that she shouldn't marry Richard. That she should marry them instead. Feeling very guilty, she reached out and squeezed Richard's hand. He returned the pressure and smiled at her. He was looking very nice this morning, and Kate ran her eyes over his dark trousers and open-necked pale blue shirt. Very smart, but very boring. Why did he never look untidy? He wasn't in court now. He was in a tiny country church in a little village in the wilds of Devon. Even the vicar was probably wearing wellies under his cassock. Richard had looked far more interesting last night when his shirt was messed up. She'd need to work on that. Not that she didn't like him looking smart, but it had its place, and he just didn't seem to be able to do casual very well. He'd never actually seen her when she was slopping around the house in sweat pants and an oversized T-shirt. When he stayed over, or she stayed at his, she always wore her best pyjamas and got dressed as soon as she got up. When he wasn't there, she could be found eating ice cream straight from the tub, her hair in a tangle, and her clothes resembling those found in most people's rubbish bins. She sneaked another glance at him. He was in for a shock after the wedding. She wasn't going to stop being her. He'd just have to put up with it.

The vicar announced the next hymn, and they all rose. Kate glanced along the pew at her mother who was standing very proudly and singing lustily, obviously very pleased that their family were the centre of attention at the service. There was another person she couldn't let down. Her mother had been waiting all her life to be able to organize a wedding for her daughter, and she was revelling in it. Since she was unlikely ever to get the chance to do the same for Vicky, Kate had better go through with hers. She looked down at the hymn book in her hand and realised she had no idea which hymn they were singing. She flicked over a few pages and pretended to mouth along, aware of a low rumble from Richard beside her. He wasn't very good at singing, but he always tried his best. She nudged him with her elbow and smiled up at him again. He did look very nice today. Maybe they could have sex again later. Since he was busy again during the week, there was a good chance this would be their last opportunity before the wedding. She would see him on the Friday for the rehearsal, but obviously they wouldn't be spending the night together. It would be bad luck for him to see her on the morning of the wedding. Or so everyone kept telling her.

The hymn finished, and the vicar said a short prayer before reading out a few notices, then dismissing the congregation. Kate filed out of the church in the wake of her mother and Richard, accepting the congratulations of the other few people there. At the door the vicar shook her hand heartily.

"Good to see you, Kate, and your fiancé. Not long now, less than a week to go. I expect you're both very excited. I'll see you all here on Friday afternoon at four, for the rehearsal. It shouldn't take long, just a formality, really." He moved on to the next person, and Kate followed her mother and Richard out into the churchyard.

"Glad that's over." She rolled her eyes. "After next Saturday I never have to go in there again."

"Really, Kate." Helen hurried her towards the gate. "You could have waited until we were out of earshot to say that."

"Oh, Mum, the vicar knows. He knew we wouldn't have been here today if it wasn't for the banns. Apart from the odd carol service, none of our family ever go to church. I shall be so glad when this is over, won't you?" She looked up at Richard.

"Well, I guess so. It'll mean we're married, so that'll be a good thing." He reached out to take her hand, but she moved slightly too far away and walked a little faster.

"Come on, let's get home. I'm starving." Kate set off at a fast pace towards their house. "Hope Dad got the lunch on."

As she opened the front gate and made her way up the path, Kate began to relax and felt really guilty about not letting Richard hold her hand. She knew full well why that had been, and she was quite ashamed. She had wanted to avoid any possibility of Sam seeing her holding her fiancé's hand. How ridiculous was that? He knew she was getting married. What possible harm could it do? But she still didn't want it to happen.

At the door she turned to wait for Richard and her mother. She caught his hand and pulled him into the house behind her.

"Just going up to my room for a minute," she said over her shoulder to Helen. "We'll be back down as soon as lunch is ready. It smells good."

She took the stairs two at a time, Richard following behind, ran into the bedroom, and jumped onto the bed.

"Come on, just time for a quickie before lunch." She grinned up at him, kicking her shoes across the room.

"What, now? Kate you're incorrigible! We can't do it now. Lunch is nearly ready."

"So what? It needn't take long. Friday didn't. Come on, don't waste time." She wriggled up the bed and held out her arms enticingly.

"Really, Kate, what's wrong with you?" Richard

reluctantly climbed onto the bed beside her and kicked off his shoes. "You're not usually like this."

"We don't usually go nearly six weeks without sex!" Kate pulled her dress over her head. "It was too long, Richard. We have a lot to make up for. And this is probably our last chance before the wedding. I assume you're too busy all week." Her bra had joined the dress on the floor, and she was lying on her back, looking up at him.

"Yes, I will be." Richard slowly undid his trousers. "But this all seems a bit forced. I'm not sure I'm in the mood."

"Not in the mood!" Kate sat up and glared at him. "Not in the mood? Your future wife is lying here offering you her gorgeous body, and you're not in the mood? What's wrong with you? Are you getting old?"

With a smile, Richard pulled off the rest of his clothes and got onto the bed beside her. "Well, if you put it like that, how can I refuse? Getting old, indeed. I'll show you."

****

"So I'll see you on Friday, then." Kate reached up and gave Richard a quick kiss on the cheek. "We have to be at the church at four."

"I know." He smiled down at her. "Behave yourself, and I'll try and call you in the week." He walked off down the path and got into his car.

Kate closed the door before he'd driven off, and wandered into the kitchen. Helen was loading the dishwasher, and she glanced up.

"Pop the kettle on, will you, love? Just fancy another cuppa."

Kate obliged, and sat down at the kitchen table.

"Think I'll see if Jen can come over," she said. "I haven't seen her for days."

"Good idea. She can come for supper, if you like. We're only having leftovers, but she's very welcome."

"Maybe." Kate shrugged and got to her feet. "I'll text her."

She fished her phone out of her bag and wrote a quick message.

D'you wanna come over? Mum says you can stay for supper.

An affirmative reply appeared seconds later, and leaving her phone on the table, Kate made her mother a cup of tea, then rummaged in the cupboard for cake. She found a tub containing two cupcakes and some flapjacks, and helped herself to one of each.

"Kate, really!" Helen straightened up from the dishwasher. "How can you eat that now, just after that enormous lunch? You're going to get fat. Or are you eating for two? You can tell *me*, darling."

"For god's sake, Mum! No, I'm not pregnant. How many times do I have to tell you? I didn't eat all that much dinner, and I like cake. Leave me alone. I'm taking these up to my room to wait for Jen. Send her up, will you?" She left the room carrying the cakes, and wandered back upstairs.

The bed was still unmade from her pre-lunch romp with Richard, and she put the cakes on her dressing table while she sorted it out.

As usual, the sex had been good, but she was feeling a little out of sorts about it. Richard's reluctance had annoyed her, and even when they were doing it she felt he wasn't totally committed to it. Pity. She had needed another really good encounter to set her up for the week and keep her reminded why she was marrying him.

The bed made, she collected the cakes and sat down cross-legged in the middle to eat them. A nice afternoon with Jen would make her feel better. They could talk about something other than the wedding. Or Richard. Or Sam. Definitely not talk about Sam. Or even think about him. Sam must not exist for the next week. Or indeed at any time after that. Kate wriggled backwards so she could lean against the wall, and stuffed the flapjack into her mouth. It would probably be better if he went off travelling again. Then in another eight years when he came back, she'd either be divorced and therefore available, or she'd be happily married with several children, and therefore immune to his charms.

She heard her mother's voice greeting someone downstairs, followed by the sound of feet coming nearer. Jenny opened the bedroom door without knocking and grinned at her.

"Hello. What's up?"

"Nothing much. Just fancied a bit of a gossip. Sorry, just ate all the cake. There's more downstairs if you want some."

Jenny sat down on the end of the bed and shook her head. "It's okay. Your mum is bringing me up a cup of tea. I've not long had lunch anyway. Has Richard gone, then?"

Kate nodded, wiping the last remaining crumbs from her mouth. "Yeah, he's back in London again this week."

"Did you do it?"

"What?"

"Sex. Did you have sex? You've been going on about it all week."

Kate laughed. "You usually don't want to know, but yes, we did. Three times."

"Good. Maybe you'll be in a better mood, then. Did it remind you why you love him?"

"Meh." Kate made a face. "Sort of. The first time, yes, and I guess the second. But this morning—he wasn't really in the mood, but I persuaded him. It was still good, but I just felt he wasn't really there. D'you know what I mean?"

Jenny wrinkled her nose. "Yeah, I guess. Maybe I really don't want to hear about this after all. But you're still marrying him?"

"Yeah." Kate sighed. "We had to go to church this morning to hear the banns again. I kept hoping someone would walk in and say we couldn't get married. Does that make me a bad person? It's just that then I wouldn't need to think about it."

Jenny looked at her in consternation. "I think that's rather worrying. Who were you hoping would walk in and say that? I really don't think you're taking this wedding seriously enough. It's not fair on Richard to marry him if you're not sure."

Kate shook her head. "No. It's not fair on Mum and Dad if I don't marry him. They've paid for this, and organised it and everything. And Granny has paid for some of it, too. I'd forgotten that. It's better I go through with it, and it may all turn out fine. I do love Richard, and we'll probably get on fine and still be married in eighty years, but if not, we can always get divorced."

"Shit, Kate, you can't go into a marriage like that!

It's meant to be forever."

"It's meant to be forever in an ideal world," Kate agreed. "But life isn't like that. I've thought about this, and I reckon it would hurt more people if I back out now than if I marry him and see how it goes. If I back out now, Richard is going to be devastated, Dad and Granny are going to be furious, and Mum will probably have a nervous breakdown and feel she has to move away. It's better this way. I'll see how it goes, and if in a year or so we're not getting on, we can split up then and no one will mind."

"And Sam?"

"What about Sam?"

"Well, Sam is the reason that any of this is happening. Before he came back, you were perfectly happy with Richard."

"Ish." Kate shrugged. "Okay, Sam made it worse, but I always had some reservations about Richard. He has some annoying habits, and I'm not really myself when I'm with him. But I always thought that didn't matter."

"But do you want to be with Sam?"

"That's not the point." Kate stood up and brushed the crumbs off her jeans. "It's not an option, is it? My way is the best. But I do need to make sure I don't see Sam again before the weekend. Just to be on the safe side." She grinned at Jenny. "Now let's go and get some cake and have a fun afternoon. No wedding talk."

Chapter 14

Wednesday 22nd July

Kate opened the gate quietly and started off towards the village. Taking a deep breath, she closed her eyes momentarily. She just had to get away from her mother. She was driving her crazy. Wedding talk all day, every day. Surely everything was organised by now. It was only three days away. She was beginning to regret taking the whole of the week off work, and was actually thinking fondly of hiding in the staff room on the pretext of making coffee. Even the company of the loquacious Holly would be preferable to that of her mother, at the moment.

She just needed to get out of the house. Didn't really matter where she went. A walk through the village would do. She stopped at the end of the cul-de-sac to check for traffic and was just about to cross the road when a vehicle appeared from the direction of the village and pulled up alongside her.

Sam wound down the window of the Land Rover and grinned at her. "Katy. I was hoping to run into you. Where are you off to? You look a bit frazzled."

Kate bent down and peered in at him. "I am. I'm trying to escape my mother. She won't shut up about the wedding, and I've got to get out."

Sam smirked. "Ah. Mothers and weddings, eh?

Isn't that her coming now?"

Kate glanced back over her shoulder just in time to see Helen emerge from their garden and stare down the road towards her. In a flash she had opened the door of the Land Rover and jumped in. She ducked down on the floor. "Drive! Just get me away from her."

Sam chuckled and set off along the road, leaving a bemused Helen wondering where her daughter had disappeared to.

After a few moments, Sam glanced over at her. "You can probably get up now. She can't see you from here."

Kate scrambled up and sat on the seat with a sigh. "Thanks. Sorry about that. I was at the end of my tether. Just needed to get out of the house for a bit. Almost wish I was at work."

"Oh, dear, it must be bad." Sam was grinning as he drove. "You can come with me, if you like. I was hoping to see you again before the big day."

Suddenly aware of her situation, Kate awkwardly licked her lips and glanced at him. "Oh. No, thanks. I'd better not." She was silent for a moment, then cleared her throat. "Well, where are you going anyway?"

"Dartmoor."

"Dartmoor? Why are you going there?"

"To deliver some barrels of beer to a pub. It's a friend of my dad. They have a supplier problem, and Dad offered to sell them some of ours to keep them going. You're welcome to come if you want. Dartmoor's nice on a day like this."

Kate thought for a moment. The idea of a day in the sun on Dartmoor, in the company of Sam Somerville, was extremely appealing. But maybe it was too appealing. She had spent the last week trying to avoid him, even to avoid thinking about him, and now here she was actually considering going on a road trip with him. Oh, what the hell. It was probably the last time she'd ever be able to do something like this. She smiled at him.

"Okay, I'd love to come. If you don't mind?"

"Fine by me." Sam shrugged. "But you'll need to do up your seatbelt if you're staying."

Kate tugged hard on the belt and managed to fasten it around herself. She smiled at him again. "Thanks. Only thing is I have nothing with me. No bag, no money, no coat. Nothing. I was just going for a walk. I only have my phone because it was already in my pocket."

"S'okay, you won't need anything." Sam shrugged. "It's a hot day, and if you do get cold, I have a jacket in the back, and I'll buy you lunch."

"I can't let you do that," Kate protested half-heartedly, feeling her face begin to get hot. Maybe this was one of those Very Bad Ideas she kept having.

"Not that again." Sam grinned. "Why, just because you're getting married? Does that mean I'm not allowed to buy you food? How's the wedding going, then? How's Robert?"

"It's Richard." Kate was aware that her face was flaming, and turned to look out the window. "It's all going well, thank you."

"Ah, yes, Richard. So where's he today, then? Shouldn't you be with him?"

"He's working. In London. I don't have to be with him all the time." Kate was defensive.

"Well, clearly not." Sam manoeuvred a tight bend.

"Otherwise you wouldn't be here with me now. You might have to be with him all the time after Saturday, though."

"Look, I think this was a bad idea." Kate started to take off her seatbelt. "Let me out here. I can walk back."

Sam put out his hand and touched her arm. "Sorry, only teasing you. Please stay. I'd love the company. I promise not to talk about the wedding or Richard. Okay? Will you stay?"

Slowly Kate did up the belt again, acutely aware of where his hand had touched her arm. "Okay, then. But no more teasing."

"No more teasing. It'll take about an hour to get where we're going. Would you like to listen to some music?"

"You have a working CD player in here?" Kate looked around in surprise.

"No need to be rude, but yes, I actually do. We're a little limited with choice, but have a rummage in that box under the seat. You may find something we both like."

"Where exactly are we going?" Kate pulled the box out and heaved it onto her knee. "Is it anywhere near the prison? I always think that looks really spooky."

"Not that close. The pub is near Hexworthy, but right in the middle of nowhere. We could go and see the prison after, if you like. Unless you're in a hurry to get back?"

"God, no." Kate picked up a CD, then discarded it. "The longer I stay out the better." She picked up another disc and smiled. "Ha, remember this? We kept playing it when we were revising for our A levels.

Fancy a listen?" She waved *In Your Honor*, by the Foo Fighters, in the air.

Sam laughed. "Go on, then, haven't heard that one for ages. That takes me back."

Kate turned on the CD player and inserted the disc. She was well aware that what she was doing was potentially dangerous, and a Very Bad Idea, but something, possibly the newly discovered misbehaving side of her, was egging her on. She managed to persuade herself that she needed a complete break from wedding things, and that this would be good for her. As the music started, she settled back in her seat and closed her eyes. In three days she would be married. She may as well have one more naughty day. And it wasn't as if it was like a date this time. There would be no opportunity for kissing.

They travelled in silence for a while, Sam concentrating on his driving and Kate on getting lost in the music, until they came to the end of the M5 and turned off down the A38 towards Ashburton.

"Not telling you what to do"—Sam glanced at her—"but should you let your mother know where you've gone? She may be worried."

Kate rolled her eyes. "I know. I thought that just now. I'm not telling her where I actually am, though. Imagine what she'd think of that? Three days before my wedding and I'm off on a jaunt to Dartmoor with another man."

"An old friend," Sam supplied. "Just tell her an old friend. Will she ask who?"

"Maybe." Kate shrugged. "I can lie." She fished her phone out of her pocket and discovered she already had a missed call from her mother. She had put the phone on silent when she left the house. With a sigh she wrote a message.

Had to get away for a bit. Gone out for lunch and a walk with a friend. Back this evening. Don't worry, it's doing me good. xx

She watched the message send, then smiled over at Sam. "There, done. Can we have fun, then?"

Sam glanced at her. "Of course. What did you have in mind? We could have a picnic again, if you like. You said you'd like that, when we met last week."

"Maybe." Kate felt suddenly awkward, and turned away. What the hell was she doing? They couldn't have another picnic. That would turn it into a date again. The very thing she had been trying to avoid for the last week. She had to make sure she didn't enjoy herself too much. She needed to keep thinking about sex. With Richard.

"Katy? Are you all right? You've gone a bit quiet."

"I'm fine." Kate smiled over-brightly. "Still feeling a bit stressed out, that's all."

"Well, we'll be there soon. Then we can have some lunch and decide what to do this afternoon. The weather's still glorious. We could go for a walk."

"Yeah, that sounds nice." Kate nodded and smiled at him. "Thank you." Her phone bleeped, and she looked down at it. "Oh, great, Mum's asking who I'm with. Need to get creative here."

"Jen?"

"No, far too easy for her to find out. Anyway…" Kate tailed off looking awkward.

"Anyway?"

"Nothing. No, I'll think of a friend she never speaks to." Kate's finger hovered over the screen, then quickly typed a message and pressed Send. "I told her I was with a girl from work. I said I bumped into her in the village."

"Okay." Sam glanced over at her. "You won't tell Jen about this, will you?"

"What?"

"You're not going to tell Jen you're with me, are you? And yet you tell her everything. Does she even know we went out the other week?"

"Why does that matter?" Kate wriggled uncomfortably in her seat. "But yes, she does know, as it happens."

"And I expect she was shocked because you 'forgot' to tell me you were getting married?"

Kate didn't reply, instead folding her arms defiantly.

"Katy, why are you here?"

Kate looked at him in surprise. "Because you invited me, and I was running away from my mother."

Sam looked at her thoughtfully for a moment, then indicated to turn off the main road and onto the moor. They drove in silence for a while, the lanes becoming more and more narrow as they neared their destination, and Kate tried to force herself to relax and enjoy the scenery.

When they finally drew up outside a tiny whitewashed building, tucked away on a bend in the road and backing onto the river, it was just on midday. Sam pulled the Land Rover into the car park and turned off the engine.

"Is this it?" Kate peered out in surprise. "This doesn't look like a pub. It's tiny."

"They've only just opened." Sam undid his seatbelt

and opened the door. "They haven't got the sign up yet. These barrels are to help get them started. You stay here a minute. I'll just go and check they're home." He slid out of the vehicle and strode off towards the plain wooden door at the back of the building. Kate watched him go, her mind in turmoil. Why did she feel so strange around him? And what on earth had possessed her to come on this ill-conceived jaunt anyway? She had managed successfully to avoid him for a week, had got things back on track with Richard—more or less—and now here she was, in the middle of nowhere, without even any money. And Sam was looking as delicious as ever. Kate screwed her eyes shut and stamped her feet in frustration. Why did she do these things? Was she actually terminally stupid? She was getting married in three days. Three days. And she was in the middle of Dartmoor with a man she should most definitely stay away from. It was not as though he was doing anything wrong. He hadn't made any moves, or even suggested they should be anything more than friends. At least not since the picnic, and that may have been in her imagination. The kiss could have just been friendly. She needed to believe that if she was going to get through the day.

Sam reappeared from behind the pub and opened the back doors of the Land Rover.

"Shall I help?" Kate twisted round to see him.

"Too heavy for you. Thanks anyway. Steve has gone to fetch a trolley. You sit tight. This won't take long."

"We're not having lunch here, then?" Kate barely kept the relief out of her voice.

"No. As I said, they've only just opened. They're

not doing food yet."

Kate watched as Sam was joined by a tall blonde middle-aged man, and between them they moved the barrels from the back of the Land Rover into the pub. When they'd finished, Kate saw the man hand Sam a large wad of notes, which he stowed in the back pocket of his jeans. Then they shook hands, and Sam came back to join her. He got into the driver's seat and did up his seatbelt.

"There, job done." He grinned at her. "Rest of the day is our own now. Where shall we go?"

"You mentioned lunch?" Kate raised her eyebrows tentatively.

"You and food." Sam laughed and started the engine. "Come on, then, I know a nice pub not far from here." He reversed back out onto the narrow lane and set off again, the sides of the vehicle brushing against the overgrown hedges to either side of them.

After about ten minutes, they drew up outside a long, low, thatched building which proclaimed itself to be the Farrier's Arms and had a large board outside advertising lunch.

"This do you?"

"Looks lovely." Kate peered out at it. "Can we sit outside? It's so hot today."

"Sounds good to me." Sam parked the Land Rover, and they made their way through the open door at the front of the building.

The interior of the pub was very dark after the bright sunshine, and Kate took a moment for her eyes to adjust. It was low-ceilinged, with a patterned carpet and wood-panelled walls, adorned with a variety of pictures and horse brasses. The beamed ceiling was hung with glasses and tankards.

"What d'you want to drink?" Sam asked.

"Diet cola would be nice, thanks." Kate stared around her, looking for a menu. There didn't appear to be one, and she found that everything was written on a chalkboard to the side of the bar. She moved away slightly to read it, and by the time Sam joined her and handed her her drink, she had decided on cauliflower cheese. They ordered the food, then made their way out to the beer garden at the back of the pub. It was fairly large, and they chose a wooden bench-style table next to the river.

Kate slid onto the seat and sighed. "This is nice. Thanks. I must pay you back."

"Don't be daft. I invited you." Sam slid in opposite her and took a long drink of his cola. "That's better. God, it's so hot today. Really heavy, too. Feels a bit like thunder." He glanced up at the clear blue sky. "Doesn't look much like it, though. At least not yet."

Kate sipped her drink and watched him over the rim of the glass. Why did he have to be quite so beautiful? He always had been, and if anything he had improved with age. As usual he was wearing old faded jeans, this time with a very old Motorhead T-shirt. He had an open blue-checked shirt on over the top, the sleeves rolled up to just below the elbow. Kate felt her stomach do a flip as she watched him. It really wasn't fair. He was far too good-looking. She found herself wondering why he hadn't got a girlfriend.

He smiled across at her. "Feeling more relaxed yet?"

"In a way." Kate made a face. "It's certainly good to be away from home and my mother anyway."

"But?"

"But I do feel a bit guilty being here with you and lying to my mother."

"Shouldn't have come, then." Sam took a long drink, his eyes never leaving her face.

"Oh, that's really helpful, Sam." Kate wriggled in annoyance. "You invited me. It was perfectly innocent and seemed like a good way to get away from Mum."

"So stop feeling guilty and just enjoy yourself." Sam shrugged and put down his glass. "All we're doing is having lunch, as old friends, in a pub on a nice afternoon. No one, not even Reginald, could object to that."

"Richard, his name is Richard." Kate frowned at him.

Sam grinned evilly at her. "If you say so. Well, not even he could object to you having lunch with an old school friend. And that's all we've ever been, isn't it, Katy?"

The food appeared just then, so Kate was saved from answering, and they both tucked into their meals with enthusiasm. Kate was very quick to devour her cauliflower cheese, and she sat back with a satisfied sigh while Sam was still finishing his sausage and mash.

"Nice?" He popped a forkful into his mouth.

"Lovely. Yours?"

He nodded. "Great. I guess you want pudding now?"

"Always." Kate grinned. "Will you join me, though? Don't want to eat alone."

"I can probably manage a little something." He scooped up the last of his potato and put down his fork.

"That was good. Shall we have a little break, or do you want the pudding straight away?"

"A little break is okay." Kate took a sip of drink. "Not too long, mind."

"So what shall we do this afternoon? D'you want to go and see the prison? We can, if you like."

"No, it's okay. It might be nice to go for a walk. Maybe by a river or something? It's so pretty round here."

"Fine. I know just the place. You'll love it." Sam looked smug, and Kate couldn't help smiling at him.

"You look so pleased with yourself," she said with a giggle. "Like a schoolboy again."

A shadow crossed Sam's face, and he picked up his plate. "Let's order pudding." He reached over and took Kate's plate. "I know what you like. Shall I order for you?"

"How very nineteen fifties." Kate grinned. "But yes, you may. I trust you." She watched him as he walked away towards the pub, wondering about the look on his face when she'd mentioned being a schoolboy. Was it still the incident with Cerys? There was something there that he wasn't telling her. Maybe today would be the last chance she'd have to find out what it was. She'd ask him when they were walking.

****

"D'you like it, then?" Sam glanced down at Kate as they strolled along the river in the shade of the overhanging beech trees.

"It's lovely." Kate sighed and smiled up at him. "Thanks. Good call. It's very relaxing. Still so hot, though."

"We could go skinny-dipping." Sam's eyes were

shining with mischief.

"Don't push it." Kate giggled. "Nice though that sounds. We could paddle, I suppose."

"Actually, not here." Sam took her arm and steered her away from the riverbank. "Look how fast-flowing it is, and how rocky. It could be rather dangerous."

Kate looked up at him quizzically. He did still have an issue with what happened eight years ago. Not surprising, really, but she wanted to know what he wasn't telling her. She took a deep breath.

"Sam?"

"Yeah?"

"The other week, when we had that picnic, you said there was some stuff about—that night—that I didn't know about. What did you mean?"

"Not now, Katy."

"It's now or never, Sam. I'm getting married in three days. I doubt we can continue these little trysts after that. I want to know what you meant. I was there that night. I know exactly what happened. What did you mean?"

Sam sighed. "Not about the night. I know you were there. Of course you know what happened then. No, I meant stuff you didn't know about, that had happened earlier. With me and Cerys."

"What stuff?"

"Not now, Katy. Let's not spoil the walk. I promise I'll tell you later. Okay?"

"Later today?" Kate stopped walking and looked up at him. "Promise?"

"I promise. We'll talk on the way back. Now look, that looks like somewhere we could paddle. See, a shallow pool. Come on." He led the way through the trees, and by the time Kate had caught up with him, he had kicked off his Converse and socks and was rolling up his jeans.

She laughed and followed suit, although her skinny jeans only allowed her to paddle in the very shallowest part. They tentatively stepped into the freezing water, and Kate caught her breath.

"God, that's cold! But so nice and refreshing." She bent down and cupped some water in her hands. "Sam!" He turned towards her, and she threw the water at his face. She missed, and it soaked his T-shirt, leaving a dark patch all down the front.

"Right, like that is it!" He grinned, scooped some water up, and expertly aimed it at her. His aim was better than hers, and it hit her squarely in the face. With a squeal, she scooped up some more and advanced towards him, hands at the ready.

"That was bloody freezing!" She flung the water at him, this time getting him on the neck.

"You started it!" Sam was laughing so much he leant against a large rock to get his breath. "It's colder than you'd think, isn't it?"

Kate joined him and vaulted up onto the rock, leaving her legs dangling down next to him. "It is. I'm soaked now. My hair's probably gone frizzy."

Sam looked up at her over his shoulder. "It looks lovely. It always does. Now come back down here. I don't think we've finished this game yet." He caught her legs and pulled her down off the rock, catching her round the waist as she landed.

She swayed as her foot slipped on a slimy rock, and leant against him for support. His arms tightened around her, and he looked down at her. "You okay?"

"Fine, thank you." Kate was suddenly acutely aware of his warm body pressing against hers, and she started to pull away. "Let me go. I'm okay now."

Sam kept hold of her, and she looked up at him. His dark eyes were burning into her, and she was shocked at the emotion she saw there. For a few seconds their gazes locked and something unspoken passed between them, and then Sam loosed his grip, and Kate stumbled back to the shore. She sat down on the grass, horrified to find her hands were shaking and her heart beating faster than normal. She bent her head and pretended to fiddle with her shoes. Sam waded out of the water and sat down a few feet away.

"Shall we go back to the Land Rover now?" He picked up a sock and attempted to dry his feet with it. "The weather looks like it might break in a minute."

Kate looked up at the sky through the canopy of leaves above them and noticed for the first time the gathering clouds. It was still just as hot, but there was the definite feel of rain coming. Silently they dried their feet the best they could, then replaced their shoes and walked back to the Land Rover in silence, carefully keeping a few feet apart. Kate's head was spinning. She was right. This had been one of those Very Bad Ideas she kept having. This might even be the worst one yet. And they were stuck in each other's company for another couple of hours.

She sneaked a glance sideways at Sam, but his face was inscrutable. Maybe if she managed to get him talking about the Cerys incident, in the car, that would keep their minds off what had just—nearly—happened. She bit her lip.

But what *had* just nearly happened? She had been

sure that if she hadn't pulled away he would have kissed her. And properly this time. And she had so wanted him to. The feel of his body pressed against hers had been electric. Oh, why had he had to come back now?

They reached the Land Rover, and Sam pulled the door open for her. She clambered in and kicked off her damp shoes. Her feet would dry much better if they were bare. Sam climbed in, and they set off in silence, Kate still struggling with the seatbelt.

The rain started to fall before they had gone a hundred yards, and the sky was turning a dark purple colour. Sam glanced in the rearview mirror.

"It's coming from behind us," he remarked. "I reckon there'll be thunder in a minute. It'd be nice to get onto a bigger road before that happens."

"How far is that?" Kate felt her voice sounded false.

"No idea. I'm actually not sure where we are." He gave a self-conscious grin. "I came here once before, but I wasn't driving, so I didn't take that much notice. I think this is the way back to the main road, though."

Kate peered out into the gathering gloom. "There don't seem to be any houses around. Are there no villages round here?"

"This is the most remote part of the moor. There are miles between villages here. Don't worry, I'll get you home."

"I know." Kate managed a small smile, and settled back in her seat.

They drove on for several miles, the rain getting heavier and the narrow road almost turning into a river. Finally they reached the top of a hill, the high hedges left behind, and the moor opening out below them. Sam stopped the Land Rover, and they both stared at the sight ahead of them. The rain was lashing down on the windscreen, and there was no habitation in any direction. The road ahead was still very narrow and winding, with no sign of a main road.

"Shit." Sam slapped his hand down on the steering wheel. "We really are in the middle of nowhere. Sorry, I must have gone wrong somewhere. Don't worry, we'll get there in the end."

"It's all right." Kate managed to restrain herself from putting her hand on his leg. "We're okay. It's not like we're out in the rain, is it? Dartmoor can't be that big. We'll find our way. Don't you have a built-in SatNav?"

Sam stared at her and laughed out loud. "Yeah, right. In this? They'd barely invented maps when this was made. SatNav indeed! No, we'll just have to find our way in the old-fashioned manner. Come on." He put the car in gear and set off down the hill, the windscreen wipers screaming as they struggled against the heavy rain. As they approached a crossroads near the bottom of the hill, Sam peered intently out the window. "I reckon we should go that way." He pointed to the right. "Just got a gut feeling about it."

Kate shrugged. "Whatever you say. You're the driver. This rain is making it difficult to see."

"Yeah." Sam was concentrating intently, his tongue slightly protruding and his eyes fixed on the road. "It is." As he spoke something suddenly leapt out from the side of the road and passed in front of them. Kate screamed and clutched at the dashboard, and Sam swerved the Land Rover to avoid it.

There was a second when the deer paused and stared in through the windscreen at them. Then it was off and across the road as quickly as it had appeared. Sam had slammed on the brakes, and the vehicle skidded on the wet road and slid rapidly towards a very deep ditch on the left-hand side.

"Hang on!" Sam yelled through gritted teeth as he struggled to control the heavy vehicle. He managed to pull it slightly round to the right, but it wasn't enough, and with a huge crash the two front wheels went into the ditch and they juddered to a halt, the back of the vehicle leaving the ground for a moment before landing with an ear-splitting crash. Kate, still gripping onto the dashboard, her knuckles white, was thrown against the side door, and Sam was thrown forward, despite his seatbelt, slamming his face hard on the steering wheel.

There was silence for a moment, apart from the lashing rain, and Kate slowly released her grip and sat back, her eyes immediately darting over to where Sam was slumped over the steering wheel.

"Sam, are you all right?" Her voice was shaking and she fumbled to undo her seatbelt with numb fingers. "Sam, speak to me." There was no reply, and she tugged at the resistant belt frantically. "Sam! Oh, god, Sam, please be all right—you must be all right."

There was a slight groan from the driver's seat, and slowly and painfully lifting his head, Sam edged back in his seat, his hand going up to his face. "Jesus, that hurts. Are you okay? Katy, I'm so sorry, there was nothing I could do…"

"I know. Of course it wasn't your fault." Her seatbelt finally released, and Kate slid along the seat towards him. "Oh, god, that looks awful! I think you need to see a doctor. We must call someone." She found to her horror that her voice was quivering and tears were beginning to fill her eyes. She rubbed at them ineffectually with her hand and tried to get her phone out of her pocket. "We need to call an ambulance."

"No, Katy, no. I'm all right. Unless you need one. Are you hurt?" With an effort, Sam sat upright and twisted round to look at her. "Katy, you're crying. Are you hurt?" There was an edge of panic in his voice, and he reached out a hand to her.

She shook her head, suddenly unable to speak, and the tears began to run down her cheeks. She took his hand and squeezed it tightly.

"No," she managed. "I'm okay. Just shocked. But you—I thought you..." She moved slightly closer to him. "Are you really all right? You look awful. Your poor face." She reached out her other hand and gently touched just above his right eye, where a dark patch was growing as she watched. A trickle of blood was running down the side of his face, and she wiped it away with her finger. "You're really hurt. That needs attention. Do you have a first-aid kit?"

Sam was watching her closely, and he caught her hand in his. "I'm fine, Katy. I'm more worried about you. And no"—he managed a small smile—"I don't have a first-aid kit. You may have noticed this vehicle is not very well equipped. Come here." He pulled her towards him and put his left arm around her shoulders. "You're shaking."

Finally giving in to her emotions, Kate began to sob in earnest and buried her face in his shoulder. "That was awful!" She hiccupped. "I thought—I thought—

you were dead."

"It'll take more than that to kill me." Sam's arm tightened around her, and he brushed his lips lightly over the top of her head. "But thank you for caring."

"Of course I care." Kate's voice was muffled by his shirt. "But are you really all right? People die from hitting their heads." She struggled upright and pulled back to look at him. "I really think you should see a doctor."

"It wasn't my head, it was my face, and I'm not going to die. I shall probably have a whopper of a black eye and a bit of a headache." He put up his hand and winced as it touched his face. "That's about all. But how about you? Did you hurt anything?"

Kate shook her head and fished in her pocket for a tissue. "I was thrown against the door, but I don't think it did me any damage." She blew her nose noisily. "What do we do now?"

Sam peered through the window, out into the gloomy afternoon. The rain was still thundering down on the roof of the Land Rover, and the sky was dark and threatening. "Well, I don't think this rain is going to let up, so I suggest we phone for help and then sit tight until someone rescues us." He felt in his pocket for his phone. "Shit, now my phone has gone. Can you see it anywhere?" Kate peered around and eventually located it under the clutch pedal. She got down on the floor and retrieved it, holding it out to Sam with a grimace.

"I think you may have trodden on it," she said sadly, noting the shattered screen. "That's a shame."

Sam took it and surveyed it philosophically. "Right. Well, that's not going to be much use. Is yours okay?"

Kate fished hers out of her pocket and nodded. "Yeah. Seems to be. Who shall I call? The AA?"

"Not a member. No, I think my dad will be the best bet. May I use it?"

Kate handed over the phone and watched as he dialled his parents' number and held the phone to his ear. Even in the whole horror of the moment, she was well aware that her presence in the car was going to cause complications for all of them. She wondered if she should try and find another way home.

"Damn, it's not connecting." Sam lowered the phone and peered at the screen. "Great, no bloody signal."

"Turn it off and on again," Kate suggested, leaning forward to look at the screen. "Might help."

Sam tried, but the signal still failed to appear. He sighed. "I guess we have three choices. One, we sit here and wait till someone comes by who can help. Two, one of us walks up the road until we find a signal, or three we abandon the car and walk to the nearest habitation." He glanced at her. "What gets your vote?"

"Shall we go and try and get a signal?" she suggested. "That seems the best idea to start with."

Sam nodded and pulled on the door handle. The door didn't move. He tried again but still nothing. "Shit. Does yours open?"

Kate pulled on the handle and pushed the door hard. It creaked slightly but didn't move. She tried again and something sounded as though it fell down inside the actual door. She shook her head.

"No. What now?" She found to her horror that her voice shook again. She really needed to get a grip.

"We'll have to get out the back." Sam jerked his thumb over his shoulder. "I've done it before, just a bit annoying. Let's hope that one isn't stuck too."

"My window opens." Kate was winding her window down, using both hands. "It's a bit stiff, but I could fit through it. Give me the phone, and I'll go and find a signal."

"You're not going on your own." Sam was firm. "We both go, or I go."

"We both go, then, 'cause I'm not staying here on my own." She wound the window down as far as it would go, slid her shoes back on, and began to climb out. "I'll come round and see if I can open your door from the outside." She jumped down into the ditch and picked her way around the vehicle until she was standing beside Sam's door. As she held onto the handle and pulled hard, Sam pushed from the inside, and eventually it gave way and creaked open just far enough for him to slide out.

Kate watched him with concern as he landed on the road and swayed dangerously. She caught his arm to steady him.

"You need to sit down. Do you feel faint?"

"No, I'm fine. Just felt a bit odd standing up suddenly. Come on, let's walk up that hill a bit, see if we can get a signal." He reached out, took her hand firmly in his, and set off up the grass onto the higher ground. Kate stumbled behind him, the rain running down her face and soaking into her thin top. She shivered despite the earlier warmth of the day. Sam looked down at her. "God, you must be freezing. My jacket's in the Land Rover. We must go back for it."

"No." Kate looked up at him, water running down

into her eyes. "I'm already soaked. No point now."

"Yes, there is." Sam turned around and slid back down the grassy slope, landing at the bottom in an ungainly heap. He grunted sharply, and Kate slithered to a stop beside him and caught the look on his face.

"You're in pain," she stated baldly. "You stay here. I'll go and find a signal. You're in no fit state to walk anywhere." She moved over to the Land Rover and, reaching inside, pulled out his khaki combat jacket. "You sit in the car, and I'll go back up the hill." She pulled the jacket on over her wet clothes and hugged it around her, the sleeves hanging several inches below her hands.

Sam looked up and grinned at her. "Suits you," he said, struggling to his feet. "But you're not going anywhere on your own. I'll be fine. Come on. That way may be better, actually." He caught her hand again and set off across the long grass.

"You wear the jacket, then." Kate puffed after him. "You're the one who's injured. You need to keep warm."

"I'm fine. Stop worrying. Right. Let's see if there's a signal here." They had reached a flat rocky area, thirty feet or so above the road, and Sam fished the phone out of his pocket and looked at the screen. "Still nothing. Damn." He looked around and pointed. "Let's go that way. I think that's the most likely way to find a house, as well."

Kate followed him doubtfully. "We'd be better sticking to the road if we want to find a house," she pointed out.

"Maybe, but we need to be on higher ground to find a signal. We can still follow the direction of the road." Sam glanced back at her. "Are you sure you're okay?"

Kate nodded and held the jacket more securely around her. Her feet in their thin flats were sodden and freezing, and her jeans were clinging to her legs. "I'm fine. Keep going. I'll keep up."

They trudged on up the hill for a few more minutes, until Sam stopped again and pulled the phone out of his pocket.

"Anything?" Kate came alongside him and peered over his shoulder.

"Nope. Not a thing. Looks like your battery is a bit low, too."

"Ah, shit." Kate took the phone from him and studied it. "It's down to ten per cent. We'd better find a signal soon. It loses charge really quickly when it gets that low."

The rain was still falling heavily, and at that moment they heard the distant rumble of thunder.

"Great. That's all we need." Sam looked up at the sky. It was covered in thick, dark, unbroken cloud, with not a hint of blue. "This isn't going to let up. Let's keep walking. I'm sure we'll eventually find some habitation." He turned back to her. "Or we could go back to the Land Rover and stay there. Could be all night, though. Your call."

"Let's keep walking." Kate screwed her eyes up against the driving rain. "At least this way we may find a signal, or a house. If we stay in the Land Rover, we could be there all night, as you say, and we don't have any food."

Sam gave a short laugh and caught her hand again. "Trust you to think of that. Good point, though. Come on, then, give me the phone, and I'll keep a check on it."

They set off again, trying to keep parallel to the road, which was now quite some distance below them. Kate stumbled on some rocks, and her hand pulled away from Sam's.

"You okay?"

"Yeah, fine, keep going. I'll catch up." She got to her feet, attempted to brush the wet grass off her knees to no avail, then hurried after him. He was just making his way across a narrow river that was rushing along a rocky bed and pouring off the high ground down towards the road. Kate stopped at the edge of the river and debated the best way to cross it. She tentatively put a foot out onto a rock in the middle, then brought her other foot up to join it.

"Careful," Sam called, his face anxious. "Those rocks are very slippery."

Kate went to step across to the next rock, but as her foot landed, the rock moved, and she was thrown off balance. With a cry and flailing arms, she fell sideways into the water and landed heavily among the rocks.

"Katy!" Sam was into the river in a flash and wading across to where she lay, gasping for breath. He caught her in his arms and hauled her unceremoniously out onto the grass, his feet slipping on the rocks so they both landed in a heap on the sodden ground. "Katy, are you all right? Are you hurt?"

Kate shook her head, still winded from the fall, and pushed her drenched hair back off her face. "No. I'm all right. Thank you for rescuing me. That was a bit scary."

"That was fucking terrifying." Sam's eyes were dark pools in the dim light. "God, Katy that was…"

Pulling her towards him, he wrapped his arms tightly around her. "Don't ever do that again."

"I don't intend to." Kate's mouth was pressed into his shoulder. "It hurt. It wasn't deep, I wasn't really in danger. Not like…"

"Not like Cerys."

Kate pulled back from him and stared into his eyes. "Tell me what you were going to tell me earlier. What don't I know about that night?"

"Now? Katy, we're soaking wet, in the middle of nowhere, and you just fell in a river. Why now?"

"Because it's coming between us. In fact, I suspect it's always come between us. Tell me. What don't I know?"

Sam stared at her for a moment, then sighed. "Okay. I'll tell you. You thought I left after that night because I was upset. Heartbroken, even. Yeah? That's what everyone thought. But that wasn't it. I left because it was my fault."

Kate pushed her hair out of her eyes again and stared at him. "No, it wasn't. You mean because you couldn't save her? But no one could."

"No, not that. It was my fault she behaved the way she did. Got so drunk and everything." He sighed again. "We broke up earlier that day. We were only pretending to be together that night, for the party. She suggested we should, and then go our separate ways the next day."

Kate stared at him and nodded slowly. "Of course. She told you about James."

"What?"

"That she was seeing James as well as you. I heard her say earlier that day that she was seeing James and she was going to break up with you. I'm so sorry. That

must have been hard. And you never said anything."
Kate frowned. "But I still don't see how that makes it
your fault. You were the one who should have been
upset."

Sam was staring at her. "She was seeing James?
She was going to break up with me? Are you sure?"

Kate nodded, her face puzzled. "Yeah, isn't that
what happened?"

"No." Sam shook his head. "I broke up with her.
That was why I thought it was my fault. I dumped *her*."

Chapter 15

June 2007, eight years earlier

Kate stretched out on the grass and closed her eyes. The sun was beating down, and she tipped her sunhat over her face.

"God, it's so hot." Jenny rolled onto her stomach and prodded Kate on the arm. "Don't go to sleep, Katy. You'll burn."

"It's pretty much the first day it's not been raining," Kate muttered from under her hat. "I'm going to enjoy it. Hope it holds out for tonight."

"It will. The gods are smiling on us today. No more exams, ever! How great does that feel?"

Kate lifted her hat and peered up at her friend. "Hardly for ever. We've still got Uni."

"Oh, you know what I mean. No more school, then. We need to celebrate."

Kate gave up trying to doze and sat up. "That's what tonight's all about. It's going to be awesome. If everyone comes."

"And by that you mean sexy Sam."

Kate giggled. "Don't call him that—someone might hear you! Of course Sam is coming."

"Are you still going travelling with him?" Jenny picked a daisy and twirled it round in her fingers. "Who else is going?"

"Me, Sam, Jon, and Rob."

"Right. You and three boys. Get real, Katy. Your mum'll never go for that! When are you meant to be going?"

"Next week. She can't stop me, Jen. I'm eighteen now. I can do what I want. You should come too. It'll be fun. Just for three months, until Uni."

"I can't. I have a job. Which is what you should be doing, not swanning around Europe spending all your money."

"Oh, don't be so boring, Jen! Once you get bogged down in work and stuff, it'll be too late to do anything like this. Seize the moment."

"Whatever." Jenny rolled onto her back. "So why isn't Cerys going?"

"Dunno. But believe me, if she was, I wouldn't be. I don't know what he sees in her. She's such a bitch. If we were American, she'd be the chief cheerleader."

Jenny laughed. "Yeah, you're right. She is a bitch. I don't really know what she has in common with Sam, either. I guess he's just been drawn in by her looks and her money, like everyone else."

"What's up, girls?" Hannah dropped to her knees beside them. "Who're you talking about?"

"Cerys."

"Ah. The superbitch. I hate her. Is she coming tonight?"

"Of course. Her father has supplied the food for the barbie. Showing off, as usual." Kate got to her feet. "I'm going home to get ready. Anyone want to come to mine? We have cake."

Jenny and Hannah got to their feet as well, and the three of them moved off towards the school building to collect the last of their belongings. The last exam was just finishing, and they were ready to party.

"Look, there's the bitch now. Who's she plotting against this time? Let's eavesdrop." Kate led the way up the path past where Cerys was holding court to a couple of her sidekicks. They were leaning against the wall of the sports hall, speaking quietly. Kate pulled Jenny and Hannah into a recessed doorway a few yards farther along, and they strained to catch her words.

"I'm going to tell him today. I can't wait any longer. I don't want him going off on his silly little jaunt thinking he has me to come back to." Cerys gave a short laugh. "I should have done this ages ago. James is much more my type. I can't be bothered to juggle them any more. I'm bored with Sam now anyway. He can go off on his little trip with his silly little friends, and I can get on with my life."

Kate caught her breath, and her hand flew up to her mouth. Cerys was going to break up with Sam. She couldn't help a little smile playing on her lips. Maybe she'd finally be in with a chance. Surely she could manage to seduce him on a three-month trip. Beckoning to Jenny and Hannah, she crept out of the doorway and headed into the school building.

"Did you hear that? She's going to break up with Sam!"

Jenny nodded. "Good. I never thought she was any good for him."

"Maybe one of us stands a chance now, then." Hannah grinned. "He is sooo sexy. He's wasted on her. She's never appreciated him."

"Hands off, girls. He's mine. I was the one he asked to go travelling." Kate tossed her hair back. "This could be my chance. D'you think she'll break up with him before tonight?"

"Even she's not such a bitch as that, is she? On the night of the hugest party of all time? Nah, she'll probably do it tomorrow."

****

"You have to tell her, Sam." Jon patted his friend on the shoulder. "I've seen the way you look at her."

Sam pulled away and stepped back, his hands thrust into the pockets of his jeans. "I can't. She might say no. And anyway, what about Cerys?"

"Break up with her, man!" Jon rolled his eyes. "You should have done that months ago. You have nothing in common, and to quote the girls, she's a superbitch. I never knew what you saw in her anyway."

Sam walked a few paces away and leaned against the wall. "She liked me. She asked me out. I wasn't going to say no." He shrugged. "No girl has ever asked me out before. Not since primary school."

"Sam, you could have any girl you want. Don't waste any more time on her. Look, this time next week we'll be in Europe. Cerys will just be a memory, and you'll have three months to spend with Katy."

"And you two losers." Sam grinned and ran a hand through his hair. "Wish I was just going with her."

"Oh, great! Ditch your best friends for a girl. And one who doesn't even know you like her. Get real, Sam. There's no way she'd go with you on your own. You need us there. But you must get rid of Cerys. Do it now, before the party. Then you can ask Katy out."

Sam looked terrified. "I can't do that." He shook his head, and his hair flopped over his forehead. "Not yet. She might say no, and then she wouldn't come travelling. I'd rather have her as a friend than not at all."

Jon inclined his head. "Okay, fair point. But for god's sake get rid of Cerys. Preferably before tonight. You're no fun when she's around. You don't even like her any more."

"Actually I never really liked her." Sam grinned sheepishly. "I was just flattered that she wanted *me.*"

A tall thin blond boy strolled over to join them. "Hey, guys, what's up?"

"Sam's gonna break up with Cerys." Jon nodded to Rob.

"'Bout time." Rob grinned. "You have to do it before we go away anyway. Can't have her thinking you're gonna come back to her. And then you can ask Katy out."

"Oh, shut up, you two. I'll ask Katy out when I'm ready." Sam looked harassed. "Or when I think she's ready to say yes. But I *will* break up with Cerys. I'll do it now. Happy?"

Both the others nodded, and Sam headed off towards the main school building, where he could see Cerys hanging out with some of her friends. As he approached, he saw her mutter something to them, and they glanced over their shoulders at him before disappearing off towards the school field. Cerys fished her phone out of her pocket and started to text, her eyes never leaving the screen when Sam joined her.

"We need to have a chat." He stopped and waited for her to look up. She finished sending her message, slipped her phone back into the pocket of her jeans, and glanced up at him.

"What?" Her pale blue eyes were hard. "I've got

somewhere to be. Can we do this later?"

Sam stared at her, her model-slim figure, her salon tan, her glossy strawberry-blonde hair with its expensive cut, and her arrogant expression, and wondered why on earth he had ever agreed to go out with her. She was not a nice person. Not like Katy. He must have been mad.

"No." He shook his head. "No, we need to do this now. Cerys, I don't want to go out with you any more."

Her head snapped up, and the icy eyes fastened onto his face. "What?"

"I'm breaking up with you. I'm sorry, but it's just not working. We have nothing in common." Sam felt he was beginning to babble but was unable to stop himself. "I'm going away next week for three months. I wanted to sort things before I went."

Cerys took a step towards him and tossed her hair back. "Let me get this straight. *You're* breaking up with *me*?"

Sam nodded, holding her gaze. "Yes. I'm sorry, but it wouldn't be fair to you to let you think we'd still be together when I got back. We'll both be off to Uni then, too. It wouldn't have worked."

She took another step towards him and stood with her feet apart and her hands on her hips. "Fuck you, Sam Somerville. Fuck you. Which is something I wish I'd never done. Right. You listen to me." She put her face up close to his. "We go to the party tonight as a couple. No one is to know this has happened. Tonight we'll be together. Then tomorrow you can fuck off. Fuck off round the world with your stupid friends and that little tramp." Sam caught his breath and clenched his fists at his sides, and Cerys narrowed her eyes speculatively. "Ah, right, so the little tramp is the reason, is she? God, you are going down in the world."

"You'll shut up about Katy!" Sam hissed the words at her, his face an inch away from hers. "It's nothing to do with her. I just don't like you any more. You're a nasty mean person, and I don't want to go out with you any more. I will do as you ask, though, and tonight we can act as though we're still together, but once the party's over, that's it."

Cerys paused for a second, then gave a brief nod and turned to walk away. "Pick me up at seven, and don't be late."

****

"Sam's not here yet." Kate strained to see past Jenny, staring over towards the entrance to the field. The party was being held in a huge marquee a mile or so outside the village, on the banks of the river. Several large gas-fired barbeques had been set up just outside the marquee, and a DJ had already got started with the music.

"Give him time." Jenny picked a piece of fruit out of her punch and sucked the alcohol out of it. "It's only just gone seven. Not many people are here yet."

"I want to see if he comes with her or not, or whether she broke up with him."

"Right, so if she broke up with him, you can spend the evening consoling him."

"Exactly." Kate grinned over her shoulder at her. "I *am* one of his best friends, after all."

"Maybe that's the problem." Jenny poured the rest of the punch down her throat. "It's sometimes hard to move from friend to girlfriend."

"I'll manage it." Kate spoke with confidence. "Oh,

here he comes. Shit, he's with Cerys. She must have decided not to tell him till tomorrow." She glanced round at Jenny. "Should we tell him what we overheard?"

"No!" Jenny caught Kate's arm. "Definitely not. Suppose she's changed her mind? It would only upset him. We need to stay out of it."

Kate sniffed with annoyance but heeded her friend's words and moved over to fetch a drink from the long table that was serving as a bar.

"Is this stuff actually alcoholic?" Kate sipped it tentatively.

"Yeah, I think it has vodka in it." Jenny was just starting on her third. "Look, Sam and Cerys are coming over."

Kate knocked back her drink in one gulp and helped herself to another, watching as Sam and his girlfriend approached them. He was looking as hot as usual in ripped jeans, a faded Foo Fighters T-shirt, and black Converse, and Cerys was wearing a skimpy yellow top, very short denim shorts, and high wedge sandals. Her long bare legs were evenly tanned, and her glossy hair swung, perfectly in place, just brushing her shoulders.

"Hi, Katy, Jen." Cerys stopped in front of them and looked them up and down. "You look—comfortable." She smirked and wound her arm around Sam's waist. "Where's the booze?"

"Over there." Jenny jerked her thumb over her shoulder. "It's only punch, but I think it has vodka in."

Cerys let go of Sam and swayed a bit. "That'll do," she said and headed over to the table. "Come on, Sam."

With an apologetic smile at Kate and Jenny, Sam

dutifully followed her over to the table and served them both with punch.

"She hasn't done it yet, then." Kate watched their progress round the marquee. "I think she's been drinking already."

"Did you see her eyes?" Jenny leaned closer and whispered, "Her pupils were huge. I don't think it's drink she's been having. I think she's taken something."

"Well, then she's even more stupid than I thought. What the hell does Sam see in her? D'you think he'll be upset when she dumps him?"

"Probably. Boys are very shallow."

"Sam's not." Kate's eyes followed him as he tailed Cerys on her social round. "We have really deep conversations. He's not just a pretty face, you know."

"I guess." Jenny shrugged. "This is getting boring. Are you just going to stand here and watch him all night, or can we go and have some fun? You'll get to spend plenty of time with him over the next couple of months. Give it a break tonight."

Kate grinned. "Sorry. Yeah, let's go and find the others and have fun. I can't believe that our school days are over. It's so weird."

"I know." Jenny caught her arm, and they headed out of the marquee towards the barbeques. "I don't feel any older."

"I don't intend *ever* to feel any older." Kate grinned and tossed her hair back. "I shall be eighteen forever. It's such a cool age. We never need to grow up and get boring and old like our parents. We can stay feeling like this always. I never want to stop having fun." She caught Jenny by the hand, and they ran over to join a group of their friends by the river.

****

"God, my head's spinning." Kate lay back on the grass and closed her eyes. The music was blaring out from the marquee, accompanied by multicoloured flashing lights, and a large number of students were dancing wildly on the grass. "Whatever's in that punch is pretty strong."

Jenny sat down beside her. "Yeah, me too. Can't believe it's only our year that are here. It looks like so many people."

"You're probably seeing double." Kate chuckled. "Well, there are fifty in our year, and I'm pretty sure they're all here. Can you see Sam anywhere?"

"Stop obsessing, Katy!" Jenny glanced around. "Yeah, he's over by the bridge with Cerys and a couple of boys. Not sure who. They're in the shadow."

Kate pushed herself up on her elbows and peered across the field in the near darkness. "Oh, that's that horrible Craig, and James. Oh, god, maybe she's telling Sam about her and James now. Let's go and find out." She got to her feet and set off towards the stone bridge that spanned the river at its widest part. Technically, it was outside the field where the party was being held, but a number of the students had ventured over there and were sitting on the bridge, dangling their feet over the edge and dropping bits of burger and sausage into the water. Kate headed towards where Sam was apparently having a heated conversation with Cerys, who was standing on top of the wall of the bridge, hands on her hips, yelling back at him.

"Katy, slow down." Jenny caught up with her and grabbed her arm. "We shouldn't interfere. I think they're having a row."

"Well, duh!" Kate glanced at her. "I bet she's breaking up with him."

"Bit public for that." Jenny kept pace with her. "We shouldn't listen."

"Shut up. They're not on their own. Look. There are at least six other people there. Come on." Kate carried on across the field, her eyes never leaving Sam as he remonstrated with his girlfriend.

"Just fuck off, Sam Somerville," Cerys was shouting at him. "You don't own me. I can do what I like. And this is what I like doing." She ran along to the end of the wall and jumped down. "See? It's not dangerous at all. You're a woose. Just a stupid little woose." She vaulted back up onto the wall, walked to the middle, and stood staring down into the river below. "Come on, Sam. Come and join me, or are you too chicken?" She tossed her head with a mocking smile.

"Cerys, come down." Sam held out his hand to her. "It's not safe. One slip and you'd be in the river. You're wearing those stupid shoes, too. It's not fucking safe. Now please get down. I get that you're upset, and I'm sorry."

Cerys spun around on one heel and wobbled precariously, putting out her hands to regain her balance. "See, chicken? It's fine. And for the record, Sammy, I'm not at all upset." She moved to the middle of the bridge and got down on her knees, peering over the edge. "It looks so good down there. I reckon we should all go skinny-dipping. Who's up for that?" She stood up and shouted to the rest of the students. "Hey, guys, who's up for going skinny-dipping in the river? Sam, come on, or are you too chicken for that?"

"Just get down, Cerys. You can go skinny-dipping

209

if you want. Just get down from the fucking wall before you fall."

"I'm not going to fall." Cerys peered over the edge again. "But you know what? I reckon I could jump down and land in the water. Shall I do that, Sammy? Shall I?" Her voice had become very high-pitched, and her eyes were shining in the dark. "Be quicker than climbing down. You come too, Sammy." She laughed loudly and threw her head back. "Like that'd ever happen." She spun round on one heel again and wobbled dangerously.

"Cerys!" Sam screamed her name as she clawed at the air with her outstretched arms, uttering an ear-splitting scream as she toppled backwards off the wall and hurtled down towards the rocky river.

There was a moment's shocked silence before everyone started screaming and running towards the river, Sam leading the way, his face ashen.

"Cerys, Cerys, no, why the hell…" He was muttering under his breath as he ran, kicking his shoes off as he reached the riverbank. Her limp body was caught against a large jagged rock, the water swirling all around, threatening to pull her away downstream. Sam and some of the other boys plunged into the water to try and reach her, but as they got close to the rock, the fast-moving water pulled her away and carried her rapidly downstream, thrashing her body against the rocks. Sam attempted to follow and could only be restrained with great difficulty by several other boys. They hauled him out of the water and held him down on the riverbank, where he struggled against them, his eyes wild as he called her name in desperation.

Chapter 16

Present day

"So all this time you've thought it was your fault." Kate stared at Sam sadly, the rain running down her face and soaking into his jacket. "And it wasn't. Not at all."

"I see that now." Sam shook his head. "I thought I'd upset her by breaking up with her and that was why she got so drunk and acted stupid. In fact, she was going to break up with me and was just annoyed that I got there first." He looked away across the rain-swept hills. "She must have really hated me. How could I have been so stupid?"

Kate reached out and touched his arm. "You weren't stupid. Every boy wanted to go out with her. You were flattered. Don't beat yourself up. And for the record, I don't think she was drunk that night. I think she'd taken something."

Sam nodded. "I guessed she had, actually. She was a bit weird all evening. I really couldn't have done anything, could I?"

"No, Sam, you really couldn't. I had no idea you were blaming yourself all these years. I, and all the others, just thought you were heartbroken at losing her. We didn't know you had broken up with her." Kate watched him as he ran a hand through his sodden hair, her mind still reeling at the reason he had broken up with Cerys. He had wanted to ask her out. She shook her head to try and rid it of the complicated thoughts that were trying to take her over, and touched his arm again. "I think we should go. I'm actually getting really cold now, and this rain doesn't seem to be letting up. I'm sorry. We can talk more about this later."

Sam's head shot up, and he looked at her with concern. "God, I'm sorry, Katy! I totally forgot where we were. We must get on." He paused for a moment, and a strange look passed over his face. "So if I *had* asked you out…would you have said yes?"

Kate looked up at him, blinking the rain from her eyes, and nodded slowly. "Yes."

They stared at each other for a long moment, then Sam took a deep breath and pulled the phone out of his pocket. "Still no signal, and very little battery. I think we need to keep walking until we find a house. You with me?"

"Yeah." Kate nodded and got to her feet. "Sounds like the best plan. It's not doing us any good getting this wet. And your face needs attention." She winced as she stretched her left leg, and Sam frowned at her.

"Are you in pain? I thought you said you weren't hurt?"

"That was before I fell in the river." Kate grimaced. "I think I may have a few bruises of my own tomorrow." She smiled up at him. "Come on, let's find somewhere to get our wounds tended, or at least phone your dad."

Sam took her hand and stared around them. "I think it might be better now if we headed down to the road. I think we should give up on the phone and just try to find habitation, and that would be the best bet. Come on." He started off down the slope towards the road, Kate clinging to his hand and trying to keep her feet on the slippery grass.

They finally reached the road and set off along what was rapidly becoming a tributary of the river, in the direction Sam thought to be the most hopeful. Both beginning to flag a little after the traumas of the last couple of hours, they trudged in silence, Kate trying hard to ignore the feelings engendered by Sam's hand in hers.

They had been walking for what seemed to Kate to be miles, when Sam suddenly stopped, and she cannoned into him.

"What is it?" She peered ahead of them through the driving rain.

"A building. Look over there, among the trees, just near that stone bridge." Sam pointed ahead of them.

Kate walked a couple of steps forward. "It is." Relief sounded in her voice. "Oh, god, I hope someone's home. Come on." She set off at a smart pace, Sam catching her up and falling into step alongside.

"Wait for me." He grinned down at her. "I hope they offer us a cup of tea."

Kate laughed. "You sound like my mum," she said. "She thinks tea cures everything. Personally, I could murder scampi and chips and a glass of wine."

Sam chuckled. "Followed by cake, no doubt."

"Well, I wouldn't want to presume." She smiled up at him. "Let's just hope they're not scared off by our appearance."

As they neared the clump of trees, it became

apparent that the building was much larger than they had originally thought. Kate stared intently at it.

"That's not just a house," she murmured. "It looks like a pub or something."

Sam caught her hand again and hurried her forward. "I think I know this place." He started to smile as they got closer. "Yes, I do. I had no idea we were here. It's a hotel. My parents know the owners. It's a really nice hotel." He grinned down at her. "Think we might be in luck."

"We can't go in a nice hotel looking like this." Kate pulled back. "We're soaked. We have nothing with us. They won't let us in."

"Of course they will." Sam had picked up even more speed, and Kate stumbled to keep up with him. "I told you. They know my family. Don't worry. This couldn't have worked out better."

As they turned up the drive towards the hotel, Kate began to shiver in earnest. She had managed to keep the cold at bay while they were walking, but now salvation was in sight, in fact almost in reach, she began to relax and felt suddenly extremely cold and extremely sore. And of course, extremely hungry. As they approached the door of the hotel, Kate hung back.

"You go in. They know you, so it won't be so bad."

"Don't be daft." Sam gripped her hand tightly. "We both go in. You look dreadful, and the sooner you can get warm and dry the better. I'm not leaving you out here. Come on." He shepherded her through the large glass doors into a spacious hallway carpeted in red. There was a reception area at the far end, and several doors leading off to either side.

Acutely aware they were actually squelching, Kate followed Sam up to the reception desk and waited while he rang the bell. After a few moments a short dark-haired lady appeared and looked at them in surprise.

"Good lord! Have you two walked here? Has your car broken down?" She walked around into the hallway and stared at them with concern.

"We had an accident." Sam nodded. "Our vehicle went off the road, and we've had to walk miles to get here. We couldn't get a signal on the phone and were wondering if we could use yours?"

The woman nodded immediately and ushered them into the office.

"Of course you can." She peered more closely at Sam. "Don't I know you?"

"You know my parents. Colin and Moira Somerville. I'm Sam."

"Of course!" She beamed at them. "I remember now. I met you some years back. Did you want to call the AA, or your parents?"

"My father." Sam nodded, unable to prevent himself from shivering. The woman looked more closely at him.

"You're hurt." She indicated his face. "We must sort that out." She turned to Kate. "Are you all right, dear? You look very cold. Are you hurt?"

Kate shook her head. "I'm fine, thank you. Just wet."

"She fell in the river." Sam spoke from where he was dialling his father. "So she's not all right. She's soaked through and probably covered in bruises." He glanced at Kate and frowned. "And I think she should sit down."

Kate glared at him. "I'm fine. Don't fuss. Honestly, I'm okay." She smiled at the woman who was ushering her towards an armchair. "I can't sit in that. I'm filthy."

The woman glanced at them both. "Okay." She seemed to come to a decision. "We need to get you dried, or you're both going to catch your deaths. Room seventeen is free. I'll take you up there in a minute, and you can get changed and dried."

"Oh, no, there's no need," Kate protested, at the same time imagining the immense joy of removing her wet clothes and getting in a hot shower. "We don't have any other clothes with us. We were only out for the day."

"That's fine. We have bathrobes in all the rooms. I'll take your clothes and get them washed and dried by the morning."

"The morning?" Kate stared at her. "But we're not staying the night. We have to get back."

"Yes, we are." Sam appeared at her side. "I've told Dad to come and get us in the morning. Sorry, Katy. You're not going anywhere tonight except to bed. And I feel as though someone is hammering continuously on my head with an iron bar, so if you don't mind, we're staying here. I have money," he added, fishing in the back pocket of his jeans and bringing out a pile of soggy notes.

The woman laughed. "Oh, dear. That's fine. Right. Let's get you upstairs and out of those clothes. I'm Barbara, by the way."

"Kate," Kate murmured, holding out her hand. "Thank you. That all sounds lovely. May I just phone home first? I told my mother I'd be home this evening."

"Of course. On you go. I expect you're both

hungry, too. Would you like some dinner sent up to the room?"

"Is that possible?" Kate could hardly keep the excitement out of her voice. "Do you have scampi? I've been yearning for scampi."

"We do." Barbara smiled. "You make your call, and I'll sort out the food with Sam."

Kate walked over to the telephone, trying not to drip on anything too important, and dialled her parents' number. To her relief, her father answered.

"Dad? It's me." She paused for a moment while she worked out what to tell him. "Dad I'm staying out tonight. I'm with a friend from work, and her car broke down, so we're booking into a hotel and will be back tomorrow…Yes, I'm fine, honestly. A bit wet, but fine. Tell Mum not to worry…No, my phone is out of battery, so she can't phone me." She took a deep breath. "Dad, I need a night away. She's driving me mad with the wedding stuff. You understand, don't you?" She smiled. "Thanks, Dad. See you tomorrow." She replaced the receiver and walked over to join Sam at the bottom of the stairs. He was holding a key and smiling at her.

"Come on. Let's go and get dry. I have to say I'm rather looking forward to this." He led the way up the wide staircase and along a corridor. "Here we go, there's fourteen…fifteen…sixteen and…seventeen." He unlocked the door and stood aside to let Kate go through first.

She walked into the room and turned on the light. It was a fairly large double room with a long window overlooking the moor, and an ensuite bathroom leading off. There was a large dressing table, an armchair, and a small table holding a television, as well as a large double bed. Kate noted the bed and decided not to think about it until she was dry. That was just too much for her brain to deal with.

"You go first." Sam pointed to the bathroom. "Don't argue, just do it, and chuck your clothes out here so I can give them to Barbara. Here, take one of these bathrobes with you." He held out a thick white towelling bathrobe that had been waiting on the bed. "That should keep you warm."

Kate took it without a word and disappeared into the bathroom. She looked around her. It was small but cosy, with a corner bath and a small shower cubicle. She eyed the bath longingly but decided it wouldn't be fair on Sam if she took too long, so she peeled off her sodden clothes, opened the door a crack, flung them back into the bedroom, and then stepped into the shower.

As she let the steaming hot water flow over her chilled flesh, Kate began to relax. She was aching all over, and a quick glance had confirmed that her whole left side was dotted with red scrape marks and bruises. She rubbed her fingers gently across a long mark that extended from her hip almost down to her knee, and winced. That was going to look dreadful in a day or so. Just in time for the wedding.

She turned the water up even hotter and stood directly underneath with her eyes tightly closed. She didn't want to think about the wedding. Not tonight. When she was spending the night in a double room with a man she was seriously attracted to, and no clothes. In fact, as she opened her eyes and moved her head out from under the water, she wasn't quite sure what she *should* be thinking about. Definitely not what she was actually thinking about. She picked up the soap and scrubbed herself clean, taking care with the bruised areas, then rinsed herself thoroughly and turned off the shower. As she got dried, she realised just how incredibly hungry she was, and hoped the scampi and chips would arrive fairly quickly.

Hanging the towel to dry on the heated rail, she slipped on the lovely warm bathrobe and went back into the bedroom. Sam was stretched out on the bed wearing the other bathrobe, his eyes closed and one arm across his chest.

Thinking he may have dozed off, Kate moved quietly around the room investigating the facilities. A small hairdryer was on the dressing table, and tea- and coffee-making things were on a table in the corner. She turned the kettle on. Just for once, she actually fancied a nice hot cup of tea.

"Nice shower?" Sam was watching her from the bed.

"Yes, thanks." Kate turned and smiled at him, feeling suddenly awkward. "I thought you were asleep."

He sat up with a painful grunt. "No. Just trying to get this headache to go off. Barbara gave me some painkillers, so hopefully it will before long."

Kate walked over and looked closely at the side of his face. "That eye looks so painful." She reached out and touched it gently. "And you still have blood on your cheek. May I clean it for you? It should probably have something put on it." She looked around the room, and her eyes lit upon a small first-aid kit on the dressing table. "Maybe there's something in here I can use." She opened it and nodded. "Yeah, this should do the trick. May I?"

Sam nodded, a small smile on his lips. "Yeah, go ahead. Be gentle. It's quite spectacularly sore."

Kate unwrapped a sterile wipe and gently dabbed the dried blood away from the long graze down the side of his face. As she leaned forward, she was acutely aware of his proximity and felt her stomach flutter. God, she was behaving like a teenager again. She was wiping blood from his face, and she was actually getting aroused. She stood up straight and took a step backwards. "That's better. If you're going to have a shower now, I can look at it again after and see if it needs a plaster or anything."

"Thank you." Sam was watching her. "You were very gentle. I'll have a shower now. Barbara said the food won't be long. You still look cold. Why don't you make us some hot drinks? I'd love a coffee."

Kate nodded. "Yes, I put the kettle on already. How d'you take it?"

"Milk and one sugar, please." He disappeared into the ensuite and closed the door.

Kate sat down on the bed and put her head in her hands. What the hell was she doing here? It was three days before her wedding, and she was spending the night in a hotel room with another man. Nearly naked. Well—she looked down at herself—the bathrobes actually covered them up very well, but she was still acutely aware they were both naked underneath. Her stomach did a little flip again, and she shook her head in despair. Oh, why had he had to come back now? Why had she accepted his offer of a day on Dartmoor? Why was she secretly glad both those things had happened? It was totally messing with her head.

Getting to her feet, she picked up the hairdryer, quickly got her hair into a more comfortable state, then went over to prepare the drinks. She emptied a sachet of coffee into one cup, popped a tea bag in the other, and poured the boiling water over them. It seemed odd to be having tea in the evening, but it was true she was still cold despite the hot shower. She felt cold on the inside. She added the milk and sugar, then carried her own cup over to the armchair and curled up in it, cradling the warm cup in her hands. She had just got comfortable when there was a knock at the door, heralding the arrival of their food, and by the time Sam reappeared from the bathroom, rubbing his hair with a towel, Kate had set the plates on the dressing table and was scattering salt and pepper on her scampi.

"Sorry, couldn't wait." She smiled at him over her shoulder. "Never been so starving."

Sam laughed and dropped the towel on the floor. "That looks wonderful. Have to say I'm pretty hungry myself." He joined her, picked up his plate, and perched on the end of the bed. Kate took hers back to the chair and curled up again.

"Still can't get warm," she remarked as she took a mouthful of scampi. "Don't know what's wrong with me."

"Probably just a reaction to the crash." Sam watched her as he ate. "We'll have to think of a way to warm you up after we've eaten."

Kate glanced up at him, but he had looked down at his plate and she couldn't see his face. What had he meant by that? She felt a tingle in her stomach as she tried to imagine, and couldn't help a tiny quiver of excitement running through her. What on earth was she thinking? In three days' time she would be married. To Richard. This was all wrong. She shovelled some more food into her mouth and chewed energetically. Or something was wrong anyway.

"This is lovely," Sam mumbled, his mouth full of scampi. "Is it as good as you'd hoped?"

Kate nodded, not trusting herself to speak, and glanced over at him. His hair, still wet from the shower, was endearingly tousled, and the rapidly burgeoning black eye and bruised face made him look rather like a small boy. He caught her eye and grinned, then winced slightly, and his hand went up to his face.

"Is it very sore?" Kate was horrified to find her voice was shaky.

"Yeah." Sam gave a rueful grin. "I won't pretend it's not. The headache is subsiding a bit, but my eye's throbbing like mad. Don't think it's going to be very easy sleeping on it, actually."

"I still think you should have seen a doctor." Kate watched him with concern. "You might have done some other damage. Promise you'll tell me if you feel sick or anything. You might have concussion."

"I'll tell you." He smiled at her again. "But I'm fine."

Kate speared her last piece of scampi and popped it into her mouth. "Okay, then. You'd better be. That was lovely scampi." She stood up and took her plate over to the table. "I think I'll have another tea to try and warm up. Would you like another coffee?"

Sam shook his head. "No, thanks. Don't actually think it's helping the headache, and I'll never get to sleep with any more caffeine." He popped the last chip into his mouth and got up. "That was really nice." He put his plate with Kate's and yawned. "God, I'm tired. What time is it?"

Kate glanced at her phone. "No idea, my phone is completely out of charge now. It was about six when we got here, so it can't be very late yet." She shivered again as she poured hot water into her cup.

"You're still cold." Sam had come up behind her, and she could feel his breath on her neck. "We need to warm you up. I don't want you to catch a chill."

"That's the sort of thing my mum says." Kate didn't turn round. "I'm not even sure what a chill is."

"Me neither." Sam put his hands on her shoulders and turned her round to face him. "But I'm sure you wouldn't want one. Especially three days before your wedding."

Kate looked away from him, her heart suddenly plummeting. Just for a few minutes she had forgotten the wedding. Sam put a finger under her chin and raised it up so she had to look at him.

"Can't send you back to Ronald with a chill. He might wonder where you got it."

"Richard."

"Whatever. Come on, we must warm you up." He took her hand and led her towards the bed, pulling back the quilt with his other hand.

Kate stared at him. "What are we going to do?"

"Warm you up. Now hop in the bed." He gave her a gentle shove and climbed in beside her. "Lie down, and I'll warm you up. Don't worry. You can keep your bathrobe on." He pulled her down beside him and drew her close, pulling the quilt over them and wrapping his arms around her. "There. That'll soon do the trick.

Come on, snuggle up and relax."

Kate let him pull her into his arms and felt herself relaxing against his warm body. She lifted her head and stared him in the eyes.

"This is nice," she murmured, "but very wrong."

"Nonsense. I'm just warming you up. Not even Rupert would object to me stopping his fiancée catching her death of cold."

Kate couldn't help a chuckle escaping, and she didn't bother to correct him this time. "I think he might, but who cares. This is actually helping. Thank you." She smiled at him, their faces so close that his breath was warming her cheek.

"It's a pleasure." He watched her, his eyes serious for once. "Did you mean what you said?"

"What?" Kate was puzzled.

"That you would have gone out with me in sixth form? And that you were worried about me when we crashed?"

"Of course!" She stared at him in surprise. "Of course I would have. And of course I was worried. You were just lying there. I thought…" She tailed off as his lips came down on hers and his arms tightened around her. She responded with a muffled moan, and their tongues gently entwined as their lips locked. Kate pressed her body closer to his, closed her eyes, and was savouring the wonderful feel of his mouth on hers when he suddenly pulled away and looked down at her, his arms still firmly around her.

"And that's all you're getting," he said with a smile. "Until you make your decision."

"What decision?" Kate's head was spinning.

"You'll know. Now just relax and try to get warm."

His arms tightened around her, and he manoeuvred her head onto his shoulder. "How's that? I need to lie on this side because of my eye."

"It's lovely," Kate murmured sleepily, wriggling even closer to him. "So was that kiss."

"Yes." Sam gently pressed his lips into her hair. "It was. Now let's try and sleep. We've had a long day."

"An' you tell me if you feel sick," Kate muttered, her eyes closed and her face buried in his shoulder. "Promise?"

"I promise."

Chapter 17

Thursday 23rd July

"Good morning."

Kate opened her eyes to find Sam's face inches from her own on the pillow. She yawned and smiled. "Good morning. Wow, did we stay in the same position all night?"

"It would appear so." He pushed a strand of hair back out of her eyes. "You look very sweet when you're asleep."

"I am very sweet." She smiled and rolled over onto her back. "Oh, god, I ache all over. How's your face? And your headache?"

"Headache's nearly gone, but my face and eye are throbbing like mad."

"I'm sorry." Kate watched him with concern. "I think I shall insist you go to the doctor."

"I might," he conceded. "It's certainly pretty bad."

She rolled over and stood up with a grimace. "Would you like a coffee?"

"Yeah, please. Are you in pain? You winced."

"Oh, just the bruises from the fall in the river. Nothing to worry about."

"Show me."

"I can't."

"Katy. Show me. There must be some on your

226

legs."

Kate rolled her eyes. "They're all down my left side. Okay I'll show you my leg." She held back the dressing gown to reveal her thigh and knee, both dotted with purpling bruises of varying sizes. "Just bruises, nothing to worry about."

"That looks really painful." Sam reached out and gently ran his hand down her leg. "You need to put something on those. They're going to be a horrible colour in a day or so."

"The ones higher up, on my ribs, feel worse." Kate was desperately trying not to react as his hand moved over her flesh. "I'll be fine." She knew she should pull away, but didn't think her legs would hold her up if she tried to move. Her whole body was tingling from his touch, and she felt suddenly lightheaded.

"Are you all right, Katy?" Sam was watching her.

"I think I need to sit down." She groped behind her and sat down abruptly on the bed beside him.

"Maybe you should see the doctor too?" he suggested, removing his hand. "You don't want to be in pain on Saturday."

"On Saturday?" Kate was momentarily flummoxed. "Why Saturday…oh. Oh, right." She turned away from him, her face beginning to get hot. She had forgotten about Saturday. She had forgotten about her wedding.

Sam got to his feet with a grunt. "I guess we'd better see if our clothes are ready. My father is coming to fetch us at ten."

Kate watched as he walked to the door and looked out into the corridor. Even covered in the thick bathrobe, his body was wonderful, and she couldn't take her eyes off him. He disappeared out of the room, and the door swung shut behind him.

Kate fell back on the bed and covered her face with her hands. What on earth was she doing? In forty-eight hours she would be dressing for her wedding. Her wedding to Richard. And she had just spent the night in the arms of a man she was pretty sure was in love with her. How she felt about *him* she wasn't prepared to consider just now, but following the surprising revelation that Sam had broken up with Cerys so he could ask her out, her mind was in utter turmoil.

"Katy? Are you sure you're all right?" Sam had returned with an armful of clean clothes and was watching her with concern.

She sat up and sighed. "Yeah, I'm okay." She looked up at him. "Tell me something, honestly. Did you really come back to get a job and settle down?"

Sam dumped the pile of clean clothes on the bed and stood looking down at her. "Why else would I have come back?"

"That's not an answer."

"Well, it's all you're getting for now. Now come on, Dad will be here in half an hour. We need to get dressed." He picked up his jeans and started to pull them on.

Kate fished in the pile of clothes, located her bra and pants, and disappeared into the bathroom to put them on. Her mind was in so much turmoil that it was actually giving her a headache. There were so many things she wanted to ask Sam, but she knew that if she did, she would be starting something she might not be able to stop.

And she really did have to marry Richard. She

would be letting far too many people down if she didn't. It was better just to let herself down. It was all her own fault anyway. If she hadn't gone out on that first date with Sam, then none of this would have happened. She wouldn't now be getting dressed in a hotel bathroom while the man she had spent the night with—albeit relatively chastely—was getting dressed on the other side of the door.

She finished fastening her bra, wincing as the elastic pressed down on her bruises, then slipped the bathrobe back on, realising she had left her jeans and top in the bedroom.

She checked her face and hair in the mirror and sighed in mild desperation. She looked like she'd been pulled through a hedge backwards, as her mother would say, and she didn't even have a hairbrush with her. She ran her fingers through her hair and vainly attempted to flatten it into some semblance of order. It defied all her efforts, and eventually she gave up and went back into the bedroom.

Sam had got dressed and was sitting cross-legged on the bed, trying to get the TV to tune in.

Kate picked up her jeans, turned her back on him, and wriggled into them under the bathrobe. As she pulled them up, she realised just how much skinny jeans and badly bruised legs didn't go together, and she couldn't help a sharp intake of breath.

"Katy? Are you okay?" Sam's voice was concerned.

"Yeah. Had forgotten how uncomfortable my jeans would be on these bruises. Wish I'd been wearing a skirt, now."

"That might have caused problems of its own."

Sam was watching her as she writhed in an attempt to pull the jeans up painlessly. "Then everyone would have been able to see your bruises. Even Rudolf."

"Richard." Kate wasn't in the mood. "But you do have a good point. I would rather avoid any awkward questions."

"Good job your wedding dress is long." Sam's voice was neutral. "At least I assume it is."

"Yes." Kate picked up her top and disappeared back into the bathroom. He was impossible. He just kept saying things to wind her up. What did he want her to say? That she wasn't going to marry Richard after all? If he wanted that, why didn't he just say so? Why did he have to be so cryptic? She pulled her top over her head and checked herself in the mirror again. But that kiss had really been something, and she was fairly sure he meant it. She turned to leave the room and paused with her hand on the door handle; she was also fairly sure that she had meant it too.

Sam looked up as she re-entered the room. "Okay? Dad will be here any minute. Are you ready to go?"

Kate nodded and slipped her phone into her pocket. "Yeah, I think so. I didn't actually have anything with me, did I?"

Sam frowned. "I think you'd better wear my jacket." He held it out to her. "Have you seen your arm?"

Kate glanced down at her left arm, and put her right hand up to touch it. "Shit. I hadn't even noticed those." Both her shoulder and elbow were turning almost as purple as Sam's eye, and she winced as she pressed her fingers against the bruises. She looked up at him, with a wry grin. "We look like we've been in a fight."

He placed the jacket gently round her and rested his hands on her shoulders. "Those may be more difficult to cover up. Will you be okay?"

"I'll cope." She looked up over her shoulder at him. "I guess I'll have to."

"Your decision." He lightly ran his fingers over her tousled hair and smiled down at her. "You look like you slept in a haystack. Now come on, let's get downstairs to wait for my dad. Probably better he doesn't find us in the bedroom together." He took her hand, and together they left the room and headed back downstairs.

Barbara met them at the bottom and smiled. "Ah, there you are. Are you having breakfast before you go?"

Sam shook his head. "We'll need to get off as soon as my father arrives," he said with a smile. "Thanks for the room. It was very comfortable."

"And thank you so much for washing our clothes," Kate added. "That was very kind of you."

"No problem. Glad you managed to get some rest." She smiled at them and carried on into the dining room.

"Shall we wait outside?" Sam glanced down at Kate. "It looks like a nice day."

"Yeah, let's." Kate nodded. "Does your father know I'm with you?"

"No." Sam pushed open the large glass door, and they walked out into the morning sunshine. "Don't worry. I'll make sure he doesn't tell anyone. He's a pretty cool dad."

"Maybe I should find another way home?" Kate suggested tentatively.

"Don't be daft. Remember where we are. The

middle of nowhere." He smiled down at her. "Don't worry. It'll be okay."

They wandered down to the end of the drive and perched on the stone wall to wait, Kate becoming more and more disturbed as she realised the possible repercussions of her night away. She took a deep breath and clenched her hands in her lap. She was going to have a lot of explaining to do.

"It'll all be all right." Sam's voice was quiet. "Don't worry. Everything will work out." He put his arm around her shoulders and pulled her closer. "Trust me."

Feeling all control over her life was slipping away, Kate gave in and rested her head on his shoulder, revelling in the feeling of safety it brought. She closed her eyes tightly and tried to think of something calming. This time even buttered toast didn't work, and she bit her lip to stop herself from crying. It was two days until her wedding, and she was the most confused she had ever been. And she had no one she could talk to. Not even Jen.

"Here's Dad." Sam pushed her upright and got to his feet. "Are you ready?"

Kate nodded and stood up, slipping the jacket on properly to hide her bruises. She stood nervously a few yards behind Sam while he greeted his father. She watched as the two men exchanged a few words, and then Colin Somerville walked over to her.

"Hello, Kate. I hear you and my son have had a bit of an adventure. I hope you're okay?"

Kate nodded. "Yes, thank you, Mr. Somerville, just a bit bruised. I do think Sam should see a doctor, though. Please, will you make him?"

Colin smiled. "Please call me Colin. Don't worry about Sam. He's pretty tough, but I rather feel his mother will share your view about the doctor. Now where did you abandon that vehicle of yours? Let's get you two home."

****

"Drop Katy here, Dad." Sam pointed to a lay-by a few hundred yards from where she lived. He glanced down at her, squashed next to him on the front seat of his father's van. "Will you be all right, Katy? Safer here than in the middle of the village."

Kate nodded silently. Her mood had become more and more agitated the closer they got to home, and she was now on the verge of a panic attack. She held Sam's gaze for a moment, and something in his eyes made her heart flutter. God, she was in a mess.

"Thanks for bringing me home." She mustered a smile for Sam's father, suddenly very aware of Sam's leg pressed against hers. It was actually her bruised leg, but she hadn't said anything in case he moved it.

"It's a pleasure, Kate." Colin pulled the van into the side of the road. "It's the least I could do, since my son managed to get you stranded in the middle of Dartmoor." He smiled at her. "Don't worry. I won't tell anyone. It'll be our secret. And before you ask again, I will do my best to get Sam to see a doctor."

Sam opened the door and slid out, holding out his hand to help Kate. She landed on the road beside him, still holding his hand, and looked solemnly up at him. "What do I do now?"

"Go home. Have a bath, tend to your bruises, and go to bed."

"That's not what I meant."

"I know." He looked down at her. "You know your temporary job?" She nodded, puzzled. "How long have you been doing that? Five years, is it? Well, just remember that sometimes things that you intend to be temporary might turn out to be more permanent, and the longer you stay there, the harder it is to leave."

Kate stared at him, her mind befuddled with his words. She frowned. "What?"

"Don't worry. It'll make sense later. Just go home and have a think about it. It might help your decision. Now go before someone sees you." He gave her a gentle push in the direction of her road, and she turned.

"When will I see you again?"

"I'll be around." He winked at her with his good eye, then climbed back into the van, and they drove off towards the village centre.

Kate stood staring after them, her heart suddenly heavy. Slowly she crossed the road, her weary brain still trying to make sense of his speech about her job. Why did he care about her job? What on earth was he talking about? God, she was tired, and hungry. She turned into the cul-de-sac and made her way towards her house. She could see that both her parents' cars were in the drive, and her heart sank. No chance of sneaking in unnoticed, then. Now the questions would start, and she was going to have to come up with a believable story as to where she'd been all night, and why she was covered in bruises. Although hopefully she could keep those concealed. She could just imagine the fuss her mother was going to make.

As she lifted her hand to open the front door, she realised she was still wearing Sam's jacket. She started to shrug it off, then paused. Which was worse, to explain a strange jacket, or to explain a badly bruised arm? She pulled the jacket back on and sighed as she opened the front door. She'd think of something to say.

"Kate! You're home!" Helen appeared in the hall. "Where on earth were you last night? It's all very well calling your father, but you didn't really tell him anything. I've been so worried. You're getting married in two days. You can't just disappear like that. It's very irresponsible."

Kate stood in the middle of the hall and felt tears welling up behind her eyes. She swallowed and looked down at her feet. She had no idea what to say.

"There you are, Kate." Her father came down the stairs and smiled at her. "Glad you're back. I bet you're hungry."

Grateful, Kate nodded and managed a small smile. "Yes. I am, actually." She took a deep breath and looked at her mother. "I'll tell you everything later, Mum, but could I just go and get changed and then have something to eat?"

Helen looked closely at her, then nodded and gave her a gentle push towards the stairs. "Go on, then. I'll get some food on for you. Cheese on toast okay?" She paused. "That's not your jacket, is it? Where did you get that?"

"I borrowed it from the friend I was with." Kate started up the stairs. "It was raining."

"It looks like a man's jacket." Helen frowned. "I thought you were with a girl from work."

"I was. It's her boyfriend's. It was just in the car." Kate carried on up the stairs without looking back and let herself into her bedroom. She quietly closed the door behind her, leant against it, and slid down until she was sitting on the floor, her knees raised. She let her arms dangle down at her sides, rested her head on her knees, and just gave in to the tears, her brain turning somersaults as she tried to make sense of the last two days and work out her feelings.

After a couple of minutes, she raised her head and wiped her hand angrily across her face. She needed to sort herself out. She had to function normally, or her parents would be suspicious. With a wince of pain, she got to her feet and gently peeled her jeans off her bruised legs. They didn't look any better, and one or two of the larger bruises were actually slightly swollen. Maybe a good long soak in the bath later would help them.

She reluctantly took off Sam's jacket, holding it close to her face for a moment before stowing it safely in her cupboard, then peeled off her strappy top. The bruises on her arm and shoulder were very visible, and turning a darker purple with every minute, and she pulled a long-sleeved shirt out of her drawer. She could wear that open over a T-shirt. That would sort the arm problem.

The legs were a different matter. Jeans were obviously out, as was a skirt, so the only option she could come up with was sweatpants. She pulled them on, then attempted to do something with her hair. Her brush wouldn't even come close to helping, so she tied it up in a loose knot and clipped it up out of the way. She would sort that later, too. Finally she splashed her face with cold water to try and get rid of the red-rimmed eyes.

Taking a deep breath, she made her way back downstairs for lunch. Her parents were in the living room, and she walked through to join them.

"There you are." Helen got to her feet. "Here you go. I thought you'd be more comfy eating in here." She handed her a plate of cheese on toast, and a steaming cup of tea. "And I just felt that maybe today you'd like a cup of tea. I'm sorry I was stressed when you got home. I was just worried about you."

Kate threw a thankful glance at her father, seeing his hand in her mother's transformation, and sat down on the sofa. "Thanks, Mum. This looks lovely, and yes, you're right, I'd love a cup of tea." She picked up her mug and took a sip. "We got soaked in the rain yesterday, and I had a hard job getting warm again. Still feeling a bit shivery even now."

"I hope you haven't caught a chill." Helen fussed around her and put a hand on her forehead. "You don't feel like you're running a fever."

"So what happened exactly, Kate?" Peter raised his eyebrows. "If you feel like talking about it."

Kate took a bite of toast and nodded. "I'll tell you. It's nothing awful. I went out for a walk yesterday morning—sorry, Mum, I just needed to get away for a bit, with the wedding stuff getting to me—and I bumped into a girl from work in the village. She was just off for a day out and asked if I'd like to go with her. On the spur of the moment I said yes, which looking back was probably a bit reckless, since all I had with me was my phone." She smiled at her mother. "But you know me, never think before I act."

Helen smiled back. "Silly girl. Never mind, no harm done. So what happened, some trouble with the car, did you say?"

"Yeah. The car broke down, and we couldn't get a

signal on the phone, and it was thundering and horrible, and we ended up walking miles until we came to a hotel in the middle of the moor."

"The moor? Where were you, then?"

"Dartmoor. It had been nice earlier. A lovely day, and we had lunch at a pub and went for a walk. Then the rain started, and we broke down." She took another sip of tea. "We were so wet by the time we got to the hotel that we decided to stay the night and get the car picked up in the morning. The hotel very kindly dried our clothes, and in the morning she called the AA and we came back."

"Sounds like a bit of an adventure." Peter smiled at her. "You look very tired. Didn't you get much sleep?"

Kate shrugged, the vision of her and Sam cuddled up together in the bed flashing unbidden into her mind. "Some. We had to walk a long way, though. If you don't mind, I think I'll just take it easy this afternoon and have an early night." She frowned suddenly. "Why aren't you at work, Dad? I just realised it's Thursday."

"Your mother insisted I stay home until you got back." Peter grinned at her. "Can't say I minded. Could do with a day off."

"Oh, god, I'm so sorry!" Kate was contrite. "I never thought you'd be worried about me. I did call you to say I was staying out."

"I wasn't worried, pet." Peter smiled. "But your mother is a bit het up over the wedding, and I think she just needed a bit of moral support."

"Well, I *was* worried," Helen bridled a little. "Not because you stayed away the night, you had told us that, but because you ran out on me earlier in the day. Is the wedding really getting to you, darling? You're not having second thoughts, are you?"

"Of course not." Kate kept her head down and carefully cut up her cheese on toast. "Bit late for that."

"Oh, thank goodness." Helen sighed with relief and fanned herself with her hand. "Would you like more tea?"

Kate nodded and held out her mug, then popped another piece of toast into her mouth as her mother left the room. She glanced up to find her father watching her.

"What?" She was horrified to feel her face begin to flush.

"Katy, if you want to talk about anything, I'm here for you. Anything at all."

Hearing him call her Katy nearly set her off again, and she felt tears pressing behind her eyes. She managed a small smile and nodded to him.

"Thanks, Dad. I'm okay."

"Well, I'm not convinced of that, but if you want to tell me, I'm here."

Helen reappeared with another mug of tea and sat down again.

"You really don't look well, Kate. Maybe it *would* be best if you had an early night. Tomorrow will be a busy day, so best rest today."

Kate looked at her in dismay. "Tomorrow will be busy? Why will tomorrow be busy? The wedding's not till Saturday."

"It's the rehearsal tomorrow, darling. Had you forgotten? And in the morning we have to go over to the hotel to make sure everything is in place there." Helen looked severely at her. "Vicky will be here in the afternoon. I really want you two to get on. Can you?"

Kate sighed. "I guess so. If she has to come. Can Jen come over too?"

"Well, she'll need to be at the rehearsal, of course, and I don't see why she shouldn't come back here afterwards. It might be nice to have another girly evening. We can all do our nails and things like that. Yes, of course she can come."

Kate smiled her thanks and finished off her lunch. She had forgotten all about the wedding rehearsal. That meant she would see Richard tomorrow. She sighed. Maybe that was for the best. She was beginning to completely lose track of why she liked him. Hopefully seeing him tomorrow would sort that out. She put down her plate and sat back.

"Thanks, Mum. That was nice. I'll call Jen in a bit and invite her over to stay tomorrow night. It would be nice if both bridesmaids were here."

"Okay, darling. Oh, and Granny will be here too, of course. She's coming in the morning."

"Oh. Okay. She's staying the night too? Where are we putting everyone?"

"Well, Jenny can go in with you, Vicky can have her old room, and I shall probably put Granny in with her."

Kate couldn't help grinning. "She'll love that."

"We all have to compromise, Kate. Planning a wedding is a big job. Now you just relax for the rest of the day, so you're full of beans for tomorrow." Helen smiled at her and patted her on the shoulder. "I'll make you pizza for tea, if you like."

"That would be lovely, Mum, thank you." Kate felt a lump forming in her throat, and reached up to capture her hand. "I love you, both of you, and I'm sorry I upset you yesterday."

"Don't be silly, darling. It's fine." Helen squeezed her hand. "You just relax, and give Jenny a ring about tomorrow."

****

Kate stretched out in the bath and let the warmth soothe her aching limbs. She had filled the water with bubbles, and they were threatening to overflow and take over the bathroom. She rested her head against the end of the bath and closed her eyes.

She had texted Jenny earlier and organised for her to come back with them after the rehearsal. Jenny had been very keen, and Kate was wondering just how much she could tell her about the ill-fated trip to Dartmoor. If it hadn't been for the bruises, it would have begun to seem like a dream rather than a real event, and Kate found herself having a hard job remembering all the details.

Except for the kiss. There was no way she could ever forget that kiss. She had never experienced anything like that before, and if she married Richard she never would again. But she still had to marry Richard. Of course she had to marry him. She couldn't bear the thought of how many people she would be letting down if she cried off now.

Better that she married him for now and sorted it out later. That's what she'd have to do. It didn't have to be for ever.

She gently rubbed the bubbles over her body, noting just how painful her ribs were. She peered down through the water at the massive bruise that extended from just below her armpit almost to her waist. At least that would be covered by her dress. But her shoulder and arm wouldn't. That was a problem that really needed addressing. She was going to have to let Jenny into the secret of the bruises and enlist her help. They would need to be very creative if they were going to find some way of covering them up.

She sighed and slid further down into the bath. And of course Richard would see all the bruises on Saturday night. But that was something she really didn't want to think about just now. In fact she didn't really want to think about it at all.

She stood up and reached for a towel. It was only eight o'clock, but she was going to go straight to bed after this. Her mother had made a lovely pizza for her tea—not as good as the one Sam had made, of course— the bath had gone some way to relaxing her, and she felt she might actually sleep. Hopefully things would seem less messed up in the morning, although at the moment she couldn't see how. She stepped out of the bath and began to dry herself carefully. She had really messed up this time, and it was all her own fault. She had given in to her emotions when she should have stayed strong. There was no way she was going to let her mess ruin the day. She had to go through with it, no matter what.

She slipped into her pyjamas and padded back to the bedroom. Her bed was turned down, ready for her, and the curtains were closed despite the fact that it was still sunny outside. Thankfully she slid under the duvet and lay back on the pillows. That felt so good. Glancing over to her left, she saw her phone, still plugged in to charge. She picked it up and stared at it for a moment, then made a decision and wrote a quick text.

Are you all right? Did you see a doctor?

She pressed Send and watched until it said it was delivered. Texting Sam was the last thing she should have done, and was probably another one of those Very Bad Ideas she seemed to keep having, but she couldn't help worrying about him and just needed to know he was all right. He probably wouldn't reply anyway, although he had messaged her earlier to let her know he had put his SIM card in an old phone, so she could still contact him if she needed.

She put the phone back on her bedside table and snuggled down under the covers, taking care not to lie on her left side. She closed her eyes and was just beginning to doze when a bleep from her phone jerked her fully awake again. Reaching for it, she pulled it under the cover and read the text.

I'm fine. Yes, Mum sent me to docs. No concussion. Hope your bruises are not too bad. x

Kate read the message three times, then carefully laid the phone back on the table. He was all right. And he had put a kiss.

Chapter 18

Friday 24th July

"Kate! Granny's here. Are you up yet?"

At the sound of her mother's voice, Kate pulled the quilt up to her chin and sighed. She really would have to get up now. She'd been awake for over an hour but had been putting off the evil moment of actually getting up and facing the rest of the world. Her long sleep had been beset with dreams about cars, deer, rain, weddings, and kissing, and in one particularly bizarre one, she had been riding a deer across a moor in the rain, pursued by Richard and Sam, both driving Land Rovers. She knew in the dream that whichever one reached her first she would have to marry, and so as not to have that decision made for her, she forced the deer to jump across a river to avoid them. That had been the point at which she had woken up, sweating profusely, her sheets in a tangle.

Wearily she swung her legs out of bed and sat up. "Won't be long, Mum," she called. "Just getting dressed."

"Well, hurry up. We're going over to the hotel in a few minutes, to check everything's ready."

"Okay." Kate stood up and stretched. She still felt very stiff and achy, and her bruises were even more painful than the day before. She pulled off her pyjamas, left them in a heap on the floor, and stood in front of the long mirror to inspect them. To her horror, the ones on her shoulder and arm were even deeper purple, but now with a yellowish tinge around the outside. They were going to be very difficult to hide. She turned to look at her side and leg and sighed. They were all beginning to turn yellow, and each one was very sore to touch. She certainly wouldn't be wearing jeans again today, or a skirt.

With a mental promise to herself that she would have a shower when they got back from the hotel, she pulled on some underwear, then opened her cupboard and surveyed the contents. It looked to be another lovely sunny day, so she needed to find something to wear that didn't draw attention. Wearing long sleeves was going to be bad enough, but sweatpants were definitely out. She rummaged for a moment, then pulled out a pair of light brown combat-type trousers. They were made of a thin cotton material and were fairly baggy, so she pulled them on and checked herself in the mirror. They'd have to do. She teamed them with a white vest top and a green checked shirt, left open. Most of her flat shoes looked completely wrong with the trousers, and it was far too hot for Converse, so she completed the outfit with a pair of leather flip-flops.

She quickly straightened her hair, put on enough makeup to cover the bags under her eyes, added some jewellery, and made her way downstairs.

"Granny."

Her grandmother was in the hallway talking to Helen, and she turned as Kate descended the stairs.

"There she is, the blushing bride to be." She stepped forward and gave Kate a hug as she reached the bottom. "You look tired. Are you not sleeping well?"

"Not really. I had some weird dreams last night." Kate smiled at her, and tried not to wince as her grandmother squeezed her ribs. "Your hair looks nice, Granny. Makes you look like Joan Baez."

"Thank you, my dear." Marion Granger smiled and patted her newly styled and dyed short dark hair. "Must look my best for your big day."

"Are you ready, then, Kate?" Helen was by the front door. "I told the hotel we'd go at eleven."

"Is Peter not coming?" Marion glanced around for her son.

"No, Marion, he had to go in to work this morning. This is more women's work anyway. Come on, we'll take my car."

Kate followed them out into the sunshine, immediately finding she was too hot in her trousers and long-sleeved shirt, and climbed into the back of Helen's Fiat. The car was even hotter, and she wound the window down in the hope of engendering a breeze.

As they drove through the middle of the village, she found her eyes drawn to the Harlequin's Arms, where she could see Sam's Land Rover sitting outside, apparently deposited there after being towed back by his father. Her stomach churned slightly, and she sank down in her seat as they passed.

The hotel was about half a mile from the centre of the village, just down the road from the church, and Helen drew up in the car park and turned off the engine.

"Hopefully we won't have to do anything this morning," she said, undoing her seatbelt and opening the door. "But we just need to check everything is there."

Kate slid out of the back and closed the door behind her, then followed her mother and grandmother into the imposing ivy-covered building that was going to be the venue for her wedding reception. She tried to imagine walking through the door with Richard on her arm, as Mr. and Mrs. Cresswell, and she very nearly turned and ran.

She felt a huge lump form in her throat, her heart began to beat faster, and she paused in the entrance hall and steadied herself against a table. She needed to get a grip. Now was not the time for a panic attack. She had to go through with this, mostly for the sake of the two women in front of her. And her father. And of course Richard.

"Kate, keep up, darling. We need you to approve the decorations."

Taking a deep breath, Kate caught up with them and walked into the huge room that was to serve as both dining room for the wedding breakfast and later as a ballroom for the dance in the evening. It was already set out with white tableclothed tables, the chairs decorated with white chair covers and pale blue ribbons to match the bridesmaids' dresses. Helen glanced around with approval.

"This all looks very nice. I think this is how we said we wanted it, isn't it, Kate?"

Kate shrugged. "I guess. It looks fine." She was beginning to feel sick and badly needed to get back out into the fresh air.

"Really, Kate, show some more interest. It *is* your wedding," Helen chided with a frown. "Now we just need to see the cake, the table decorations, and the favours, and then we can probably go back." She led the way to a side room, where the four-tier square cake was currently residing, surrounded by the homemade wedding favours that she and Kate had spent hours making a few weeks earlier. "Ah, yes, that all looks fine too. Isn't the cake splendid, Marion?" Helen turned to her mother-in-law. "My friend Jane, in the village, made it for us."

"It's lovely, Helen." Marion inspected the cake, with its mass of blue and mauve sugar flowers cascading down the tiers, and the silver horseshoe topper. "Very impressive. Kate, are you all right? You look very pale."

Kate shook her head. "Not really, Granny. I feel a bit sick, actually. I think I'll go back outside to get some air, if that's all right."

Helen glanced at her sharply and nodded. "On you go, darling. We'll be out in a moment. I just need to find out where they've put the table decorations. By the way, I don't think you dressed very wisely this morning, Kate. Those clothes look a bit heavy for a day like this."

Kate made her way back out to the car and leant against it with her eyes closed. She was well aware that her behaviour was probably making her mother even more convinced she was pregnant, but she really couldn't help it. She felt on the edge of panic, her bruises were all hurting, and instead of being excited for the following day, she had an overwhelming feeling of doom. That was no way to go into a marriage, but she could see no other option.

She pressed her hands over her eyes and uttered a long shuddering sigh. She had to talk to someone, and she supposed that someone would need to be Jen. She would make her feel better. She pulled her phone out of her pocket. It was still only eleven thirty. Jen wouldn't be over until four for the rehearsal. She would need to find some way of getting through the rest of the day until then, and avoid too much conversation with her mother or grandmother. Even her father wasn't at home to be her ally.

"Kate, do you still feel sick?" Helen appeared at her side and put a hand on her arm.

"No, I'm okay now." Kate mustered a smile. "It's just the heat, I expect."

"Hmmm." Helen looked at her closely. "If you say so. Come on, then, let's get back home and have a cuppa. And you can take those silly trousers off. Far too hot for today."

They drove back to the house in silence, and Kate followed her mother and grandmother to the kitchen. Helen immediately filled the kettle, and Marion sat down at the table.

"Do go and get changed, Kate." Helen glanced over her shoulder at her. "You'll feel much better if you're cooler. Would you like tea?"

"Okay." Kate shrugged. "If you like. And cake too, please."

She turned and started slowly up the stairs. They were insisting she change her clothes. That was a bit of a problem. She opened her cupboard again and stared at the contents. As far as she could see, her only other option was a long multi-coloured Indian cotton skirt she had bought during her hippy phase, which had lasted all of two weeks in the summer after she left school. She pulled it out and held it up against her. It came down just far enough to cover the bruises on her ankle bone, so she stripped off the trousers and slipped it on.

She looked in the mirror. Of course it didn't go with the green checked shirt, so she pulled that off too and tossed it onto the bed. The only long-sleeved top that worked with it was a white peasant blouse, so she pulled that on over her vest top. She looked in the mirror and grimaced. She looked ridiculous and not at all like herself. But it did look more summery, so it would hopefully keep her mother quiet.

Rummaging in her handbag, she pulled out a card of Paracetamol and popped two in her mouth, washing them down with a gulp of rather stale water from beside her bed, then made her way back downstairs.

Helen and Marion had moved into the conservatory and had the door to the garden open. Helen looked up as Kate entered.

"Ah, that's better, darling. You look much cooler. I don't think I've seen that skirt before."

"It's very old." Kate sat down in a wicker chair. "I never usually wear it."

Marion looked over at her. "It reminds me of the sort of things we used to wear in the sixties," she said with a reminiscent smile.

Kate looked at her grandmother in surprise. "Were you a hippy, Granny?" she asked with a smile.

Marion took a sip of her tea. "I think we all were for a while. It was the summer of '67, the Summer of Love they called it. Your father was just five, and I spent the summer hanging out at festivals and took him with me. It was a lovely time."

Helen stared at her. "Marion! I never knew any of that. What about Douglas? Did he go to the festivals too?"

Marion looked slightly guilty. "He had to go to work. I was a stay-at-home mum, as they call them now, so I was able to spend the whole summer doing what I liked. We very nearly fell out over it, actually. I was rather selfish back then."

Kate looked at her with a new respect. Her grandmother had hidden depths. "That sounds such fun. Did Dad enjoy it?"

"I doubt he remembers much about it." Marion gave a cheeky grin. "In fact, I rather hope he doesn't! I did a few things that summer that not many people know about. I think he might be a little shocked if he knew what his very respectable mother got up to."

"Granny!" Kate giggled and curled her legs up under her with a wince of pain. "Why are you telling us now?"

"Well, a lot of time has gone by, Douglas is dead now so can't be hurt by it, and at seventy-five I reckon I can get away with having an interesting past." She looked keenly at Kate. "Are you all right, Kate? You looked like you were in pain."

"I'm fine." Kate wriggled into a more comfortable position. "Just got a little bruise on my hip."

"Good job it's only on your hip," Helen said. "That will be well covered by your dress. How did you do that?"

"Oh, I don't know." Kate tossed her head impatiently. "I think I bumped into a table or something. Now back to Granny…what on earth did you get up to that Granddad wouldn't have liked?"

Marion sighed. "Oh, nothing much by today's standards, I suppose. It's just that he was rather a respectable man—you know, he worked in a bank—and

I think he was rather embarrassed that his wife was going round draped in flowers and hanging out with hippies. I married too young, I think. I was only just twenty-two when Peter was born. I felt very trapped and not really ready to settle down, and 1967 was about letting my hair down and being young again. Douglas was nearly ten years older than me, of course, and he just didn't understand it. He was of a different generation, really."

"Granny, I never knew any of this!" Kate was enthralled. "Did you do anything really naughty?"

"Kate! Really." Helen frowned. "I'm not sure you should ask that."

"It's fine." Marion chuckled. "I've started telling you, so you may as well hear it all. Nowadays I doubt you'd think much of it, but I smoked dope a fair bit. Never at home, of course, but I was rather naïve and didn't realise how much my clothes smelled of it. So Douglas found out, and that was when we had the really big row." She sighed. "I'm really not sure we were suited at all. These days, I wouldn't have married him. I would have gone off travelling while I was still young." She glanced over at Kate and looked as though she was about to speak, then changed her mind. "My rebel phase only really lasted for that summer, but it was a summer to remember. I'm very glad it happened."

"Wow, that's really weird, Granny!" Kate was watching her with awe. "I had no idea you were so interesting. I'm sorry."

"No reason why you would have. I don't usually talk about it."

"Well, I must say I'm very surprised, Marion." Helen got to her feet. "We've always thought you seemed so respectable."

"I am now. Have been for years. Once that summer was over, I conformed to what Douglas wanted me to be. We were happy enough, and I had Peter, of course, but I often wondered…" She tailed off and stared out into the garden.

"Right. I'm going to make some cakes for later." Helen stroked Kate's hair as she passed. "You look a bit pale, darling. Are you still feeling sick?"

"No, I'm fine now, Mum. Don't fuss. I'm just going to stay here and talk to Granny for a bit."

Helen nodded and went out to the kitchen, leaving Kate and Marion alone. Marion looked over at Kate. "Come out in the garden with me, Kate. I have something more to tell you that I'd rather your mother didn't hear."

Intrigued, Kate got to her feet, biting her lip as she banged her leg against the chair. She followed her grandmother out the French windows, and they began to stroll down the lawn towards the few apple trees at the end of the garden.

"What is it, Granny? Something else naughty you got up to?"

"Yes, it is." Marion glanced at her and took her arm. "I didn't want your mother to hear this, just in case she felt she should tell your father, and I really don't want him to know." She walked over to the shade of a tree. "Shall we sit down, or are your bruises too sore to sit on the ground?"

Kate looked at her in surprise. "I'm fine to sit on the ground," she said, feeling her face begin to get hot. "I said it was just one bruise."

"What you said and what you actually meant are

not necessarily the same thing." Marion sank gracefully to the ground. "That's better. Come on, sit down. We need a chat."

Nervously Kate sat on the grass and stretched her legs out in front of her. "What about?"

"You and me. I think we're rather alike. I think we both do things because we want to please other people, and sometimes forget about ourselves." She fixed Kate with a stern stare. "But first, before we go any further, I want you to be honest with me. These bruises you have, or bruise, if you prefer—did someone hurt you?"

Kate shook her head vigorously. "No. No, nothing like that, Granny, I promise you. I bumped into a table, like I said."

"Kate, I wasn't born yesterday. You don't have to tell me the truth, of course, but I just want to know that you're not about to marry someone who hits you."

Kate nearly laughed. "God, no, Granny. Richard would never do anything like that. He's a very good person. He never does anything wrong."

"But you didn't bump into a table, did you?"

"No, I didn't. I fell in a river, but that's all I'm telling you." Kate glanced at her. "And please don't tell Mum or Dad."

"I won't. Why do you think I brought you out here?" Marion leant back against a tree and folded her arms. "And might I hazard a guess that you weren't with your fiancé when this accident occurred?" Kate didn't respond. "I shall take that as a yes. Don't worry, I'm not going to pry, it's your secret. But I just wanted to tell you a little story. Way, way back in 1960, when I was just twenty, I met your grandfather. He already had a very successful job and very good prospects, while I was just working in a dress shop. We started going out together, and my parents were over the moon. He was a real step up the social ladder for me, and they did everything they could to encourage the relationship. To be honest, they didn't need to do very much. I was quite taken with Douglas. He was very good-looking, older than me, and he had enough money that he was able to take me to places none of my friends had been. So when he proposed, I naturally said yes. Just like you, I got swept along in the wedding preparations, not really thinking about what it meant. That I would be committed to the same person for the rest of my life. That from that moment on I would be a wife, and in those days, before women's lib got going, that was rather a menial thing to be. It wasn't until just before the wedding that I began to have doubts. Realised that I probably wouldn't get to do any of the things I had dreamed about as a girl. Travelling to the Himalayas, visiting Australia, seeing the Pyramids. Douglas was kind, and had a good job, but his idea of a fun holiday was two weeks in Bournemouth. He had no desire to travel the world, to see or experience new things. To be honest, he was very boring."

Kate's head shot up, and she looked suspiciously at her grandmother. Had someone been talking to her? How did she know what she was feeling?

Marion continued. "I suddenly realised I was being very rash marrying him, and it might well be the biggest mistake of my life. But this was just days before the wedding, and it was all organised and paid for. There was no way I could pull out—my parents would be devastated. As would Douglas. I may have been having doubts, but he was devoted to me.

"So I went ahead with it, with the tiny idea at the back of my mind that if I was really unhappy I could get divorced. My parents, who were very old-fashioned, would have been horrified, of course, but the option was still there. Not at all the way to go into a marriage, eh?"

Kate slowly shook her head.

"Things were actually all right for a while. Douglas and I did get on, and although I got a bit bored at home—he made me give up my job—once I fell pregnant with your father, I had something to occupy me. Then when Peter was nearly five I met some new friends and got caught up in the hedonistic atmosphere of the summer of love. It was wonderful, Kate. You would have loved it. I don't remember the weather ever being bad, either. I behaved very irresponsibly. I took Peter to festivals and parties, I stayed up all night, smoked far too much dope—and I fell in love."

She glanced at Kate. "Really fell in love. I'd thought I was in love with Douglas, but this was quite different. He was so different, so exciting. He had travelled all over the world, and he was going off again to see even more places. He told me he'd take me to India, to Australia, to South America. Everywhere. I was completely lost. And he loved Peter, too."

Kate found her mouth had gone dry. "What did you do?"

"Nothing. It was too late. I had committed myself to Douglas, and I was too afraid of hurting people to leave him and follow my heart. And of course I had Peter. I was afraid someone might take him away from me if I left. So at the end of the summer I went back to being a boring housewife, and kept everyone happy."

"Except you."

"Except me." Marion looked at Kate. "I didn't think I mattered."

"What happened to your lover?"

"That sounds strange." Marion's eyes were wistful. "Hearing him called that. He went away. He went off travelling again. Last thing I heard, he had settled in Australia."

"Was he sad? Did he ask you to go with him?"

"I think he was sad, and I know he would have loved me to go with him, but no, he didn't try and persuade me. He knew I had to decide for myself. I had a husband and child. He may have been an adventurer, a free spirit, but he didn't want to make me feel guilty if I didn't go with him. I guess that was because he *was* a free spirit." She sighed. "But I suppose I wasn't as free as he was, and I just couldn't bring myself to hurt the people I would leave behind."

"And did you regret your decision?" Kate wasn't sure she wanted to hear the answer.

"Every day."

Kate was silent, her hands distractedly plucking at the grass. Her head was reeling from her grandmother's revelations, and she couldn't help wondering what had prompted them. "Why did you tell me?"

Marion leaned forward and took Kate's hand. "I just want to make sure you don't make the mistakes I did. I can sense a disquiet about you, and I'm sure all is not well. You certainly don't have the demeanour of a girl who is marrying the love of her life tomorrow. Just don't forget about yourself in all this. You are just as important as the people you think you will be letting down."

Kate pulled her hand away and stood up. "I don't know what you mean, Granny. I'm fine. There's no problem." Her voice shook as she spoke, and to her horror she could feel tears welling up behind her eyes. "I'm fine. Everything is fine." She turned and ran back to the house, going straight upstairs and throwing herself face down on the bed.

Oh, why had Granny told her that story? How could she see through her like that? She buried her face in the pillow, her mind whirring with thoughts. Granny could tell she was unhappy; Granny had even sussed that the story about the bruise was a lie. What was she suggesting she do? Pull out of the wedding now? The day before? Leave Richard at the altar? What did she think she should do?

However much it was hurting her, she couldn't do that. She couldn't do that to her parents, to Richard, even to her friends and relatives who were making the effort to come to the wedding. To the lady who had made the cake. The people she would be letting down were too numerous to mention. She just couldn't do it.

It wasn't even as if Richard had done anything wrong. She had nothing real that she could complain about. She just wasn't sure she loved him any more. She rolled onto her back and stared up at the ceiling. She would have to be strong. Be strong and believe it needn't be forever. It wouldn't be forever. It was easy to get divorced these days.

A sudden bleep from her phone made her jump. She reached out for it and peered at the screen. It was from Sam. For a moment, Kate considered deleting it without reading it. Then her curiosity got the better of her, and she opened the message.

Are you okay today? How are the bruises? x

She stared at it blankly for a moment. There was that kiss again. She closed her eyes and gripped her phone tightly. She really should just ignore it. She opened her eyes and read it again, then wrote a short reply.

Pretty bad. Hope your eye is getting better. Her finger hovered over the Send button. Then she added a quick *x* and sent it before she could change her mind.

Chapter 19

"Kate why on earth are you dressed like that?" Jenny stared at her in amazement. "I haven't see that skirt for eight years!"

Kate caught Jenny by the hand and pulled her to the back of the church. "I needed something to cover my legs," she whispered, pulling the skirt up slightly and holding out her leg. "Look."

"Kate! What on earth have you done? How did that happen?"

"I'll tell you back at the house." Kate glanced up to the front of the church, where the vicar was chatting to her parents. "And I need your help. I have some more on my arm. But Jen, not a word to my parents, or Vicky."

"Of course not." Jenny squeezed her arm. "I can imagine the fuss your mother would make. But I'm most intrigued as to how you got them. They look really sore."

"They are." Kate started down the aisle towards her parents. "Very."

"Kate, do you know where Richard has got to?" Helen was looking a little harassed. "He's usually on time for everything. It's ten past four, and the vicar can't stay for ever."

"Don't know." Kate shook her head. "I haven't heard from him today."

"Well, could you ring him, darling? See if he's got held up."

"I didn't bring my phone."

"Kate, you never go anywhere without your phone!" Helen sighed. "Here, use mine. I need to know he's on the way. And of course Vicky hasn't arrived, either."

"That's no big surprise, or loss," Kate muttered, reluctantly taking Helen's phone and dialling Richard's number. She pressed it to her ear. "Straight to voice mail." She handed it back to Helen. "I'm sure he'll be here in a minute."

As she spoke, the door of the church opened, and Richard and Vicky both appeared.

"Sorry I'm late." Richard walked over and gave Kate a kiss on the cheek. "The traffic was dreadful. I've come straight from London. Are you okay, darling? I've never seen those clothes before."

"You haven't seen all my clothes," Kate snapped, turning away. "Now come on, the vicar can't stay much longer."

"I'm just late." Vicky grinned at her parents. "I left late."

"Right." Helen nodded briskly. "Now we're all here, let's get the practice over with, and then we can go back home and have something to eat. Kate, are the flower girls not coming?"

"Didn't see the point." Kate shook her head. "All they do is walk down the aisle with Jen and Vicky. They can tell them when to stop and start."

"Okay, then, let's get started." Helen clapped her hands, and everyone got into their positions. "Richard, where's your best man?"

"Oh, he can't come. Don't worry. He knows what to do."

"Right. No best man, no flower girls, I'm not sure why we're bothering with this." Helen was beginning to let the stress show. "At least Kate is here. From the look of her earlier, I wasn't sure she would be."

Vicky gave her sister an inquisitive glance and got a dark look in return. "You look really weird in those clothes, Kate. Is that your new look? Very retro."

"No, now shut up and let's get this over with." Kate gripped her father's arm as they prepared for the walk down the aisle. "I want to get back to the house. Mum has made cakes."

As they started down the aisle on the instruction of the vicar, Peter squeezed Kate's hand. "Are you okay, pet? You look a bit sad."

"I'll be okay, Dad." She smiled at him, realising again that she couldn't let him down. "I'll be okay."

****

By five o'clock, they were all heading back to the house, the rehearsal having gone reasonably well and everyone being confident that they knew what they would be doing the next day.

Richard left to go to his parents' house for the night, and the rest of them headed back to Kate's for the girly evening that Helen had organised. Peter was being banished to the bedroom after dinner so the three girls and Helen and Marion could have girly chatter and do their nails. Kate was actually dreading it. She wanted to escape to her room with Jenny and confess all her worries and misdoings, but she wouldn't be able to do that until they went to bed. Unless they could escape for a few minutes.

When they got back to the house, Helen shepherded them all into the living room and insisted on making tea. Kate found herself on the sofa with Jenny, her grandmother sitting opposite them. Vicky was nowhere to be seen.

"Where did Vicky get to?" Jenny looked round. "Maybe she's gone home."

"No such luck." Kate scowled. "Mum told her she had to stay the night."

"Vicky wanted to pop to the village shop on the way back." Marion had overhead them. "She shouldn't be long."

"Pity."

"Here we go, ladies, tea and cake. Tuck in." Helen breezed in and placed a loaded tray on the coffee table. "Peter, you can join us for this. It's only later, when we do our nails, that you have to go to bed."

Despite her mood, Kate couldn't help but laugh. "Mum! That's so mean. Why can't you let him stay?"

"It's okay, Katy." Peter ruffled her hair as he passed by. "I don't think I want to spend the evening so horrendously outnumbered. I really don't want to paint my nails, either."

A sound from the hall made Kate look round, and Vicky appeared in the doorway. "Sorry, just had to get something from the village." She walked in and bounced down onto the chair next to her grandmother, a wide grin on her face. "And guess who I bumped into?"

"No idea." Kate rolled her eyes.

"Sam Somerville."

"So?" Jenny shrugged. "You knew he was back. You saw him in the pub."

"Yeah, but this time he has a huge black eye." She

grinned evilly. "He told me he got it crashing his car into a ditch on Dartmoor, but I reckon someone hit him."

"Don't be ridiculous, Vicky," Jenny jumped in. "Who on earth would want to hit Sam? Why would he be lying?"

"Dartmoor?" Helen looked up in surprise. "Wasn't that where you went with your friend, Kate? Maybe you were there at the same time."

"No, Mum." Kate could feel five pairs of eyes on her. "We went to Exmoor. I told you."

"No, darling, I'm sure you said Dartmoor. Didn't she say Dartmoor, Peter?"

Kate turned and looked at her father. Without hesitation he shook his head.

"No, Helen, it was Exmoor."

"Oh." Helen looked confused. "I could have sworn…oh, well. I suppose I am rather stressed. I probably wasn't listening properly. Have a cake, Vicky, before Kate eats them all."

She handed the plate to Vicky, then disappeared out to the kitchen to replenish the tea.

Kate took a bite of her cake, still aware she was being watched. Out of the corner of her eye she could see Vicky's grinning face, and next to her she felt Jenny shift in her seat.

"Can we go up to your room in a minute, Kate?" Jenny asked suddenly. "There's something I want to run by you."

"Of course." Kate nodded, and caught her father's eye. She was fairly sure she detected a slight wink, then he finished his tea and took his cup back to the kitchen. "Let's go now. Back in a minute, Granny." Kate got up, pulled Jenny with her, and headed for the stairs.

Once in her bedroom, she shut the door and sat on the bed. Jenny stared at her.

"Kate? What the fuck was that all about? Dartmoor? Exmoor? Sam? Have you been really stupid again?"

Kate nodded miserably, and felt her eyes fill up with tears. "Yes. I've really done it this time, Jen." She looked up at her. "And I don't know what to do. Let me show you something first, though." She lifted her skirt so Jenny could see the whole length of her leg and the extent of the bruising, then pulled off her blouse to reveal her arm and shoulder. "And there's more on my ribs."

Jenny stared in horror at the purpling bruises. "Kate, how the hell… Were you with Sam? Was this from his car crash?"

Kate shook her head. "Well, yes, I was with Sam, but it wasn't from the car crash. He got his black eye in the Land Rover—he hit the steering wheel—but I got my bruises when I fell in the river. He rescued me."

Jenny sat down on the edge of the bed, her eyes wide. "Kate, I'm gobsmacked. When was this?"

"Wednesday. Jen, it was an accident. I just went with him to escape Mum. It was just supposed to be for a few hours, but everything went wrong."

"So how long were you out?" Kate was silent. Jenny peered at her suspiciously. "Kate, how long?"

"All night."

"All night? You spent the night with Sam Somerville, three days before your wedding? Where were you?"

"In a hotel."

"Oh, dear god." Jenny was lost for words. She was staring at Kate when the door suddenly opened, and Vicky stepped into the room. She took one look at Kate's bruised arm and realisation flooded over her face. She closed the door behind her and grinned at them.

"Next time you lie to Mum and Dad, make sure you've covered your tracks," she said. "I can give you some tips. I perfected it years ago. Now what the hell are you going to do about that?" She reached over and gently touched Kate's arm. "That looks really sore. Just like Sam's eye."

"There's more." Jenny pointed to Kate's skirt. "She's got bruises all up her leg and on her ribs."

"Shit, Kate. Are you okay?" Vicky sounded genuinely concerned.

Kate stared at her in surprise. "Not really. But why do you care?"

"Because you're my sister, and you've suddenly got a whole lot more interesting." She grinned again. "So spill. You were on Dartmoor with Sam Somerville, and you had a car crash? What were you doing there? And why did Dad back you up? Does he know?"

"No, he doesn't." Kate shook her head. "That surprised me too. He's been giving me some funny looks lately."

Vicky sat down on the bed next to Jenny. "So why were you with Sam? Have you been seeing him?"

Kate put her hands up to cover her face and groaned. "Don't tell Mum and Dad."

"I won't."

"I've been really stupid. I went out with him when he first got back, just as friends for a catch-up. All very innocent, but it sort of turned into a date, and I didn't tell him about Richard."

Vicky was grinning widely. "Ah, I get it now. That was before the Hen night, wasn't it? Then I really dropped you in it."

"Yep. You did." Kate sat down on the bed and wriggled up so she could lean against the pillows. "But then I went out with him again, supposedly to explain why I hadn't told him, but that was even more like a date, and he kissed me."

Vicky laughed. "Did you know about this?" she asked Jenny.

Jenny nodded. "Eventually. She didn't tell me about the kisses straight away, though. But after that she decided to try and avoid him 'cause we realised it would be a very bad idea for her to see him again." Jenny glanced over at Kate. "That didn't go too well. She went out for a drink with him last week, but managed to avoid him for a week, until this Dartmoor debacle."

"You still like him, then?" Vicky watched her. "Obviously. So how did you happen to go to Dartmoor? That seems a bit random."

"I was trying to get away from Mum on Wednesday." Kate rolled her eyes. "She was driving me crazy with wedding stuff, so I went out for a walk. I had just got to the end of the road when Sam pulled up in his Land Rover and spoke to me. While we were talking, Mum appeared at the gate, and I jumped into the Land Rover to escape her. He was going to Dartmoor to deliver some beer and asked if I wanted to go with him." Kate sighed. "I was so desperate to get away that I said yes."

"Okay." Vicky shrugged. "Doesn't sound too bad yet. How come you crashed the car?"

"A deer jumped out in front of us in the rain, and he swerved to avoid it. We went into a deep ditch, and Sam hurt his face."

"And your bruises?"

"That was when I fell in the river when we were walking to try and find a phone signal."

Vicky stared at her silently. "And now you're covered in bruises you can't explain to Richard or Mum and Dad, and which are going to show under your wedding dress." She looked at Kate thoughtfully. "Or are you not going through with the wedding?"

"I have to." Kate looked so miserable that Jenny reached out and grabbed her hand. "It's all arranged and paid for. I can't let Mum and Dad down. Or Richard. I have to go through with it." A strange look crossed her face, and Jenny squeezed her hand.

"What is it, Kate?"

"Well, this was the really weird thing. Granny spent ages, earlier, telling me a tale about her youth, and I think she was telling me not to marry Richard unless I was really sure. And she knows about the bruises."

"Granny does?" Vicky stared at her in surprise. "However did that happen? And what stories?"

"I can't tell you the stories, that's up to her to tell you if she wants to. It was all very personal. Long story, but I had to admit to her and Mum that I had a bruise on my hip and said that I walked into a table, and Granny took me aside and asked if Richard had been hitting me."

Vicky burst out laughing. "Seriously? God, that's

hysterical. But how come she knows about the other bruises?"

"She guessed. I don't know how. I told her I fell in a river, but didn't tell her any more."

"So." Vicky moved further up the bed. "Are you in love with Sam?"

"No. Yes." Kate hugged her knees and buried her face in them. "I don't know. Maybe. I don't know what to do. I spent Wednesday night in a hotel with him. Three days before my wedding. I've really messed up this time."

"And did you sleep with him?" Vicky was watching her with interest.

"No. Well, not what you mean." Kate looked up briefly. "We slept in the same bed. There was only one. But we didn't do anything."

"Nothing?" Jenny leaned forward.

"Nothing." Kate felt her face get hot.

"You always were a dreadful liar, sis."

"He kissed me. That's all."

"That's all?" Jenny narrowed her eyes. "A proper kiss this time?"

Kate nodded. "Yeah. But that's all. He didn't ask me not to get married or anything."

Vicky kicked off her shoes and pulled the clip out of her hair. She had come straight from work and was still wearing her suit. She shook her head, and her hair fell down around her shoulders. "Well, he probably wouldn't, would he? He must know it's all arranged."

"Vick, have you had your hair cut?" Jenny was watching her.

"Yeah, d'you like it?" Vicky ran her hand over it and posed.

269

"It's much shorter. Looks nice, actually," Kate admitted. "Just remembered I'm really pissed with you."

"You usually are. Why this time?"

"Richard's Stag do."

Vicky laughed. "Yeah, thought you'd hate that. I tried to get in on as many photos as possible, just to piss you off."

"Well, you succeeded. I had a real go at him over it, too."

"Well, to be fair, he didn't invite me." Vicky grinned. "I just turned up, but he didn't seem to mind. It was a good night, actually. He can be fun."

"How long did you stay?" Kate watched her closely.

"Oh, pretty much until the end. They went to several clubs, and I stayed with them until about two. Then they went on somewhere I wasn't keen on, so I stayed put." Vicky grinned at Kate. "Richard's not so boring when he's out on the town, you know."

Kate felt her head begin to spin. So Richard had lied to her. He had told her Vicky had only been with them when they took the selfies. He said she had gone off with her friends after that.

Why would he lie? Vicky had been happy enough to say she'd been there. Obviously there was nothing between them, so why had he lied? Was it just because he knew how much she hated her sister? She glanced at Vicky. Or she had done, until tonight. Tonight she was actually being nice.

"Didn't Richard tell you Vicky left after those photos we saw?" Jenny frowned.

"Yes." Kate nodded. "He did. He lied to me."

"Probably feared for his life if he told you." Vicky stood up and took off her jacket. "He knows how much we don't get on." She grinned at Kate. "Anyway, who are you to talk? You've been lying to him for weeks."

Kate took a deep breath. "Right. I'm finding this all way too stressful to cope with. I'm going to have to go through with the wedding. I can't let Mum and Dad and everyone else down now." She wriggled off the bed and stood up. "So what the hell can we do about these bruises on my arm? My dress is sleeveless."

Jenny got up and looked closely at the arm. "Maybe we could use makeup?"

Vicky joined her. "Fake tan?"

"It would need to be nearly black to cover this." Kate felt the tears threatening to return. "There must be something we can do."

"Have you got a dark foundation?" Jenny was rummaging through Kate's makeup bag. "That might be worth a try." She found a tube and squeezed a little onto her finger. "May I rub it on, or would you rather do it?"

"You can do it." Kate gritted her teeth and held her arm out.

Gently, Jenny smoothed a little foundation over the centre of the bruise, where it was the darkest purple. "It's not covering it at all." She stood back and inspected it. "That won't do. We need to think of something else."

"Stage makeup!" Vicky suddenly announced. "That should do it. That's really thick and covers anything."

"Okay." Kate stared at her. "Do you have any?"

"No."

"Well, that's no bloody good, then."

"But I'm sure we can get some. Think! Do you know anyone who might have some? There used to be a drama group in the village. They'd have some."

"There did!" Jenny's eyes lit up. "You're right. Our neighbour, Mr. Freeman, belonged to it. He used to play the dame in the pantomime."

"Oh, I remember him." Vicky laughed. "He was good."

"Does he still do it?" Kate's voice was tearful. "Can we really get some?"

"I don't know if he does it now, but he'll know who does." Jenny headed for the door. "I'll pop home now and try and find out. Will you be okay, Kate?"

"I'll look after her." Vicky nodded. "Don't worry, I'll be nice. Just go, and hurry up. I'll tell Mum you had to go home for something you forgot for tomorrow. Otherwise she'll fuss."

As the door closed behind Jenny, Kate looked at Vicky. "Why are you being nice?"

"I told you, you've just become more interesting." She shrugged. "Anyway, I don't actually want you to be unhappy, and I think you are."

Kate sat down on the bed again and sighed. "Yeah. This should be the most exciting time of my life, and I just feel like crying all the time. I've really messed this up, Vick. Big time."

Vicky sat down beside her. "Not necessarily. Maybe this was meant to happen. Maybe Richard is not who you're meant to be with."

"Well, it's a bit bloody late to find out." Kate fell backwards onto the bed and covered her face with her hands. "This wedding has cost Dad and Granny thousands. I can't just change my mind now. And it would destroy Mum."

"True." Vicky wrinkled her nose. "But think what it's doing to you. They'd be pissed off with you for a while, but you might be about to ruin your whole life."

Kate opened one eye and looked up at her sister. "I can't do it, Vick. However much this is tearing me apart, I have to go through with it. There are too many people who'd get hurt." She rolled onto her stomach. "It doesn't have to be forever."

"Kate, you can't go into a marriage thinking like that!" Vicky stared at her. "That's not fair to Richard."

"And me dumping him the day of the wedding would be?" Kate shook her head. "No, I just can't do it. It's not like he's even done anything wrong."

"He did lie to you about the Stag do." Vicky raised her eyebrows. "If you want an excuse."

"That's hardly worth breaking up over." Kate sat up miserably. "But thanks for trying. I almost wish he *had* been having an affair."

Vicky raised her eyebrows. "Did you think he was?"

"Not really. It's just when I was in London I saw him going into a restaurant with his arm round a woman." She sniffed. "Turns out she was with his clients, and he was just guiding her through the door."

Vicky frowned and a strange look passed over her face. "When was that? I didn't know you'd been to London recently."

"Tuesday of last week. I went up to surprise him, but he was working. I saw him for about five minutes, and then he had to go out to some lunch and later a dinner with some clients. I happened to see him going into a restaurant when I was on my way back to the station." Kate glanced at her sister and managed a small smile. "I actually skived off work to go. Never done that before."

"You *are* getting naughty." Vicky got up and walked over to the window. "Hope Jen doesn't take too long. Mum's going to start fussing if we stay up here."

"And there was this weird thing too." Kate was still thinking about London. "Some old guy at the court thought he'd met me at some parties in London. He mentioned one in Mayfair a few weeks ago. I accused Richard of taking other women to parties, and he got quite upset. He, and Jen, pointed out that loads of people look like me. It was a bit odd, though."

"Jen's back." Vicky was still looking out the window, her back to Kate. "I think I'd better go back downstairs. Mum'll be getting suspicious if I'm up here with you too long. She'll be expecting us to be fighting."

Kate watched her as she walked over to the door. "Vick? Thanks. You've been nice. I kinda think you understand."

Vicky glanced over her shoulder and shrugged. "Don't get used to it. But I don't want to see you ruin your life." She opened the door just as Jenny arrived triumphantly waving a tube of cream in the air. "I'll leave you to it. I *am* on your side."

Jenny came into the room and shut the door behind her. "You and Vicky all right?"

"Yeah, she was actually being nice. I think." Kate gave a wry grin. "Only because I'm likely to be in trouble this time rather than her."

"Not if this stuff works." Jenny held up the cream. "Apparently it covers anything. Shall we give it a go?"

****

"Well, now this is nice." Helen beamed at her daughters. "Everyone getting on together."

"Don't get used to it," Vicky warned from her corner of the sofa. "I'm only being nice to her because she's a condemned woman."

"Vicky, what a thing to say!" Helen frowned at her. "It's the most exciting moment of a woman's life."

"If you say so." Vicky glanced at Kate and raised her wine glass to her. "I hope you're right."

"What colour are you doing your nails, Kate?" Marion changed the subject. "Are you going for a pale colour, or a contrast?"

"Don't know." Kate shrugged, studying her nails with disinterest. "Does it really matter? No one will be looking at my hands."

"Well, actually, they might," Jenny pointed out apologetically. "They may want to see your ring."

"Oh, whatever. Top my wine up, Vick." Kate held her glass out. "I'm too tired to care. Can I go to bed soon, Mum?"

"Oh, Kate, must you?" Helen looked at her sadly. "This is supposed to be such a fun evening. It's only nine o'clock. Can't you stay up a bit longer? At least do your nails first."

"If I must." Kate snatched up the nearest bottle of nail varnish. "Will this do?"

"Maybe not." Jenny gently relieved her of it. "I'm not sure black is very apt for the bride. Why not try this nice pearly one? Shall I do it for you?"

Kate shrugged and took a swig of wine. "If you like." She held out her hand. "Hurry up, then."

"Kate, what's the matter, darling?" Helen moved

over and sat down next to her. "Do you feel ill? Are you feeling sick again?"

"No, Mum. I'm not feeling sick. I'm not feeling ill in any way, and for the last time, I'm not pregnant. I'm tired. That's all, bloody tired." To her horror, Kate felt her eyes start to fill with tears, and she turned away. "Just leave me alone. Jen, you can do my nails, and then I'm going to bed."

Helen patted her on the arm. "Okay, darling. I'm sorry to have been hassling you. Vicky, fill up your sister's wine glass. And do Granny's at the same time."

Marion was watching Kate closely. "An early night will do you good, Kate," she said quietly. "Time to reflect on tomorrow. It's a big step you're taking."

Kate glanced at her. What did her grandmother mean? Was that another suggestion that she shouldn't be getting married? Well, to be honest, she didn't need anyone to tell her that. She had realised it was actually the biggest mistake of her life, and in fact a Very Bad Idea. Even worse than the other ones she had been having lately. But she was stuck with it. She had made her bed and had to lie in it. She felt her whole body go cold. Richard's bed. Which up until now she had been happy to lie in.

Right now she couldn't think of anything worse, and that brought up even more worries about the wedding night. Since the night in the hotel with Sam, she couldn't imagine spending the night with any other man. The way he had held her close…the amazing kiss… How could she even be considering going through with the wedding? It was madness. It was a total nightmare, and she was stuck firmly in the middle of it. If only she could wake up.

"Kate?" Marion's voice cut through her reverie. "Are you all right?"

She shook her head. "No. No, I don't think I am. Sorry, Mum, I have to go to bed now. I'll see you all in the morning." She glanced at Jenny. "Come up when you're ready, Jen. What time do we need to get up, Mum?"

"About eight should be all right." Helen was watching her anxiously. "The ceremony is at one, so that should give us enough time. Darling, what's wrong?"

"Nothing. Like I said, I'm tired. I'll be fine in the morning." She left the room without looking back and made her way slowly up the stairs. As she started to open her door, she became aware of someone watching her and turned to find her father standing in his bedroom doorway.

"Dad."

He held out his arms, and without a moment's hesitation she turned and ran into them. As her tears started to flow, Peter gently stroked her hair and muttered soothing words. She buried her face in his shoulder and tightened her arms around his waist.

"Sorry, Dad," she hiccupped, her voice muffled. "I'm so sorry."

"Don't be daft, love." He continued to stroke her hair. "You let it all out. If you want to tell me what's wrong, I'm here, and if you don't, that's your choice. But Katy"—he pulled back slightly and looked down at her—"remember I love you, no matter what, and I always will. And so does your mother."

"Thank you, Dad." Kate raised her head and wiped her hand across her wet eyes. "I know you do. I think I just need to go to bed. I'll be fine in the morning."

"If you say so." Peter watched her closely. "But you know where I am."

Kate reached up and kissed him on the cheek, his words, the same ones Sam had used after their second date, ringing in her ears. She turned and went into her room. This was all Sam's fault. Why had he had to come back and complicate things? If he hadn't, she would be about to marry Richard, happy in the knowledge that he was the love of her life and very good in bed.

She sat down on the bed and pulled her socks off. Instead, she was about to marry Richard, knowing he wasn't the love of her life and constantly wondering whether someone else would be even better in bed. That was no way to start a marriage. That was no way to live a life. How could she plan to sleep with Richard every night knowing she would be thinking of Sam?

She had to face the facts: she was absolutely, completely, and definitely in love with Sam. And from what she had learned the other day, she was fairly sure he felt the same. But not completely sure. Why had he not tried to persuade her not to marry Richard? If he really cared, would he not have done that? Instead, the last thing he had said to her had been some strange waffle about her job.

She slid under the covers and lay flat on her back. And he stopped the kiss before it really got going. Why had he done that? She tried to rack her brains to remember what he'd said when they were cuddling on the bed, but she'd been so tired it had slipped her mind.

There was something, though, and she couldn't help feeling it might be important. She would try and remember in the morning. Closing her eyes, she slid a little further down under the covers, determined to be asleep when Jenny joined her. She wasn't in the mood for talking, even to her best friend.

She was just beginning to doze when she was startled by her phone bleeping. Almost nervously, Kate reached out from under the cover and picked it off her bedside table. It was from Sam. She stared at it, hardly daring to read it.

Are you all right? xx

Two kisses this time. Kate stared at the screen. Why now? Why was he texting her now? What did he mean? What should she reply? In fact, should she reply? She read it again, then wrote a single word.

No.

She thought for a moment, then added two kisses and pressed Send before she could change her mind. She put the phone under her pillow for easy access should he text again. She was just beginning to drift off when it bleeped again.

I'm sorry. Wish we were still on Dartmoor. xx

Shit, now he was really messing with her head. What should she reply to that? Why didn't he just say, "Don't marry Rudolf"? That would be enough. She lowered the phone and stared up at the ceiling. But she had to go through with it. People were depending on her. She couldn't let them down. What did he want her to do? Or say? She knew exactly what she wanted to say to him: "I love you, Sam Somerville, I have loved you for nearly ten years, and I will love you forever." So why was she still marrying Richard?

She rolled onto her stomach and stared at the screen again. She had no idea how to reply. She had no idea what he meant. She had no idea what to do.

Carefully she turned the phone off, replaced it on her bedside table and slid back under the covers. This was something she really couldn't deal with now. Not when she was getting married in the morning.

Chapter 20

Saturday 25th July

"Morning."

Kate opened her eyes and found Jenny sitting on the edge of the bed with a mug of tea. "Morning."

"Thought you might like this to wake you up."

"Thank you." Kate struggled into a sitting position and took the mug. "That's nice. What time is it?"

"Just gone eight. Your Mum said I had to wake you. Everyone is really worried about you."

"Yeah. They're not the only ones." Kate sipped the tea.

"Are you…" Jenny looked away.

"Am I still going through with it? Yeah. I have to. You know that."

"You must think about you. This is your life you're talking about." Jenny looked distressed. "I've never seen you look so unhappy, Kate. And don't tell me it doesn't have to be forever. You can't go into a marriage thinking it's only temporary."

Kate frowned as something tugged at her memory. "Say that again."

"You can't get married viewing the marriage as temporary. It's not fair on either of you."

Kate shook her head as the memory eluded her. "It's fairer than if I dump him this morning. Imagine

281

how he'd feel. And it's not his fault I've gone off him. No, it's better this way."

"So you really have gone off him?" Jenny stared at her. "Oh, Katy, you can't do this! It's all wrong."

"Well, that's as may be, but it's happening." Kate swung her legs out of bed and winced. "Shit, these bruises aren't getting any better." She picked up her phone and turned it back on. It immediately bleeped.

"Who's that from?" Jenny asked.

"No one." Kate kept the phone in her hand. "Just someone wishing me well."

"Kate, you're lying."

"Well, we both know I've been doing a lot of that lately." She got to her feet, the phone still clutched in her hand. "And I shall be telling the biggest lie of all later."

"That's from Sam, isn't it?"

"Maybe. Look, it really doesn't matter any more."

"Kate, in less than five hours you'll be married to Richard. Of course it matters. You're in love with Sam. Just admit it."

"Okay. Yes, I'm in love with Sam. I've always been in love with Sam. Happy now?" Kate scowled at Jenny. "Oh, yeah, and guess what? On the day of the party at the end of school, he broke up with Cerys."

Jenny gasped.

"They were only pretending to be together for the party. And do you know why he broke up with her? To ask me out." She tossed her phone onto the bed and shook her head violently. "He's spent the last eight years thinking he was to blame for her death. I've had all that to deal with, too. Jen, I really just can't think straight any more. Nothing is as I thought it was."

Jenny was staring at her in horror. "Kate, no! Is he in love with you, then?"

"I don't know." Kate sat down on the bed again. "I think so. But he hasn't asked me not to marry Richard, so maybe not. Surely he would have done that. He must know I'm having doubts. I kissed him, for fuck's sake! And he was the one who stopped it."

"What?" Jenny frowned. "He stopped the kissing? Why?"

"I don't know. It was lovely, and he suddenly pulled back and said that was all for now. Or something. He said something else too, but I was really tired and very turned on, and I can't remember what it was."

"Try. I think it might be important."

"I told you, my brain just can't deal with this. I can't remember anything properly. Like he waffled on about my job and I have no idea why. He told me to think about it. It made no sense at all." She stood up again. "I have to get ready. You and Vicky will have to help me dress. I have to do this. It's too late not to, now. But it doesn't have to be forever."

Jenny was watching her sadly. "But will Sam wait for you?"

"It's a chance I have to take." Kate walked into the bathroom and closed the door.

She stripped off her pyjamas, turned the shower on full, and stepped under it. The hot water flowed all over her aching body, stinging the bruised areas. She gently massaged soap all over and let the water rinse it off. No way the shower was going to help her sort out her problems today. There *was* no sorting out this problem. She was stuck with it.

****

"Stand still, Kate, I'm getting this stuff everywhere." Jenny sighed in frustration as she applied the stage makeup to Kate's shoulder. "It's not hiding it as well as it did yesterday. What am I doing wrong?"

"Let me try." Vicky joined her and gently smoothed the greasy paste over the bruise. "You do realise we have to do her whole arm, right? Otherwise it's going to be blotchy."

"Then one arm will be darker than the other." Kate twisted round to try and see what they were doing. "You can't do that."

"Kate, we're doing the best we can. Next time you get married, don't go gallivanting on Dartmoor with your lover just three days before the wedding."

"Ha, ha, very funny." Kate scowled at Vicky. "He's not my lover."

"Well, he should be." Vicky stood back and surveyed her handiwork. "He's much more your type than Richard. D'you think that'll do, Jen?"

"I think it might have to. I suppose it's quite dark in the church. So long as it doesn't actually look purple, we should get away with it."

Kate turned and looked at herself in the mirror. She was wearing her underwear, and the enormous bruise on her ribs was an almost shiny purple colour. Her leg was basically mottled purple and yellow, but the ones on her shoulder and elbow had nearly disappeared. Her whole arm looked slightly more orange than the other one, and she held them out to compare them.

"Maybe you'd better put some on my right arm, too. Just so they match."

"We could, but it's so sticky I'm worried it's going

to get on your dress, so the less we use the better." Jenny stood behind her and looked in the mirror. "I don't think anyone will notice. We do, because we know it's like that."

"Okay." Kate was unconvinced. "Better get the dress on now, then."

"Not yet. Your hair's not ready." Jenny picked up the flowers that were to be pinned in her hair. "D'you want me to do it?"

"I s'pose so." Kate sighed and sat down on the bed. "Let's get it over with. I don't want it to look fancy."

"Kate, if you're insisting on going through with this, you must do it properly. Otherwise Richard will notice that something's wrong."

Kate closed her eyes as Jenny started brushing her hair back from her face. Why couldn't she remember what Sam had said after they kissed? Why did she feel it was important? And she still couldn't make sense of his comments about her job. Where did that come into anything? She sighed. She just wished her brain didn't feel so addled. And then there was Granny and her story. There was something Granny had said that she felt she should have taken more notice of. Why couldn't she remember that either? Maybe she should speak to Granny again.

"How does that look?"

Kate opened her eyes and stared at her reflection in the hand mirror Jenny was holding out. Her hair was swept back from her face and fastened behind her left ear with a spray of cream roses. It looked very nice, but she was shocked by the sight of her face. Her eyes were red, and she had dark shadows surrounding them. Her cheeks were hollow, and she just looked really miserable.

"I look dreadful," she stated dully. "Not my hair, that's nice, thanks, Jen, but my face. I look ill."

"You look sad." Vicky looked over her shoulder into the mirror. "A bride shouldn't look sad. This is all wrong, Kate. It's not too late to stop it."

"Yes, it is." Kate pushed the mirror away and stood up. "Why don't you understand? It's way too late. I can't let Mum and Dad and Richard down. And Granny. It's all my own fault, and I can't let them suffer for my mistake."

"Okay, you don't care about yourself, but what about Sam? Aren't you letting him down?"

"No. He hasn't asked me not to marry Richard. I don't know what he wants." She glanced down at her phone, realising she hadn't actually read his latest message. Hesitantly she picked it up and swiped the screen. The message had been sent the night before after she had turned it off. It was simply a question mark followed by two kisses. She stared at it in dismay. Now that was even more confusing. What the hell did that mean? "I want to speak to Granny."

"Do you want her to come up here?" Jenny looked doubtful. "She might see what we've been doing with your bruises."

"That doesn't matter." Kate shook her head. "She guessed I had more bruises. But I need to ask her something."

"I'll fetch her." Vicky went to the door. "Come with me, Jen. Kate needs to do this alone."

The two girls left the room, and Kate sat very still on the bed. She just needed to ask her grandmother one thing. It was too late, but she just needed to know.

She reached out and took a swig of the water that she had beside the bed, trying hard to fight the sick feeling that was churning in her stomach. This was not how she had imagined her wedding day.

There was a light tap on the door, and Marion's head appeared. "May I come in?"

"Yes, Granny, come and sit down. I just wanted to ask you something." Kate patted the bed beside her.

Marion sat down next to her and took her hand. "Kate, you look dreadful," she said bluntly. "Something's obviously not right."

"Granny…" Kate ignored her words. "After Granddad died, did you try and see your lover again?"

Marion sighed. "No, darling. Your grandfather only died five years ago. That was more than forty years since I last saw…him. It was too late."

"Was it? Surely if you loved each other it wouldn't matter how long it was."

"Life's not really like that, Kate." Marion's face was sad. "I lost him the day I made my decision to stay with Douglas. There was no going back. He moved on. I couldn't expect him to hang around in case I came to my senses and changed my mind. As I said, real life isn't like that."

Kate stared down at her hands, clasped together in her lap. No going back, her grandmother had said. No going back.

She glanced up at her. Marion was sitting with a faraway look in her eye, and Kate touched her gently on the arm.

"I'm sorry, Granny. You must be very sad."

"I'm used to it now. But yes, I was very sad, for a very long time." She picked up Kate's hand and gave it a squeeze. "And I want to make sure you don't make the same mistake. I know you're not going to tell me anything, but just remember your whole life hangs on your decision today. And you have to stop worrying about everyone else. You need to put *you* first. And also you need to consider whether you might be letting someone else down; not me, or your parents, or even Richard."

"What do you mean?"

"You know perfectly well what I mean. Now whatever you decide, I need to go and get ready, or your mother will be hassling me." She stood up and put her hand on Kate's shoulder. "Your parents would get over it, Kate."

Dismally Kate shook her head. "I'm not so sure, Granny. I'm not so sure. And I'm not sure whether…" She looked away.

"It's your decision." Marion bent and dropped a light kiss on her head. "I'll see you in a bit. Shall I send the girls back up?"

"Yes, please." Kate nodded, feeling the tears welling up behind her eyes again. Far from helping her, the chat with her grandmother had confused her even further. There was no going back. It was her decision. Something tugged at her memory again, and she frowned in concentration. Had she heard that somewhere before? If so, where?

The door opened, and Jenny and Vicky came in.

"Are you okay?" Jenny sat on the bed next to Kate. "What were you asking your grandmother?"

"Nothing important." Kate shook her head. "It didn't help. Now I'm even more confused. If only Richard had done something wrong, then I wouldn't feel so guilty. But he hasn't, so I have no reason to hurt him like that."

"He lied about the Stag night," Vicky reminded her.

"That's not really important. No, I still have to do this. Help me on with my dress, and let's get it over." Kate stood up. "You two look very nice, by the way. How long till your car comes?"

"Half an hour." Jenny held the dress out so Kate could step into it. "Kate, please…"

Kate held up her hand. "Don't. Just let it go. What will be will be."

Jenny pulled the dress up, and they manoeuvred Kate's injured arm through the narrow armhole. Then Vicky carefully zipped it up, trying to avoid any pressure on her ribs.

"What jewellery are you wearing?" Jenny glanced over at Kate's dressing table. "And where's your engagement ring?"

"I'm wearing those pearls, there, in that box, and the earrings that match them. My ring is in my bedside drawer."

"Bracelet?" Vicky moved over to help.

"No idea."

"This one would go well." Jenny held up a pearly bangle, and Kate shrugged.

"Whatever." She held out her wrist, and Jenny slipped it on.

Jenny and Vicky stepped back to look at her, and Jenny sighed. "You look lovely. This should be a wonderful moment, but I've never seen you look so sad."

"I'll be okay." Kate lifted the hem of her dress and

slipped her feet into her white satin shoes. "I have to be. Shall we go downstairs?" She picked up her phone from the bed and clutched it tightly.

"You won't be able to take that." Jenny frowned slightly. "Maybe your mother could take it in her bag?"

"I need it." Kate shook her head. "Find me somewhere to put it."

"Kate, you can't!"

"I'm not going without it." Kate was firm. "Find me somewhere to put it."

"I'll take it," Vicky offered. "I can find somewhere to put it, but there's no way you can have it with you. If I have it, it'll never be far away from you. You can keep it until we get to the church, then give it to me before Jen and I walk down the aisle."

Kate hesitated for a moment, then nodded. "Okay. Thank you. I know you think I'm crazy, and to be honest I probably am, but thank you anyway."

"Let's go downstairs. The cars will be here any minute." Jenny opened the door, Vicky straightened the train of Kate's dress, and the three of them made their way slowly down the stairs.

"Darling, you look wonderful!" Helen was in the hall attempting to get her hat to stay on. "Peter, come and see. She looks so beautiful."

Peter appeared in the doorway of the living room and stared up at his daughter. He nodded and smiled at her. "Yes. She looks lovely. Very beautiful."

Kate reached the bottom step and turned to flick her train round. "Thank you." She watched her mother's face and could see the glint of tears in her eyes. She really couldn't let her down. It would destroy her. "Where's Granny?"

"She's already left for the church. The car for me and the bridesmaids is already here, so if you two are ready, we should probably get going." Helen gave up on the hat and picked up her bag. "Do I look all right?"

"Mum, you look lovely." Kate was fighting to keep the tears in. "Really nice. That colour really suits you."

"Well, this may be my only chance to be mother of the bride." She fixed Vicky with a stern glare. "I may as well make the most of it. Come on, girls, let's go." She stepped forward and kissed Kate on the cheek. "See you in a little while, darling."

Kate stood very still as she watched them leave, Jenny glancing back over her shoulder with an agonised look before closing the door behind them. Her mother's only chance to be mother of the bride. How could she spoil that for her? God, people kept making things more and more difficult.

"Katy? Come and sit down for a minute." Peter held out his hand to her. "We don't need to leave for a few minutes."

She followed him into the living room and carefully sat down, trying not to crease her dress. She was acutely aware of the still slightly sticky makeup on her arm, and tried to avoid bumping it on the chair.

"You look nice too, Dad." She managed a smile. "Very smart."

"Thank you." Peter watched her, his head on one side. "Do you want to talk about anything before we go?"

"No. Thank you." Kate looked away. "Maybe we could just go now. Drive round the block a bit or something? The car is here, isn't it?"

"Of course, if that's what you want." He got to his

feet and helped her organise her train. "Come on, then. Have you got your bouquet?"

Kate collected the blue-and-mauve bouquet from the hall table and waited while her father opened the front door. The old-fashioned white Rolls Royce was waiting in the road, and several of the neighbours had come out into their gardens to watch Kate leave. Summoning up a smile for them, Kate waved her hand as she climbed into the back of the car and arranged her dress around her. She leaned back against the leather seat and closed her eyes. It was really happening. This should be the happiest day of her life, and all she wanted to do was leap out and run as far away as possible. She was possibly about to ruin her life.

Her father slid in beside her and leant forward to speak to the driver. "Go to the left at the end of the road. We'll take the long way round to the church. Take your time."

"Dad? That's going to take ages." Kate looked at him in surprise.

"I think we need to talk."

"No, I'm fine." She shook her head and turned to look out the window, her face feeling suddenly hot.

"Well, now, I have to say I don't think you are." Peter settled back in his seat and watched her. "You are, quite honestly, the saddest bride I have ever seen. And I don't like to see my little girl like that."

Kate turned towards him, her eyes swimming with tears. "Oh, Dad, I've really messed up."

"Well, I thought you might have." Peter smiled slightly. "Do you want to talk about it?"

Kate shook her head miserably. "No. Nothing to talk about. It's my mess, and I need to sort it."

Peter narrowed his eyes and folded his arms across his chest. "And how are you going to do that?"

Kate was silent. How could she answer that? By marrying Richard and then leaving him in a few months time? Was that really what she was thinking of doing? What sort of plan was that? What had Granny said? Not at all the way to go into a marriage—that had been it. And it was her decision. Why did that still stir a memory? Why was that important? Who had said that?

"Kate?"

"Dad, it's all right. I know what I'm doing. I love you."

"I know. And I love you. We both love you, and whatever you decide, we always will." He paused and looked thoughtful for a moment. "I just—I just don't want you to make the same mistake my mother did."

Kate's head shot up in surprise. "You know about that?"

Peter smiled sadly. "I just know how sad my mother was when I was young. She tried not to let it show, but I knew. We were very close. She used to take me everywhere with her, and I got to recognise how she was feeling. Even when I was very young. My father was rather a cold man. He didn't really deal with feelings very well, and I dare say he never noticed, but I knew."

"Granny talked to me the other day." Kate spoke quietly. "She told me things about her life. Sad things, but she said you didn't know."

"I have a very good memory." Peter smiled. "I remember a very hot summer when I was about five, when Granny took me to lots of parties. She was happy and laughing all the time. She had lovely friends who played with me. There was one in particular. Looking back on it, I suspect there was something between them. Then one day it was all over. We never saw them again, and after that my mother always seemed just a little bit sad." He caught Kate's hand in his. "I don't want you to be sad, Katy. Don't make the wrong decision. Don't make a decision you'll regret all your life."

There it was again. Decision. Everyone kept saying it was her decision. Granny, Dad, and Sam. Sam! She stiffened in her seat. That was what Sam had said after they kissed. That was all until she had made her decision. He was making her decide. Just like Granny's lover had made her decide. She went all hot and cold, and her head began to spin. He hadn't told her to leave Richard because it had to be her decision. Not because he didn't love her. He had been telling her he loved her, but trying to tell her she had to make her own decision. How could she have forgotten? How could it have taken her this long to figure it out?

She turned to her father, her eyes wide. "Dad. I love you. Can we go straight to the church now?"

"Of course." Peter looked at her closely, muttered something to the driver, and the car turned right, heading towards the village and the church. Kate found her heart was beating at double speed, and beads of sweat were beginning to form on her forehead. Oh, why had she been so stupid? But it was still too late to cancel—how could she do this to Richard? Or to her Mum? Whatever her Dad said, she knew her Mum would be devastated. How could she do that to her? And poor Richard, he really hadn't done anything wrong except be boring. And not be Sam.

As they drew up at the church gate, Kate saw Jenny, Vicky, and the two flower girls waiting for her. Vicky was looking quite agitated and came straight over to the door when the car stopped.

Kate stepped out onto the path and heaved her train with her.

"Kate, I need to speak to you. Now." Vicky caught her arm. "Dad, wait over there. I need to speak to her alone."

Peter nodded and stood to one side as his daughters moved over to the gate.

"Kate, you can't go through with this, and there's something you need to know about Richard. He's lied to you about other things." Kate raised her eyebrows. "Remember the girl at the restaurant? That was me. I was also the girl at the party in Mayfair."

Kate stared at her, realisation dawning on her face. "Of course. I thought the girl at the restaurant looked familiar, but you had had your hair cut and I hadn't seen it like that. But why? What's been going on?"

"We're not having an affair." Vicky shook her head. "It's not like that. He's been representing one of our clients in that big case in London, and I had gone with them. That's why I was having dinner with them." She hesitated. "The party was a bit different, though. I was in London on business, and when Richard found out, he asked if I'd like to go to a party with him. It was in Mayfair, and I must say I jumped at the chance. It didn't really occur to me that it might seem odd, or that he wouldn't tell you. He actually said you weren't into those sorts of things, which if I'd cared to think about, might have seemed odd." She took a deep breath and wrinkled her nose slightly. "Don't freak out, but he actually made a pass at me."

Kate stared at her in horror. "Richard made a pass at you? How, why? What did you do? Why didn't you tell me?"

Vicky looked distressed. "I didn't tell you 'cause I thought it would upset you. I told him where to go, of course. I wouldn't do that to you, however much we fight. He was a bit drunk, and he hadn't seen you for ages, so I just put it down to a stupid moment. He apologised afterwards. I'm sorry, Kate. I should have told you."

Kate caught her sister's hand. "Thank you for telling me now. That's kinda shocked me in several ways, actually. I honestly thought he wouldn't do something like that with anyone, let alone my sister, and you say he was drunk? I've never seen him drunk. I always thought he was way too boring to misbehave. And did he honestly say I wouldn't like to go to a party in Mayfair? I've been asking him to take me to things like that for ages. He always says I'd get bored. I think he believes I'd let him down in front of his snooty friends." She narrowed her eyes at her sister. "Did he say that?"

Vicky shook her head. "No." She made a face. "He did keep saying how well I fitted in with everyone, though. It got a bit creepy, actually. It was just after he'd said that for the dozenth time that he made his move. He tried to kiss me and said how much fun I was."

Kate took a deep breath. "More fun than me, I guess?"

Vicky gave an apologetic shrug. "Well, he didn't actually *say* that, but I kinda thought that's what he meant. But please believe me when I say I told him where to go. And it was only the one party I went to. Did you say that man thought he saw you at several?"

Kate nodded. "Yes, he did. I suppose he could have been mistaken, but maybe not. Now I know what he tried to do with you, maybe he has been taking other women out too. I do believe you, by the way. Thank you. I wish you'd told me sooner, even yesterday when I mentioned the party thing, but never mind. I reckon I've got enough there, and it makes me feel a lot less guilty."

"And there's the skydiving," Vicky added.

"What?" Kate was confused.

"He told me he wanted to go skydiving. Remember, I told you? I wondered if he'd do it for the Stag? Well, he never told you that. You don't tell each other things, and if you loved each other enough to get married, then you *would* tell each other things, and neither of you would have felt the need for anyone else."

"Vicky, why are you doing this?"

"Because I've never seen you so sad. I know we don't usually get on, but I don't want you to be sad, and I really meant it when I said Sam is better suited to you. Don't ruin your life, Kate. Make the right decision. There's still time. I can make it right with Mum and Dad."

Kate squeezed Vicky's hand. "I know. Thank you. Maybe we can be better friends after this. Right. Shall we?" She smiled at Vicky's expression. "Trust me. Here take my phone, and keep it handy."

She turned and started up the path towards the church door. As she and Vicky approached, Jenny left the flower girls and came to meet them.

"Kate? What's happening? You're not going through with it, are you? Didn't Vicky tell you?"

"Trust me, Jen, I know what I'm doing." Kate managed a grin. "Are we ready to go in?"

"Kate, this isn't like your job."

"What?"

"Pretending it's temporary. That wouldn't work. You can't go into it like that." Jenny shook her arm gently.

Kate's face broke into a smile. "Oh, that's what he meant! God, why did he have to be so cryptic? I shall have words about that. Don't worry, Jen, it'll all be okay. You two go and take the flower girls. Dad and I will be just behind you. Trust me."

With a puzzled look at her friend, Jenny took the smaller flower girl by the hand and walked into the church. Vicky followed with the other flower girl, and Kate heard the music start up. She turned to her father and took a deep breath.

"Okay, Dad. Are you ready?" She took his arm, and they moved to the door. The bridesmaids were slowly making their way down the aisle, the flower girls carefully scattering their petals in front of them, and over their heads Kate could just make out Richard and his best man standing at the front.

She took a deep breath and held tight to her father's arm. As the music began to swell and they took their positions in the doorway, Kate murmured in her father's ear, "I'm sorry, Dad. Please forgive me. I tried to do it for you and Mum, but I can't. I'm sorry. I love you both."

Peter squeezed her hand. "I love you, Katy. We

just want you to be happy. Should we be walking down the aisle, though?"

"I couldn't take that away from you. This may be your only chance to walk one of your daughters down the aisle." Kate gave him a small smile.

"You may do this again." Peter was watching her closely.

"Not like this." Kate shook her head. "If I ever do decide to marry someone else, it won't be in a church. It'll be on a beach, or up a mountain, or on a boat. This is our only chance to walk down an aisle. Shall we?"

Peter nodded and kissed her on the cheek. "Good luck, Katy. I hope it all works out. You deserve to be happy."

"Not sure about that." Kate grimaced. "But thanks."

The music reached a crescendo, and they stepped into the church and started down the aisle towards the altar. Kate was uncomfortably aware of the smiling faces watching her, and very nearly lost her nerve when she caught her mother's eye. Helen was already crying, dabbing at her eyes with a tissue, Marion beside her, an inscrutable look on her face.

As they arrived at the front of the church, Peter let go of her arm and took a couple of steps backwards, leaving her standing a few feet away from Richard. She glanced sideways at him, then took a deep breath and leaned forward to the vicar.

"May I have a word with Richard, please?"

"Of course." The vicar looked from one to the other of them in surprise. "Would you like to go to the vestry?"

"No. Here is fine."

"Kate?" Richard's voice had a slight edge to it. "What are you doing?"

"I need to ask you a couple of questions." Kate turned to face him, aware that the congregation had gone silent. "Do you want to go skydiving?"

"What, now?"

"No, not now. Don't be ridiculous. You told Vicky you would like to go skydiving. Is that true?"

Richard glanced nervously across the church to where the bridesmaids were standing. "Well, yes. I do quite fancy it. Kate, what is this?"

"Richard, why didn't you tell me?" Kate's voice was sad. "That's a big thing. Something one would normally share with a fiancée. But you didn't tell me. You let me believe you were even more boring than you actually are." Richard started to speak, but Kate held up her hand. "No, wait. I haven't finished. I haven't told you everything, either. You actually thought I liked being a secretary, and that was my fault because I never told you I didn't. I hate that job. It was only ever temporary. I should have told you that, but we never talk about things like that, do we? Richard, don't you think that people who are going to spend the rest of their lives together should tell each other things? I do."

Richard was staring at her, a look of incomprehension on his face. "Kate, why are you saying all this? We can get past this. We can start talking more."

"No, Richard, I don't think we can." Kate stared at him sadly. "I'm really sorry, but I don't think we can. We've also been lying to each other, and people in love don't do that." He was staring at her in horror, his face beginning to go red. "If I didn't know it wasn't the case, I could be forgiven for thinking you were having an affair with my sister."

He made a strangled sound, and Kate held up her hand.

"Wait. I know you're not, but you lied to me. She was the woman I saw you with at that restaurant. You told me she didn't stay for long at your Stag party. She stayed all evening. And she also told me you took her to the party in Mayfair, and what happened while you were there. We won't go into that now, but I am sure you can see why I might be bothered by that?"

Kate looked up at him. "And that friend of yours mentioned other parties he thought he'd seen me at. Vicky says she only went to one, so who were the other women who looked like me? I'm sorry, Richard, but I really don't think we should get married. I'm sorry."

She was aware of a low moaning sound behind her that she was rather afraid was coming from her mother, and she almost faltered.

Richard was staring at her nervously. "I'm sorry. I don't know what came over me at that party. It's you I want, Kate."

"I'm not sure you do, actually. If we were as in love as we need to be to get married, then you wouldn't have done what you did, and neither would I." She saw his frown and held up her hand. "I'll explain that in a minute. And if you really think I wouldn't enjoy one of those parties in London, then you don't know me at all. My guess is you think I'd embarrass you, and you found Vicky and maybe some other people were more sophisticated companions. And—let's be honest—what do we really have in common? You said I wouldn't be any good as an explorer. I want a man who will let me be myself, and if I want to be an explorer, or an astronaut, then I expect his support. Not someone who tells me I'd be a better secretary."

"But Kate, why would you want to be an explorer? That's just not you. We can go abroad if you like. We're going to Barbados for our honeymoon."

"To a five-star hotel. That's not the same. I don't actually want to be an explorer, but I want to travel to places. To experience the real place, not just their best hotel. I want to go camping. You hate things like that." She looked him in the eye. "We've been lying to each other, Richard. You didn't tell me about Vicky, and I didn't tell you I'd been out for a couple of drinks with an old school friend."

"What's wrong with that?"

"An old male school friend. And I didn't tell him I was engaged. And I didn't tell you I'd been. And I found I was enjoying his company more than yours. And I let him kiss me. That's no way to start a marriage. I'm sorry, Richard, but I can't marry you." She gently eased her engagement ring off her finger and held it out to him. "Please forgive me. I thought it would be okay, I'd convinced myself it would be okay, but this morning I realised it wouldn't."

Richard took the ring from her and held it in his hand. "I understand." He sighed and ran a hand over his hair. "We're not as close as we could be. We do have different aims in life. We do want different things. I thought that didn't matter, but maybe it does. Maybe we *are* too different. I shouldn't have lied to you, it was very silly, as was some of my behaviour, and from the sound of it you haven't been perfect either. I'm sorry it's come to this, but I think I understand."

"Thank you." Kate stepped forward and kissed his cheek. "I'm sorry to do this here, too, but I thought everyone should understand. We can talk more later in private, if you want to." She turned and faced the open-mouthed, silent congregation, who were watching the scene playing out in front of them. Her mother was sobbing quietly onto Peter's shoulder, and Jenny and Vicky were both trying to conceal smiles. Kate stared around at them all and was suddenly tongue-tied. A hand on her arm made her jump. Her grandmother had joined her.

"It's okay, Kate. That was a difficult thing to do, but I think it was the right thing to do. You made the right decision. Go and enjoy your life."

Kate leaned over and kissed her cheek. "Thanks, Granny. Can you look after Mum and Dad?"

Marion nodded, and Kate turned back to the congregation. "I'm going to go now, but there's a big party arranged, and paid for—sorry, Dad—over at the hotel, and it would be a huge waste if it didn't all get eaten, so please all still go and enjoy that. I'm sorry to have wasted everyone's time, but at least it's nice for you to have a get-together. Mum, I hope you understand and forgive me. I love you." She turned to the bridesmaids. "Thanks, girls, you were great, couldn't have made it this far without you both. Vicky, have you got my phone?" Vicky handed her the phone, and Kate held it tightly in her hand. She had started to walk back up the aisle towards the door when she noticed the astonished face of Holly, her young co-worker. She paused and tossed her bouquet to the girl. "Thank you, Holly, and I hope you find your astronaut one day. Oh, yes, and tell James I quit." Then, with as much dignity as she could muster, Kate walked back up the aisle and pushed open the heavy oak door at the end.

She emerged into the sunshine and immediately shaded her eyes as it dazzled her. She took a deep breath and stepped onto the path. Sam was sitting cross-legged on a raised stone tomb. They stared at each other.

"You took your time. I was beginning to get worried."

"Next time you don't want me to marry someone, please just tell me, don't make me work it out." She glared at him. "And you shouldn't be sitting on that. It's someone's grave."

"That's okay. It's my great-granddad's. He doesn't mind. He's dead." Sam slid down off the stone and walked towards her. His eye had gone a mixture of purple and yellow, and the scratch down his face still looked raw. "You're not married, then? What did you do with Roderick?"

"*Richard* is still in the church, with all the rest of my friends and relations. And no, I'm not married, but no thanks to you. Why couldn't you have just said, 'Don't marry Richard'? I would have understood that."

Sam had reached her and stood looking down at her. "If you worked it out, then you know why. You had to make the decision for yourself."

"I know that now." Kate sighed. "But if it hadn't been for Granny and her story, I might not have done. I was so hung up on not letting everyone down that I was going to go through with it and sort it out afterwards."

"Which I realised. Hence the warning about temporary jobs."

"Again, I know that now, but I only worked that one out after I got here! Honestly, Sam, if this is going to work, you're going to have to stop being so cryptic. It does my head in."

He moved even closer. "Well, you got there in the end. What do you want to do now?"

She looked up at him. "Finish that kiss we started in the hotel?"

"Sounds good to me." He smiled down at her. "I love you, Katy Granger. I hope you finally realise that."

"I love you too, Sam Somerville. I love you too."

A word about the author...

Rachael Richey writes Women's Fiction. She lives in Cornwall, England, with her husband, son, and daughter.
You can visit Rachael's website at:
http://rachaelricheybooks.weebly.com/